THE UNCOLLECTED WORKS
OF
LOUISA MAY ALCOTT

VOLUME ONE

SHORT STORIES

THE UNCOLLECTED WORKS

OF

LOUISA MAY ALCOTT

VOLUME ONE

SHORT STORIES

With an Introduction by Monika Elbert

IRONWEED AMERICAN CLASSICS
IRONWEED PRESS · NEW YORK

Ironweed Press, Inc.
P.O. Box 754208
Parkside Station
Forest Hills, NY 11375

Manufactured in the United States of America.

Ironweed American Classics books are printed on acid-free paper.
For maximum durability, this book is Smyth-sewn
and case-bound in Arrestox® vellum.

Library of Congress Cataloging-in-Publication Data

Alcott, Louisa May, 1832–1888.
  [Selections. 2001]
  The uncollected works of Louisa May Alcott / with an introduc-
tion by Monika Elbert.
    p.   cm. — (Ironweed American classics)
  Includes bibliographical references (p.).
  Contents: v. 1. Short stories
  ISBN 0-9655309-9-X (v. 1 : acid-free paper)
    I. Title.   II. Series.
PS1016.E45   2001
813'.4—dc21   2001024531

CONTENTS

APPENDIX

ACKNOWLEDGMENTS

Special gratitude is owed to the following individuals and institutions for the courtesies extended: Philip Lampi, Dennis Laurie, and Russell Martin, Newspapers and Periodicals Department, American Antiquarian Society; Gregory Eiselein and Anne Phillips, Kansas State University; Microtext Department, Boston Public Library; McNichols Library, University of Detroit Mercy; and Library of Congress.

INTRODUCTION

In the stories in this volume Louisa May Alcott (1832–1888) displays her remarkable versatility as a storyteller. Most of the stories were written during the last two decades of her life, when she had already established herself as a successful commercial writer, accomplished in a variety of genres. Although her affinity for the Gothic does occasionally surface, Alcott largely eschews the sensational and instead affirms and celebrates middle-class ideals and aspirations, tempered by Transcendentalist precepts and old-fashioned Protestant values.

The adult stories in this collection are, thematically and structurally, an outgrowth of Alcott's earlier stories and owe much to the narrative examples of her literary precursors. "Lost in a Pyramid; or, The Mummy's Curse" (1869), with its occult and Egyptological subject matter, is reminiscent of Edgar Allan Poe's "Some Words with a Mummy" (1845). The probing scientist, the victimized "vivacious little creature, half child, half woman," and the poisonous flower also call to mind Nathaniel Hawthorne's "Rappaccini's Daughter" (1846). Similarly, the wayward pastor in "John Marlow's Victory" (1878) is a composite drawn from a cast of ministers, literary and real, most prominently Arthur Dimmesdale from Hawthorne's *The Scarlet Letter* (1850) and Theodore Parker, a charismatic abolitionist preacher and acquaintance of Alcott's, who was known to have a wandering eye.

The didacticism of Alcott's philosopher father, Amos Bronson Alcott, is readily discernible in her "Mrs. Gay" stories. Mrs. Gay's prescription for domestic bliss—fresh air, good nutrition, cleanliness, and order—adheres to the Transcendentalist lifestyle promoted at Bronson's utopian community, Fruitlands. Above all, the Thoreauvian principle of simplicity reigns supreme in Mrs. Gay's idealized household. Conversely, Alcott deplored the materialism and idleness of the leisured class. In "Romance of Chicago, the Ruined City: Through the Fire" (1872), a story attributed, at least in part, to Alcott, the status-conscious young woman who chooses a rich suitor over a poor one must literally endure a trial by fire to learn the value of work and true love.

Alcott, who in her youth had aspired to be a playwright and actress, published a number of stories about female artists and performers, beginning with her first thriller, "The Rival Prima Donnas" (1854). As these stories attest, she struggled to reconcile the image of the traditional "True Woman" with that of the emancipated "New Woman," but proved unable to achieve a satisfactory synthesis, her feminism often stymied by her New England conservatism. The price of creativity for Alcott's artist heroines is often the "spinster's" life, which permits a great deal of independence and freedom but also results in emotional isolation, a quandary with which Alcott must have been well acquainted. In "Victoria: A Woman's Statue" (1881), Alcott seems to suggest that women must ultimately forgo artistic ambition to fulfill their maternal mission: "The talent that might have rendered the womanly heart hard and selfish was sacrificed to a higher art, and the life that was full of effort, disappointment, solitude, and pain for her was help, sunshine, courage, and devotion for others." This same self-sacrificing impulse is again exhibited by her female artists in *Diana and Persis,* an unfinished story on which Alcott had worked earlier, during the winter of 1878–79. Although Alcott never fully resolves a woman's conflict between self-abnegation and self-realization, her stories underscore the cultural dilemma faced by women in the nineteenth century.

Alcott's juvenile stories hark back to a strain of Puritanism, but one that has been reinterpreted from a secular vantage point, free of the didacticism and dogma of the popular Sunday-school tracts and the Christian children's magazines. Though a traditionalist in some respects, Alcott rejected the earlier models of children's fiction, perhaps the best-known of which is the Rollo series by Jacob Abbott, who sought principally to instill propriety and obedience to authority. Nor did she fall back on the narrative formula of the popular Victorian girls' stories of the time, such as the Elsie Dinsmore series, written by Martha Finley and published during the same period as *Little Women* (1868, 1869). The Elsie Dinsmore books were socially and morally conservative and reinforced Victorian values and gender stereotypes. Although Alcott herself was not averse to a certain amount of finger-wagging moralism, she also celebrated daring, adventurousness, and independent thinking in her child and adolescent protagonists. *Golden Hours: A Magazine for Boys and Girls,* a Christian periodical for children, warned that *Little Women* was not a "religious book" and therefore "should not be read on Sunday," but did characterize the book as "lively, entertaining, and not harmful."

The appeal of Alcott's juvenile fiction lay partly in its depiction of ordinary children who, despite their curiosity and mischievousness, have the capacity to balance impetuosity with rationality. Her Little Women series rivaled in popularity the Oliver Optic books by William T. Adams, a best-selling adventure series for boys. It was the success of the Oliver Optic books that convinced Thomas Niles of Roberts Brothers to commission Alcott to write a similar line of books for girls. Alcott's purpose was both to entertain and instruct, as the Optic series did. Although her fiction was similarly fast-paced and engaging, Alcott challenged Adams's philosophy of writing for children, attacking his plots as sensational and implausible. To Alcott, the Optic books, with their accounts of encounters with pirates and other improbable adventures, seemed farfetched, and she decried in particular his positive portrayals of criminals. Not surprisingly, Alcott was not a contributor to Adams's *Oliver Optic's Magazine* (1867–75).

Alcott did find a ready market for her children's stories, however. A plethora of juvenile periodicals appeared after the Civil War, and many of those founded before the war enjoyed their heyday during the postbellum period. From 1868 to 1870, Alcott edited *Merry's Museum,* one of the preeminent children's journals of the nineteenth century, to which she also contributed stories, including "Milly's Messenger" (1869), as well as the "Merry's Monthly Chat with His Friends" column (1868–69). *Merry's Museum* ran two of Alcott's serials that were later published as books: *Will's Wonder Book* (1870), a group of stories about the wonders of nature and God, and part of *An Old-Fashioned Girl* (1870). Alcott's stories in *Will's Wonder Book* were probably inspired by the Peter Parley stories of Samuel Griswold Goodrich, the founder of *Parley's Magazine* (1833–44) and *Merry's Museum;* like Goodrich, she sought to promote the values of industry, probity, and nationalism.

During her tenure at *Merry's Museum,* Alcott wrote *Little Women,* and as a result of its success, she did not feel compelled to dedicate herself to the magazine, and resigned in 1870. (*Merry's Museum* failed in 1872 and was absorbed by the *Youth's Companion.*) Alcott went on to establish a long-standing relationship with *St. Nicholas;* among her many contributions to that prestigious publication were the serialized novels *Eight Cousins* (1875) and *Jack and Jill* (1880). *St. Nicholas* was then under the stewardship of the progressive, feminist editor Mary Mapes Dodge, the author of the children's classic *Hans Brinker* (1865). Dodge's reputation as an editor enabled the journal to attract the works of such luminaries as Mark Twain, Sarah Orne Jewett, Bret Harte, Helen Hunt Jackson, Robert Louis Stevenson, and Rudyard Kipling. Two of Alcott's most important posthumous publications, "Lu Sing" (1902) and "The Eaglet in the Dove's Nest" (1903), appeared in *St. Nicholas*.

"Lu Sing," a story Alcott had intended to submit to *St. Nicholas* shortly before her death, is drawn from her experiences as a surrogate mother to her niece, Louisa May "Lulu" Nieriker, the daughter of Alcott's sister May, whom Alcott adopted after the death of the child's mother. In the story, set in imperial China, the willful, disobedient Lulu is represented by Lu Sing and Alcott and her sister Anna by Lu Sing's long-suffering aunts Ah Wee and Ah Nah. "My poor baby," Alcott writes in a May 1883 journal entry, "has a bad time with her little tempers and active mind and body." On one occasion Alcott spanked Lulu—a desperate act, considering Alcott's disavowal of corporal punishment—and promptly regretted her action: Lulu's "bewilderment was pathetic, and the effect, as I expected, a failure. Love is better, but also endless patience." This incident, one may assume, inspired "Lu Sing." In the animal fable "The Eaglet in the Dove's Nest," Mrs. Dove takes into her nest an ill-tempered eaglet foundling and teaches him lessons in gentleness and kindness so that he may learn to "rule his temper" and "guide his will." The fetishized white feather from Mrs. Dove, which the eagle continues to carry under his wing, is a tribute to maternity; perhaps this story represents a wish fulfillment for Alcott in her role as surrogate mother to little Lulu.

During Alcott's time, holiday stories written for Christmas

and New Year's issues were particularly anticipated. In the final decade of her life, when she was at the height of her fame, Alcott wrote a handful of such stories, three of which are included in this volume: "Grandmama's Pearls" (1882), "Bertie's Box: A Christmas Story" (1884), and "Little Robin" (1886). "Grandmama's Pearls," the story of three young cousins who learn the importance of "modesty, obedience, and self-denial," appeared in *St. Nicholas* and "Bertie's Box" and "Little Robin" in *Harper's Young People.* Founded in 1879, *Harper's Young People* was modeled on Harper Brothers' successful adult journals, *Harper's Monthly, Weekly,* and *Bazaar.* Harper Brothers had ventured into the field of children's publishing back in the 1850s, producing children's textbooks and readers, including Abbott's Rollo books. The fiction in *Harper's Young People* tended to be mildly moralistic and sentimental. In "Bertie's Box," the child Bertie reminds his elders of the true spirit of Christmas when he attempts to send his most prized possessions to a destitute family in Iowa. The story ends with a Dickensian blessing, "God bless our dear little Santa Claus and send him many Christmases as happy as the one he has made for us!" "Little Robin," loosely based on "The Babes in the Wood," is the story of two children who lose their way in the woods one Christmas Eve while on a sledding jaunt. But before any harm can befall them, they are saved by the resourceful "Little Robin" of the title. Following her typical narrative pattern, Alcott allows her disobedient child protagonists to place themselves in danger, but never to the point of plunging them into the nightmarish world of folk fairy tales.

Another children's journal with which Alcott had an enduring affiliation was the *Youth's Companion* (1827–1929), perhaps the most successful juvenile periodical of the nineteenth century. In its early years the journal had a rigid Christian framework; but by the time Alcott wrote for the journal, in the 1870s and 1880s, it had become considerably more flexible and less didactic, and its high literary tone also attracted a sizable audience of adult readers. Of the eleven children's stories in this collection, five appeared in the *Youth's Companion*. The first two stories deal with conflicts between children and adults, who are compelled to rethink their attitudes toward children and recognize the limits of their own authority. In "Uncle Smiley's Boys" (1870), a tribute to Bronson Alcott's pedagogical methods, the teacher Uncle Smiley rehabilitates misbehaving students by appealing to their sense of fairness and brotherly love rather than by disciplining them with corporal punishment. In "Mother's Trial" (1870), two children, a brother and sister, grouse bitterly about schoolwork and chores until their mother decides to give them a dose of their own medicine by feigning indolence and leaving them to their own devices. For the want of their mother's care and supervision, the children soon grow miserable, finding that they are unable to take care of themselves, and realize "how much happier it makes us, old and young, to bear and forbear, to deny ourselves for others and make duty pleasant by a willing heart." For the maternal audience of the *Youth's Companion,* the idea of a mother forsaking her responsibilities, if only for a day, must have been both shocking and liberating.

In the later stories "Bonfires" (1873) and "A Little Cinderella" (1874), Alcott demonstrates her skill in creating narratives with broad appeal as well as social critical content. "Bonfires" offers an implicit critique of the Victorian model of femininity, illustrating the functional superiority of such "unfeminine" attributes as courage and self-reliance to those which Alcott's contemporaries prized in young girls, such as docility and physical beauty. "A Little Cinderella" is Alcott's feminist retelling of the familiar fairy tale. In Alcott's version Phoebe, the "little Cinderella," is saved from a life of drudgery not by a prince but by two female guests at her aunt's farmhouse.

For all her social radicalism, Alcott was in some ways quaintly reactionary. In the *Youth's Companion* pieces she often betrays her deep-seated prejudices against the poor—undoubtedly shared by the predominantly middle-class readers of the magazine—and appears to legitimize gross class inequalities. The charity shown Phoebe is, in reality, a type of noblesse oblige, and in the end she makes no attempt to rise above her class station but is content to live out her life as a servant, "the happiest little maid who ever loved and served a gentle, generous mistress." Alcott's paternalistic attitude toward the poor is again evident in "Number Eleven" (1882). In what may be interpreted as an act of self-mutilation, the youthful protagonist, Johnny, has his hand tattooed to remind himself to heed his conscience, as "we poor folks get tempted dreadfully, and it's hard to keep from taking things when we need 'em so much." "Number Eleven" seems to imply that the poor are by nature criminally inclined.

Surprisingly, Alcott had a low opinion of her juvenile fiction, in an unguarded moment even referring to it as "moral pap." Reading through her journals and letters, one has the distinct impression that Alcott looked on writing as a joyless chore: "Mr. Niles [of Roberts Brothers] wants a girls' story, and I begin *Little Women*. Marmee, Anna, and May [Alcott's mother and sisters] all approve my plan. So I plod away, though I don't enjoy this sort of thing. Never liked girls or knew many." But Alcott reveals an entirely different attitude when speaking of her first novel, *Moods* (1865, 1882). In an uncharacteristic display of creative passion, she confided in her journal in August 1860, "*Moods*. Genius burned so fiercely that for four weeks I wrote all day and planned nearly all night, being quite possessed by my work. I was perfectly happy and seemed to have no wants. . . . Daresay nothing will ever come of it; but it *had* to be done, and I'm the richer for a new experience." Some four years later a chapter of the novel appeared as a short story, "A Golden Wedding:

and What Came of It," in the Boston weekly *Commonwealth*. Alcott fully reworked the excerpted chapter at least twice: first for the 1865 edition of *Moods* and then for the 1882 edition. Although the first edition of *Moods* was not critically well received, an anonymous reviewer for the British *Reader* singled out the "Golden Wedding" chapter for praise: "There is a description of a Golden Wedding in a farmhouse of New England that has a subtlety of humor and wit not unworthy of [the British writer and critic] Charles Lamb, alternating with passages of pathos and true feeling, which warrant the largest hope from the author."

In following the progression of the "Golden Wedding" text, one can trace Alcott's development as a writer and a proponent of women's rights. "A Golden Wedding: and What Came of It" mirrors Alcott's own negative reaction to her sister Anna's marriage and, in comparison to the two later versions, seems mean-spirited and acrimonious. Throughout the story Kate, the "old maid," expresses only grudging happiness on the occasion of her best friend Sallie's wedding. Although both vowed to remain single, Sallie becomes enticed into marriage when she and her boyfriend, David, chance upon a "golden wedding" anniversary celebration and are captivated by the blissful domestic scene they witness. With ill-disguised bitterness and envy, Kate warns Sallie, "Ten years hence I'll ask you how you like that new world; for golden glories have a tendency to fade, and wedded life is not all a summer-morning walk." In the revision for the first edition of *Moods*, Alcott dispenses with the character of Kate and renames the best friend Sylvia and the boyfriend Adam. She also infuses the narrative with more passion and romance, adding to the beginning an encounter with a group of swashbuckling Cubans and closing with Sylvia's reverie of love as she sleeps under the stars and a "canopy of boughs." In the final version, the earlier Gothic framework is discarded and the opening dialogue rendered in a less stylized and more natural manner. At the end Sylvia is still pondering the possibility of wedded life with Warwick, but in this version she ends up sleeping in "Phebe's bed in the old garret" instead of outside in nature, though connected to it "by the pleasant patter of the rain upon the roof." Stylistically the 1882 "Golden Wedding" is the superior, suffering from neither the awkward narrative structure of the original nor the Romantic excesses of the second.

With each revision Alcott modifies her view of marriage. In the short story, marriage is regarded as a betrayal of sisterhood, as an exclusionary relationship in which the couple sever old ties and begin life anew as an isolated pair. Then, in the 1865 *Moods,* it is sentimentalized and idealized. Finally, it is presented as a more encompassing form of love, one that enlarges the couple's social circle and strengthens communal bonds. "Having learned the possibility of finding happiness after disappointment and making love and duty go hand in hand," Alcott disavows the austere feminism and overblown Romanticism of the earlier versions and embraces and apotheosizes domesticity, choosing "a wiser, if less romantic, fate" for Sylvia. Perhaps in this last "Golden Wedding" Alcott is reviewing her own past and acknowledging that she is at last comfortable and at peace with her life alone as an artist.

Monika Elbert
Montclair State University

STORIES

A GOLDEN WEDDING:
AND WHAT CAME OF IT

"How I should like to see one of these family festivals. Be sure to invite me to yours, Sallie," said I, laying down the paper from which I had been reading an account of a golden wedding to my friend as we sat sewing on her bridal gear.

"I will, if I ever have one, and I hope it may do some young Beatrice and Benedick as much good as the first one I ever saw did me and my spouse that is to be. Do you know, Kate, I never should have had any wedding at all if it had not been for that 'family festival,' as you call it."

"That is challenging me to ask all about it, so tell away while I finish these everlasting frills. Thank heaven, I shall never have to do the like for myself."

Sallie smiled a superior smile, and sat rocking and recalling some pleasant experience so busily that she quite forgot me, till I reminded her that her audience was ready and the work would get on much faster if the needles kept time to nimble tongues.

"You remember a conversation we had a year ago, Kate?" she began, with a look in which malice, mirth, and embarrassment were ludicrously blended.

"Yes—and I also remember that though we both agreed that marriage was slavery, that liberty was better than love, and that neither of us would ever change our opinion, one of us has already turned traitor, and not only exults in her perfidy but tries to beguile others into bondage."

"I'll thank you not to pucker my work in your indignation, dear," placidly answered my recreant friend, adding, with the matronly air brides so soon acquire, "We thought ourselves very wise, but we shall both discover that Nature is wiser still, and be glad to mind her, as dutiful daughters should."

"Don't moralize, Sallie, but tell your story, and convince me if you can."

"You won't own it if I do. Our vows of celibacy were taken in the wintertime, when hearts, like plants, are apt to lie asleep or grow very slowly and only blossom in artificial heat. But as spring comes on, all manner of unsuspected longings begin to stir, pale hopes grow green again, fresh aspirations begin to climb and affections to stretch out little tendrils groping for something strong to lean upon."

"Which means that you wanted someone to love. Why don't you say so plainly and not meander about, spouting rigmaroles and budding what's-their-names, like a metaphysical gardener? Everyone ferments in the spring, and it's a mercy they do, for what would become of hotel keepers and mountain guides if your 'green longings' and 'climbing aspirations' did not set people to walking to and fro upon the face of the earth?"

"Persons situated as I am must be allowed to romance in all things and meander at their own sweet will. If you keep interrupting, you will never hear the story, for I am to go out with David at five. Last June I went, as you know, to spend the summer with my old schoolmate up among the Berkshire hills. Gay times we had; for Mary's brother was at home, and a certain friend of mine, who had a habit of appearing at places where I went, quite accidentally and very opportunely happened to come there as a quiet place in which to study."

"So your affectional tendrils fell to twining, and the gentleman cheerfully made himself a trellis for your sake, instead of studying his books, as he should have done."

"Thank you for giving me a lift over that trying part of my story, Kate. You see, we had been friends for a long while and never thought of anything else till that summer. Even then, we did not 'philander,' as you say, though we soon found that we had changed to one another. I was troubled when I discovered how much I liked my friend, and took occasion, as young people are fond of doing, to air my opinions upon marriage and my firm determinations never to change them. David did not agree upon that point, but in various twilight chats we all had together, he showed me that he was afraid of poverty, and dared not marry till he had made his fortune. I should have been relieved on hearing that; but I regret to say I was not, and I found myself thinking his views rather sordid, while my own began to look rather selfish. Neither said anything about love, but tried to enjoy the present, forget the future, and ignore the time when we should part, David to make his fortune, I to enjoy my liberty, and both to live our lives alone."

"Sensible persons; I respect you there. It's a pity you ever changed your minds."

"I would not have you for my bridesmaid if I thought you really meant so, Kate. I have hopes of you, however, since I have seen you adore a year-old lord of creation and submit to his petty tyranny, and feel assured that when your David comes, you won't say, 'Go away, I'm busy.'"

"Two yards and a quarter; you'll want some more cambric. Don't forget it when you go out."

Sallie laughed till the tears stood in her merry brown eyes at the only reply vouchsafed her, and Sallie's friend, with somewhat testy dignity, begged her to go on.

"Well, my love, we had a very happy summer, leading the lives of gypsies and enjoying such entire freedom that I, for one, got rather tired of it—the freedom, not the summer nor the society. One breezy September day we four set out on a ten-mile walk to visit several green nooks and say good-bye to them, for our holiday was nearly over. Just as we had turned our faces homeward in the early afternoon, a heavy shower blew up, drenching us completely but by no means dampening our spirits. We took council while the flood descended, and Fred, Molly's brother, as leader of the troop, decided that it was best to go to a house not far off, whose owner he chanced to know. Being in just the mood for adventures, we splashed away, a moist and mirthful party, and after a mile of mud found ourselves before a red farmhouse standing under a pair of ancient elms with a patriarchal air which promised hospitable treatment and good cheer—a promise speedily fulfilled by the lively old woman who came trotting out with an energetic 'Shoo!' for the speckled hens congregated in the porch and a hearty welcome for the weather-beaten travelers.

"'Sakes alive!' she said. 'You be in a mess, ain't you? Come right in and make yourself ter hum. Abel, take the menfolks up chamber and fit 'em with anything dry you kin lay your hands on. Phebe, see to these poor little creeters and bring 'em down lookin' less like drownded kittens.'

"These directions were given with such vigorous illustrations, and the old face shone with such friendly zeal, that we all submitted at once, sure that the kind soul was pleasing herself in serving us. Abel, a staid farmer of forty, obeyed his mother's order regarding the 'menfolks,' and Phebe, a pretty girl of sixteen, led Molly and me to her room and offered us her best. While repairing damages, we made a discovery that added much to the romance and enjoyment of our adventure. A smart gown lay outspread upon the bed, suggesting that some festival was afoot, and a few questions elicited these facts from Phebe. Grandpa had seven sons and three daughters, all living, all married, and all blessed with flocks of children. Grandpa's birthday was always celebrated by a family gathering. But today being the fiftieth anniversary of his wedding, the various households had decided to keep it with unusual ceremony, and all were coming for a supper, a dance, and a 'sing' at the end.

"Upon hearing this, Molly and I proposed an immediate departure. But Grandma Blake would not hear of it; for the shower had settled into a steady rain, our clothes must be dried, the horses were both away to bring the children home, and she insisted on our all staying to enjoy the fun in a neighborly way. Taking the matter into our own hands, we said we would; and arrayed in two of Phebe's second-best gowns, with white aprons and a rustic ornament stuck here and there to hide misfits, we went down to join the gentlemen. They were in the solemn best parlor, but greeted us with a laugh, for both were *en costume*. David's height put Abel's wardrobe out of the question, and Grandpa, taller than any of his seven goodly sons, supplied him with a sober suit, roomy, square-skirted, and venerable, which became him and with his beard produced the curious effect of a youthful patriarch. Fred, with an eye to effect, had laid hands on an old uniform, in which he looked like a volunteer of 1812. They agreed to stay, without a murmur, and all of us entered into the spirit of the hour with a heartiness which won the family and placed us in friendly relations at once.

"Fred went out somewhere with Abel; Mary and I helped Phebe lay a long table to receive the coming feast; and David, begging Grandma to consider him one of her own boys, fell to work with us, while little Nat tumbled about in everyone's way, quite wild with excitement, and Grandma stood in her pantry like a culinary general, swaying a big knife for a baton as she issued orders and marshaled her forces, the busiest and merriest of us all.".

II

"When we had trimmed the table with such common flowers as could be got, hung green boughs about the room, with candles here and there to give a festal light, and added several other unusual touches, which caused the old lady to thank her stars we came, she went up to dress; Molly followed to preside over Phebe's toilette; and David and I began to talk with little Nat, hoping to shorten the trying half hour before the 'party came in,' as he expressed it. He was a cripple, yet seemed one of those household blessings which in the guise of an affliction keep many hearts tenderly united by a common love and pity. A cheerful creature, always chirping like a cricket on the hearth as he sat weaving baskets or turning bits of wood into useful or ornamental articles for such as came to buy them, and hoarding up the proceeds like a little miser for one more helpless than himself.

"'What are you making, Nat?' I asked, for David presently fell into a brown study.

"'Them are spoons, ma'am—'postle spoons, they call 'em,' said the boy. 'You see, my mother reads a sight, and she found something in a book about spoons with the head of a 'postle on each. She guessed they'd sell, bein' new, so I got Grandpa's big Bible with pictures in it and worked till I got the heads good; and they do sell, and I'm savin' up a lot. It ain't for me, you know. There wouldn't be no fun in that. It's for Mother, 'cause she's wors'n I be, and I like to give her things.'

"'Is she sick?' I asked, watching his thin face kindle with the happy knowledge that he was a little providence to one he loved.

"'Oh, ain't she, though,' he answered. "Why, she hasn't stood up this ten years. We were tipped over in a wagon when I was a baby. It done something to my legs, but it broke her back and made her no use, only jest to pet folks and keep 'em good and stiddy. Ain't you seen her? Don't you want to?'

"'Would she like it?' said David.

"'She admires to see folks and you'll make her laugh, so I guess you'd better go in. But first I want to give you one of my spoons, 'cause you seem to like 'em so much,' added the little fellow, as I reluctantly laid down the one with the handsome head of Saint John upon it. Nat looked at it, then at David, then at me, and gave it back with a knowing smile that brought color into two pairs of cheeks as he said:

"'It does look like him, specially the nice baird and curly hair. You'd rather have that one, I guess, and when you are married, I'll make a whole set if you'll let me know.'

"I said nothing as I pocketed my spoon, and David bespoke and paid for a set before he remembered that there was to be no marriage. Then Nat took up his crutches and hopped away to the room where a plain, serene-faced woman lay knitting, with her best cap on and her clean handkerchief and large green fan laid out upon the coverlet. This was evidently the best room of the house, and as we sat talking, I saw many traces of that refinement which comes through the affections. Nothing seemed too good for the invalid. Birds, books, flowers, and pictures were plentiful here, though visible nowhere else in the homely house. Two easy chairs beside the bed showed where the old folks oftenest sat; Abel's home corner was there by the antique desk covered with farmer's literature; Phebe's workbasket stood in the window, Nat's lathe in the sunniest corner of 'Mother's room'; and from the speckless carpet to the canary's clear water glass, all was exquisitely neat, for love made labor light.

"Finding that neither mother nor son had any complaints to make, nor any sympathy to ask, we amused them with an account of our adventures, over which they laughed so heartily that before I knew it, I found myself complimenting Patience Blake upon her cheerfulness.

"'Bless you, my dear, why shouldn't I be cheerful, with such a many comforts as I have?' she answered brightly. 'My life may not look a happy one to folks that don't know me, but it is, for when a woman has a good husband and loving children, she finds troubles come light and the world a pleasant place to be in, even if her share of it is shut in by four walls like mine.'

"I stole a glance at David to see how he received this statement, and found him looking straight at me, evidently with the same purpose; which discovery caused me to ask hastily if Mrs. Blake didn't think some women were happier single.

"'Not many, miss. Them that are have a starved sort of a look and don't seem so kind of finished off as the married ones do. I guess the good Lord planned things right, and when they go wrong, it ain't His fault. I rather think it's best for all to marry, for if we are poor, it's pleasant helping one another; if we are rich, it makes fine things twice as comfortable enjoying them together; if there's trouble, it ain't so heavy bein' shared; if there's happiness, it seems sweeter when there's someone to rejoice with you; and if there's partings, those that are left find that it makes Heaven seem homelike and death easy, to remember that they'll still be a family when they all meet again.'

"I had nothing to say to that, and sat watching the woman softly beating some tune on the sheets, with her quiet eyes turned toward the light. Many a sermon had been less eloquent to me than the look, the tone, the cheerful hope and resignation that made her plain face beautiful. David said, 'Thank you,' but got no farther, for Nat cried out, 'Hooray! There they be,' and clattered away, to be immediately absorbed into the embraces of a swarm of relatives, who now began to arrive in a steady stream. Old and young, rich and poor, coming with overflowing hands or trifles humbly given, all were received alike—all hugged by Grandpa, kissed by Grandma, shaken half breathless by Abel, welcomed by Patience, and danced around by Phebe and Nat till the house seemed like a great hive of hilarious and affectionate bees. At first David and I stood apart, feeling rather in the way, but Phebe told the story of our mishap and introduced us with such goodwill that the family circle took us in at once.

"The young people soon went to romp in the barn, and the men, armed with umbrellas, turned out en masse to inspect the farm and stock and compare notes over pigpens and garden gates. But I was so enraptured with the wilderness of babies that I followed the matrons to Patience's room and gave myself up, body and soul, to the small people, who swarmed over me, tugging at my hair, exploring my eyes, covering me with moist kisses, and keeping up a babble of little voices, more delightful to me than the discourse of their mamas. A very pretty scene we made of it, for each baby was laid on Grandma's knee, its small virtues, vices, ailments, and accomplishments rehearsed; its beauties praised, its strength tested, and the verdict of the family oracle pronounced as it was cradled, kissed, and blessed on the kind old heart which had room for every care and joy of those who called her 'Mother.' It was a sight I never shall forget, for just then I was ready to receive and profit by it. Our best lessons seldom come from books, Kate, and I learned one then, as I saw the fairest success of a woman's life while watching this happy grandmother with fresh faces framing her faded one, daughterly voices chorusing good wishes, and the harvest of half a century of wedded life beautifully garnered in her arms."

Sallie sewed quietly for many minutes, and I gave no sign of disapproval or impatience, for she looked so earnest, womanly, and sweet, it was too pretty a picture to spoil by a word. I was just sinking into a little daydream of my own when romance was effectually routed by my friend's continuing abruptly:

"The fragrance of coffee broke up the maternal conclave, and the babies were extinguished in blankets, where they were expected to simmer till called for. The women unpacked baskets, brooded over teapots, and kept up a harmonious clack while the table was covered with pyramids of cake, regiments of pies, quagmires of jelly, and bread and butter ad libitum. I really believe every article of food, from baked beans to wedding cake, found a place upon that board, which certainly had a good excuse for groaning. Finding that there were hands enough, I ran away to the barn, in which chaos seemed to have come again. The offshoots had been as fruitful as the parent tree, and some four dozen young immortals were in full riot, the boys whooping, the girls screaming, as if their spirits had reached an explosive pitch and must find vent in noise. Fred was in his element—introducing new games, joining in the old, and keeping the fun a-going—for rosy girls were abundant, and the ancient uniform and its wearer found favor in their eyes. David sat on a milking stool, with a flock of children about him listening with breathless interest to the fairy tales he told. I thought he had never looked so well or happy as he did sitting there, with a little lass on either knee and one, more confiding than the rest, with an arm about his neck, a curly head upon his shoulder, for Grandpa's clothes seemed to invest the wearer with a passport to their affections."

"Of course you joined that party and made a fairy tale to suit yourself, which ended, as all such nonsense usually does, 'and so they were married and lived happily all the days of their lives,'" said I.

"Something very like that, Kate, though I scolded myself all the while and was glad when the toot of a horn sent the whole flock streaming into the house like a brood of hungry chickens. By some process known only to mothers of large families, everyone was wedged close about the table, and the feast began. This was none of your stand-up, wafery-bread-and-butter teas, but a thoroughgoing, sit-down supper, and all settled themselves with a smiling satisfaction prophetic of great appetites and a firm determination to gratify them. I joined a detachment of girls drawn up behind Grandma to act as waiters and did my best to be 'a neat-handed Phillis,' though at first rather bewildered by the gastronomic performances I beheld. Babies ate pickles; boys sequestered pie with a rapidity that made me wink; women appeared to swim in tea and the men to bolt everything edible with a tranquil voracity that took my appetite away, while the host and hostess beamed upon one another and their robust descendants with an honest pride beautiful to see.

"'That Mr. What's-his-name don't eat scursely anything, but jest sets lookin' round, sort of 'mazed like. Do go beg him to fall to on something, or I shan't take a mite of comfort in my supper,' said Grandma, as I went to her with an empty cup. She meant David, and suspecting how he felt, I answered as one having authority:

"'He is enjoying himself with all his heart and eyes, ma'am, and can't find time to eat, for he never saw such a fine sight as this before. However, I'll take him something he likes, and make him eat it, for the poor fellow must be very hungry.'

"'Bless me! You're to be Miss What's-his-name, be you? Well, now, I'd no idee of it,' said the old lady, quick to catch the change in my voice as I spoke of David. So I said primly:

"'Nor I. We are only friends, ma'am.'

"'Oh!' and the monosyllable was immensely expressive as the old lady confided a wise little nod to the big coffeepot into whose depths she was peering.

"When I came to David, he looked up with an expression I had never seen upon his face before, and through the cordial interest of his tone there seemed to flow an undercurrent of regret as he said, glancing down the table:

"'This is a sight worth living eighty hard years to see, and I envy this old couple as I never thought to envy anyone. To rear ten virtuous children, to put ten useful men and women into the world and give them health and courage to work out their own salvation, as these honest souls will do, is a work to be proud of, a fortune to enjoy here and hereafter. Let us drink their health and take example by them.'

"He put the glass of milk I had brought him to my lips, drank what I left, and turned to help a clamorous boy to his seventh piece of pie, while I walked away, feeling, as he looked, in a half-pleasurable, half-painful mood of doubt and desire, hope and regret."

III

"All things must have an end, even a family feast, and by the time the last lad's buttons peremptorily declared, 'Thus far shalt thou go and no farther,' all professed themselves satisfied, and a general uprising followed. The surplus population were herded in parlor and chamber, while a few brisk hands cleared away and left Grandma's premises as immaculate as ever. It was dark when all was done, so the kitchen was made ready, the candles lighted on the walls, the door of Patience's room set open, and little Nat established in an impromptu orchestra, made of a table and chair, whence the first squeak of his fiddle announced that the ball had begun.

"Everybody danced. The babies, piled on Patience's bed or penned behind chairs, sprawled and pranced in unsteady mimicry of their elders. Ungainly farmers, stiff with labor, tramped their best and swung their wives about with kindly pressures of the hands that had worked so long together. Little couples toddled gravely through the figures or frisked promiscuously in a grand conglomeration of arms and legs. Gallant cousins kissed pretty cousins at exciting periods and were not rebuked. Fred brought several of these incipient lovers to a pitch of despair by his devotion to the comeliest damsels and the skill with which he executed unheard-of evolutions before their admiring eyes. My David led out the poorest and the plainest women with a kindly courtesy that caused their homely faces to shine and their scant skirts to be forgotten. I danced with sticky-fingered boys, drowsy with repletion but bound to last it out; rough-faced men who paid me paternal compliments; and one ambitious youth who confided to me his burning desire to work a sawmill and marry a girl with yellow hair. While perched aloft, little Nat bowed away till his pale face glowed, till all hearts warmed and all feet beat responsive to the good old tunes that have put so much health into human bodies, so much happiness into human souls. I wish you'd been there, Kate; it would have just suited you.

"At the stroke of nine the last dance came. All down the long kitchen stretched two smiling rows—Grandpa and Grandma at the top, the youngest pair of walking grandchildren at the bottom, and all between fathers and mothers, uncles, aunts, and cousins, while such of the babies as were still extant bobbed with unabated vigor, as Nat struck up the Virginia Reel and the old couple led off as gallantly as the young one who came blundering up to meet them. Away they went, Grandpa's white hair flying in the wind, Grandma's impressive cap awry with excitement, as they ambled down the middle and finished their tuneful journey with a kiss, amid great applause from those who regarded that as the crowning event of the day.

"When all had had their turn, a short lull took place, with refreshments for such as still possessed the power of enjoying them. Then Phebe appeared with an armful of books, and all settled themselves for the family 'sing.' I have heard much fine music, but never any that touched me more than this, for, though often discordant, it was hearty, with that undertone of feeling which adds power to the simplest air and is often more attractive than the most florid ornament or faultless execution. Everyone sang, as they had danced, with all their might—shrill children, soft-voiced girls, lullaby-singing mothers, gruff lads, and strong-lunged men. The old pair quavered, and still a few indefatigable babies crowed behind their little coops. Ballads, comic songs, popular airs, and hymns followed each other in rapid succession; and when they ended with that song which should be classed with hymns for association's sake and, standing hand in hand about the room, with the golden bride and bridegroom in their midst, sang 'Home,' I listened with dim eyes and a heart too full to sing.

"Still standing so when the last note died, the old man folded his hands and began to pray. Kate, I never heard a prayer like that before; for, though ungrammatical, inelegant, and long, it seemed a quiet talk with God—manly in its confession of shortcomings, childlike in its appeal for guidance, fervent in its gratitude for all good gifts, chiefly the crowning one of loving children. As if close intercourse had made them familiar, this human father turned to the Divine as those sons and daughters turned to him, as free to ask, as confident of a reply when all afflictions, blessings, cares, and crosses were laid down before Him and the work of fifty years submitted to His hand. There were no sounds in the room but the one voice, often tremulous with emotion and with age, the coo of some dreaming baby, or the low sob of some mother whose arms were empty, as the old man stood there with the old wife at his side, a circle of children girdling them around, and in all hearts the thought that as the former wedding had been for time, this golden one at eighty must be for eternity.

"'Now, my children, you must go before the little folks are tuckered out,' said Grandpa, in the pause that followed his amen. 'Mother and I can't say enough toe thank you for the presents you have fetched us, the dutiful wishes you have give us, the pride and comfort you have allers ben toe us. I ain't no hand at speeches, so I shan't make none, but jest say straight out from my heart, ef any affliction falls on any of you, remember Mother's here to help you bear it; ef any worldly loss comes toe you, remember Father's house is yourn while it stans; and so the Lord bless and keep us all.'

"'Three cheers for Gramper and Gramma!' roared a six-foot scion as a safety valve for sundry unmasculine emotions which oppressed him, and three rousing hurrahs made the rafters ring, struck terror to the heart of the oldest inhabitant of the rat-haunted garret, and summarily woke all the babies. Then the good-byes began; the flurry of wrong baskets and bundles in wrong places; the sorting of small folk, too sleepy to know or care what became of them; the maternal cluckings and paternal shouts for missing Kittys, Bens, Bills, and Mary Anns; the piling into vehicles, with much ramping of indignant horses unused to such late hours; the last farewells, the roll of wheels, as one by one the happy loads departed and peace fell upon the homestead for another year.

"'I declare for't, I never had such an out-and-out good time sense I was born into the world,' exclaimed Grandma, as we lingered around her. 'Come, Moses, let's set down and talk it over with Patience 'fore we go to bed.'

"The old couple got into their chairs, and as they sat there side by side, Mary crept behind them and, in that splendid voice of hers, sang the fittest song for time and place—'John Anderson, My Jo.' It was too much for Grandma: The old heart overflowed, and reckless of the cherished cap, she laid her head on her 'John's' shoulder, saying, through her tears:

"'That's the cap sheaf of the hull, and I can't hear no more tonight. Moses, lend me your hankchif, for I don't know where mine is and my face is all of a drip.'

"Before the red bandanna had gently performed its office in Grandpa's hand, Mary was gone. But as I lingered on the stairs, while Phebe brought a candle, I saw David bend his tall head and kiss the white-haired bride as if she were his mother."

"Then you went to bed and dreamed delightfully about your own golden wedding, didn't you, Sallie?"

"I did not dream because I did not sleep. But I saw my great mistake, repented of it, and soon received my reward.

Next morning, when we left the kind old people, to walk home in the early dawn, I found Mary so uncommonly fond of her brother that she took him to herself and kept so far before us that David and I were quite alone. We talked freely of the happy family and the pleasant home scene we left behind, till both of us grew enthusiastic in our praise of domestic life, entirely forgetful of former conversations. The lovely morning, full of sweet sounds, dewy freshness, and rosy light, seemed to soften and allure us both; and when David looked down at me, saying, with the smile that always made his grave face so benign, 'Sallie, I think we have both changed our minds,' my heart began to beat, but I looked up and answered soberly:

"'I think we have.'

"Neither of us spoke for several minutes as we paused on a little knoll to watch the sun climb up behind the hill. As the great ball of fire wheeled into sight, bathing earth and sky in a golden glory, David turned to me with a look that needed no words, and offered me his hand. I put mine into it, and holding each other fast, we stood together very quiet, very happy, while the sun rose on a new world for us."

"Ten years hence I'll ask you how you like that new world; for golden glories have a tendency to fade, and wedded life is not all a summer-morning walk, Sallie."

My words brought no shadows to my friend's happy face as she looked out with a trustful, hopeful glance upon the lover waiting for her at the gate and answered tranquilly:

"David will be with me."

"Go to your David, then, and leave the buttonholes to me. That is all old maids are good for."

LOST IN A PYRAMID;
OR, THE MUMMY'S CURSE

"And what are these, Paul?" asked Evelyn, opening a tarnished gold box and examining its contents curiously.

"Seeds of some unknown Egyptian plant," replied Forsyth, with a sudden shadow on his dark face as he looked down at the three scarlet grains lying in the white hand lifted to him.

"Where did you get them?" asked the girl, inhaling the soft and subtle perfume which seemed to come from them.

"That is a weird story, which will only haunt you if I tell it," said Forsyth, with an absent expression that strongly excited the girl's curiosity.

"Please tell it. I like weird tales, and they never trouble me. Ah, do tell it. Your stories are always so interesting," she cried, looking up with such a pretty blending of entreaty and command in her charming face that refusal was impossible.

"You'll be sorry for it, and so shall I, perhaps. I warn you beforehand that harm is foretold to the possessor of those mysterious seeds," said Forsyth, smiling even while he knit his black brows and regarded the blooming creature before him with a fond yet foreboding glance.

"Tell on, I'm not afraid of these pretty atoms," she answered, with an imperious nod.

37

"To hear is to obey. Let me read the facts, and then I will begin," returned Forsyth, pacing to and fro with the far-off look of one who turns the pages of the past.

Evelyn watched him for a moment and then returned to her work, or play, rather, for the task seemed well suited to the vivacious little creature, half child, half woman.

"While in Egypt," commenced Forsyth slowly, "I went one day with my guide and Professor Niles to explore the Cheops. Niles had a mania for antiquities of all sorts and forgot time, danger, and fatigue in the ardor of his pursuit. We rummaged up and down the narrow passages, half choked with dust and close air, reading inscriptions on the walls, stumbling over shattered mummy cases, or coming face-to-face with some shriveled specimen perched like a hobgoblin on the little shelves where the dead used to be stowed away for ages. I was desperately tired after a few hours of it, and begged the professor to return. But he was bent on exploring certain places, and would not desist. We had but one guide, so I was forced to stay; but Jumal, my man, seeing how weary I was, proposed to us to rest in one of the larger passages, while he went to procure another guide for Niles. We consented, and assuring us that we were perfectly safe if we did not quit that spot, Jumal left us, promising to return speedily. The professor sat down to take notes of his researches, and stretching myself on the soft sand, I fell asleep.

"I was roused by that indescribable thrill which instinctively warns us of danger, and springing up, I found myself alone. One torch burned faintly where Jumal had stuck it, but Niles and the other light were gone. A dreadful sense of loneliness oppressed me for a moment; then I collected myself and looked well about me. A bit of paper was pinned to my hat, which lay near me, and on it, in the professor's writing, were these words:

"'I've gone back a little to refresh my memory on certain points. Don't follow me till Jumal comes. I can find my way back to you, for I have a clue. Sleep well, and dream gloriously of the Pharaohs. —N. N.'

"I laughed at first over the old enthusiast. Then I felt anxious, then restless, and finally resolved to follow him; for I discovered a strong cord fastened to a fallen stone, and knew that this was the clue he spoke of. Leaving a line for Jumal, I took my torch and retraced my steps, following the cord along the winding ways. I often shouted, but received no reply, and pressed on, hoping at each turn to see the old man poring over some musty relic of antiquity. Suddenly the cord ended, and lowering my torch, I saw that the footsteps had gone on.

"'Rash fellow, he'll lose himself, to a certainty!' I thought, really alarmed now.

"As I paused, a faint call reached me, and I answered it, waited, shouted again, and a still-fainter echo replied.

"Niles was evidently going on, misled by the reverberations of the low passages. No time was to be lost, and forgetting myself, I stuck my torch in the deep sand to guide me back to the clue and ran down the straight path before me, whooping like a madman as I went. I did not mean to lose sight of the light, but in my eagerness to find Niles I turned from the main passage and, guided by his voice, hastened on. His torch soon gladdened my eyes, and the clutch of his trembling hands told me what agony he had suffered.

"'Let us get out of this horrible place at once,' he cried, wiping the great drops off his forehead.

"'Come, we are not far from the clue. I can soon reach it, and then we are safe.' But as I spoke, a chill passed over me, for a perfect labyrinth of narrow paths lay before us.

"Trying to guide myself by such landmarks as I had observed in my hasty passage, I followed the tracks in the sand till I fancied we must be near my light. No glimmer appeared, however, and kneeling down to examine the footprints nearer, I discovered to my dismay that I had been following the wrong ones, for among those marked by a deep boot heel were prints of bare feet. We had had no guide there, and Jumal wore sandals.

"Rising, I confronted Niles with the one despairing word 'Lost!' as I pointed from the treacherous sand to the fast-waning light.

"I thought the old man would be overwhelmed, but to my surprise, he grew quite calm and steady, thought a moment, then went on, saying quietly:

"'Other men have passed here before us. Let us follow their steps, for if I do not greatly err, they lead toward the great passages where one's way is easily found.'

"On we went, bravely, till a misstep threw the professor violently to the ground with a broken leg and nearly extinguished the torch. It was a horrible predicament, and I gave up all hope as I sat beside the poor fellow, who lay exhausted with fatigue, remorse, and pain, for I would not leave him.

"'Paul,' he said suddenly, 'if you will not go on, there is one more effort we can make. I remember hearing that a party, lost as we are, saved themselves by building a fire. The smoke penetrated further than sound or light, and the guide's quick wit understood the unusual mist; he followed it and rescued the party. Make a fire, and trust to Jumal.'

"'A fire without wood?' I began, but he pointed to a shelf behind me, which had escaped me in the gloom, and on it I saw a slender mummy case. I understood him, for these dry cases, which lie about in hundreds, are freely used as firewood. Reaching up, I pulled it down, believing it to be empty, but as it fell, it burst open, and out rolled a mummy. Accustomed as I was to such sights, it startled me a little, for danger had unstrung my nerves. Laying the little brown chrysalis aside, I smashed up the case, lit the pile with my torch, and soon a light cloud of smoke drifted down the three passages which diverged from the cell-like place where we had paused.

"While busied with the fire, Niles, forgetful of pain and

peril, had dragged the mummy nearer and was examining it with the interest of a man whose ruling passion was strong even in death.

"'Come and help me unroll this. I have always longed to be the first to see and secure the curious treasures put away among the folds of these uncanny winding sheets. This is a woman, and we may find something rare and precious here,' he said, beginning to unfold the outer covers, from which a strange aromatic odor came.

"Reluctantly I obeyed, for to me there was something sacred in the bones of this unknown woman. But to beguile the time and amuse the poor fellow, I lent a hand, wondering, as I worked, if this dark, ugly thing had ever been a lovely, soft-eyed Egyptian girl.

"From the fibrous folds of the wrappings dropped precious gums and spices, which half-intoxicated us with their potent breath; antique coins; and a curious jewel or two, which Niles eagerly examined.

"All the bandages but one were cut off at last, and a small head laid bare, around which still clung great plaits of what had once been luxuriant hair. The shriveled hands were folded on the breast, and clasped in them lay that gold box."

"Ah!" cried Evelyn, dropping it from her rosy palm with a shudder.

"Nay, don't reject the poor little mummy's treasure. I never have quite forgiven myself for stealing it, or for burning her," said Forsyth, painting rapidly, as if the recollection of that experience lent energy to his hand.

"Burning her! Oh, Paul, what do you mean?" asked the girl, sitting up with a face full of excitement.

"I'll tell you. While busied with Madame la Momie, our fire had burned low, for the dry case went like tinder. A faint, far-off sound made our hearts leap, and Niles cried out, 'Pile on the wood; Jumal is tracking us! Don't let the smoke fail now, or we are lost!'

"'There is no more wood. The case was very small and is all gone,' I answered, tearing off such of my garments as would burn readily and piling them upon the embers.

"Niles did the same, but the light fabrics were quickly consumed and made no smoke.

"'Burn that!' commanded the professor, pointing to the mummy.

"I hesitated a moment. Again came the faint echo of a horn. Life was dear to me. A few dry bones might save us, and I obeyed him in silence.

"A dull blaze sprang up, and a heavy smoke rose from the burning mummy, rolling in volumes through the low passages and threatening to suffocate us with its fragrant mist. My brain grew dizzy, the light danced before my eyes, strange phantoms seemed to people the air, and in the act of asking Niles why he gasped and looked so pale, I lost consciousness."

Evelyn drew a long breath and put away the scented toys from her lap, as if their odor oppressed her.

Forsyth's swarthy face was all aglow with the excitement of his story, and his black eyes glittered as he added, with a quick laugh:

"That's all. Jumal found and got us out, and we both forswore pyramids for the rest of our days."

"But the box—how came you to keep it?" asked Evelyn, eyeing it askance as it lay gleaming in a streak of sunshine.

"Oh, I brought it away as a souvenir, and Niles kept the other trinkets."

"But you said harm was foretold to the possessor of those scarlet seeds," persisted the girl, whose fancy was excited by the tale and who fancied all was not told.

"Among his spoils Niles found a bit of parchment, which he deciphered, and this inscription said that the mummy we had so ungallantly burned was that of a famous sorceress, who bequeathed her curse to whoever should disturb her rest. Of course I don't believe that curse has anything to do with it, but it's a fact that Niles never has prospered from that day. He says it's because he has never recovered from the fall and fright, and I daresay it is so. But I sometimes wonder if I am to share the curse; for I've a vein of superstition in me, and that poor little mummy haunts my dreams still."

A long silence followed the last words. Paul painted mechanically, and Evelyn lay regarding him with a thoughtful face. But gloomy fancies were as foreign to her nature as shadows are to noonday, and presently she laughed a cheery laugh, saying, as she took up the box again:

"Why don't you plant them and see what wondrous flower they will bear?"

"I doubt if they would bear anything after lying in a mummy's hand for centuries," replied Forsyth gravely.

"Let *me* plant them and try. You know wheat has sprouted and grown that was taken from a mummy's coffin—why should not these pretty seeds? I should so like to watch them grow. May I, Paul?"

"No, I'd rather leave that experiment untried. I have a queer feeling about the matter, and don't want to meddle myself or let anyone I love meddle with these seeds. They may be some horrible poison, or possess some evil power, for the sorceress evidently valued them, since she clutched them fast even in her tomb."

"Now, you are foolishly superstitious, and I laugh at you. Be generous; give me one seed, just to learn if it *will* grow. See, I'll pay for it," and Evelyn, who now stood beside him, dropped a kiss on his forehead as she made her request, with the most engaging air.

But Forsyth would not yield. He smiled and returned the embrace with loverlike warmth, then flung the seeds into the fire, and gave her back the golden box, saying tenderly:

"My darling, I'll fill it with diamonds or bonbons, if you please, but I will not let you play with that witch's spells. You've enough of your own, so forget the 'pretty seeds' and see what a Light of the Harem I've made of you."

Evelyn frowned, and smiled, and presently the lovers were

out in the spring sunshine reveling in their own happy hopes, untroubled by one foreboding fear.

II

"I have a little surprise for you, love," said Forsyth, as he greeted his cousin three months later, on the morning of his wedding day.

"And I have one for you," she answered, smiling faintly.

"How pale you are—and how thin you grow! All this bridal bustle is too much for you, Evelyn," he said with fond anxiety, as he watched the strange pallor of her face and pressed the wasted little hand in his.

"I am so tired," she said, and leaned her head wearily on her lover's breast. "Neither sleep, food, nor air gives me strength, and a curious mist seems to cloud my mind at times. Mama says it is the heat, but I shiver even in the sun, while at night I burn with fever. Paul, dear, I'm glad you are going to take me away to lead a quiet, happy life with you, but I am afraid it will be a very short one."

"My fanciful little wife! You are tired and nervous with all this worry, but a few weeks of rest in the country will give us back our blooming Eve again. Have you no curiosity to learn my surprise?" he asked, to change her thoughts.

The vacant look stealing over the girl's face gave place to one of interest, but as she listened, it seemed to require an effort to fix her mind upon her lover's words.

"You remember the day we rummaged in the old cabinet?"

"Yes," and a smile touched her lips for a moment.

"And how you wanted to plant those queer red seeds I stole from the mummy?"

"I remember," and her eyes kindled with sudden fire.

"Well, I tossed them into the fire, as I thought, and gave you the box. But when I went back to cover up my picture and found one of those seeds on the rug, a sudden fancy to gratify your whim led me to send it to Niles and ask him to plant it and report its progress. Today I hear from him for the first time, and he reports that the seed has grown marvelously, has budded, and that he intends to take the first flower, if it blooms in time, to a meeting of famous scientific men, after which he will send me its true name and the plant itself. From his description, it must be very curious, and I'm impatient to see it."

"You need not wait. I can show you the flower in its bloom," and Evelyn beckoned with the *méchant* smile so long a stranger to her lips.

Much amazed, Forsyth followed to her own little boudoir, and there, standing in the sunshine, was the unknown plant. Almost rank in their luxuriance were the vivid green leaves on slender purple stems, and rising from the midst, one ghostly-white flower, shaped like the head of a hooded snake, with scarlet stamens like forked tongues, and on the petals glittered spots like dew.

"A strange, uncanny flower! Has it any odor?" asked Forsyth, bending to examine it and forgetting, in his interest, to ask how it came there.

"None, and that disappoints me. I am so fond of perfumes," answered the girl, caressing the green leaves, which trembled at her touch, while the purple stems deepened their tint.

"Now, tell me about it," said Forsyth, after standing silent for several minutes.

"I had been before you, and secured one of the seeds, for two fell on the rug. I planted it under a glass in the richest soil I could find, watered it faithfully, and was amazed at the rapidity with which it grew when once it appeared above the earth. I told no one, for I meant to surprise you with it; but this bud has been so long in blooming, I have had to wait. It is a good omen that it blossoms today, and as it is nearly white, I mean to wear it, for I've learned to love it, having been my pet so long."

"I would *not* wear it, for in spite of its innocent color, it is an evil-looking plant, with its adder's tongue and unnatural dew. Wait till Niles tells us what it is, then pet it if it is harmless. Perhaps my sorceress cherished it for some symbolic beauty—those old Egyptians were full of fancies. It was very sly of you to turn the tables on me in this way. But I forgive you, since in a few hours I shall chain this mischievous hand forever. How cold it is! Come out into the garden and get some warmth and color for tonight, my love."

But when the night came, no one could reproach the girl with her pallor; for she glowed like a pomegranate flower, her eyes were full of fire, her lips scarlet, and all her old vivacity seemed to have returned. A more brilliant bride never blushed under a misty veil, and when her lover saw her, he was absolutely startled by the almost unearthly beauty which transformed the pale, languid creature of the morning into this radiant woman.

They were married, and if love, many blessings, and all good gifts lavishly showered upon them could make them happy, then this young pair were truly blessed. But even in the rapture of the moment that made her his, Forsyth observed how icy cold was the little hand he held, how feverish the deep color on the soft cheek he kissed, and what a strange fire burned in the tender eyes that looked so wistfully at him.

Blithe and beautiful as a spirit, the smiling bride played her part in all the festivities of that long evening, and when at last light, life, and color began to fade, the loving eyes that watched her thought it but the natural weariness of the hour. As the last guest departed, Forsyth was met by a servant, who gave him a letter marked "Haste." Tearing it open, he read these lines, from a friend of the professor's:

Dear Sir:

Poor Niles died suddenly two days ago while at the Scientific Club, and his last words were, "Tell Paul

Forsyth to beware of the Mummy's Curse, for this fatal flower has killed me." The circumstances of his death were so peculiar that I add them as a sequel to his message. For several months, as he told us, he had been watching an unknown plant, and that evening he brought us the flower to examine. Other matters of interest absorbed us till a late hour, and the plant was forgotten. The professor wore it in his buttonhole—a strange white, serpent-headed blossom with pale glittering spots, which slowly changed to a vivid scarlet till the leaves looked as if sprinkled with blood. It was observed that instead of the pallor and feebleness which had recently come over him, the professor was unusually animated and seemed in an almost unnatural state of high spirits. Near the close of the meeting, in the midst of a lively discussion, he suddenly dropped, as if smitten with apoplexy. He was conveyed home insensible, and after one lucid interval, in which he gave me the message I have recorded above, he died in great agony, raving of mummies, pyramids, serpents, and some fatal curse which had fallen upon him.

After his death, livid scarlet spots, like those on the flower, appeared upon his skin, and he shriveled like a withered leaf. At my desire, the mysterious plant was examined, and pronounced by the best authority one of the most deadly poisons known to the Egyptian sorceresses. The plant slowly absorbs the vitality of whoever cultivates it, and the blossom, worn for two or three hours, produces either madness or death.

Down dropped the paper from Forsyth's hand; he read no further, but hurried back into the room where he had left his young wife. As if worn out with fatigue, she had thrown herself upon a couch, and lay there motionless, her face half hidden by the light folds of the veil, which had blown over it.

"Evelyn, my dearest! Wake up and answer me. Did you wear that strange flower today?" whispered Forsyth, putting the misty screen away.

There was no need for her to answer, for there, gleaming spectrally on her bosom, was the evil blossom, its white petals spotted now with flecks of scarlet, vivid as drops of newly spilled blood.

But the unhappy bridegroom scarcely saw it, for the face above it appalled him by its utter vacancy. Drawn and pallid, as if with some wasting malady, the young face, so lovely an hour ago, lay before him aged and blighted by the baleful influence of the plant which had drunk up her life. No recognition in the eyes, no word upon the lips, no motion of the hand—only the faint breath, the fluttering pulse, and wide-opened eyes betrayed that she was alive.

Alas for the young wife! The superstitious fear at which she had smiled had proved true: The curse that had bided its time for ages was fulfilled at last, and her own hand wrecked her happiness forever. Death in life was her doom, and for years Forsyth secluded himself to tend with pathetic devotion the pale ghost, who never, by word or look, could thank him for the love that outlived even such a fate as this.

MRS. GAY'S PRESCRIPTION

Bang, bang, went the front door as Mr. Bennet and the boys hurried off to store and school, leaving Mrs. Bennet to collect her wits and draw a long breath after the usual morning flurry.

The poor little woman looked as if she needed rest but was not likely to get it. For the room was in a chaotic state; the breakfast table presented the appearance of having been devastated by a swarm of locusts; the baby began to fret; little Polly set up her usual whine of "I want sumpin' to do"; and a pile of work loomed in the corner waiting to be done.

"I don't see how I ever shall get through it all," sighed the despondent matron, as she hastily drank a last cup of tea. Two great tears rolled down her cheeks as she looked from one puny child to the other and felt the weariness of her own tired soul and body more oppressive than ever.

"A good cry" was impending when there came a brisk ring at the door, a step in the hall, and a large, rosy woman came bustling in, saying in a cheery voice, as she set a flowerpot down upon the table, "Good morning! Nice day, isn't it? Came in early on business and brought you one of my Lady Washingtons—you are so fond of flowers."

"Oh, it's lovely! How kind you are. Do sit down, if you can find a chair. We are all behindhand today, for I was up half the night with poor Baby and haven't energy enough to go to work yet," answered Mrs. Bennet, with a sudden smile that changed her whole face, while Baby stopped fretting to stare at the rosy clusters and Polly found employment in exploring the pocket of the newcomer, as if she knew her way there.

"Let me put the pot on your stand first. Girls are so careless, and I'm proud of this. It will be an ornament to your parlor for a week"; and opening a door, Mrs. Gay carried the plant to a sunny bay window where many others were blooming beautifully.

Mrs. Bennet and the children followed to talk and admire, while the servant leisurely cleared the table.

"Now, give me that baby, put yourself in the easy chair, and tell me all about your worries," said Mrs. Gay, in the brisk, commanding way which few people could resist.

"I'm sure I don't know where to begin," sighed Mrs. Bennet, dropping into the comfortable seat, while Baby changed bearers with great composure.

"I met your husband, and he said the doctor had ordered you and these chicks off to Florida for the winter. John said he didn't know how he should manage it, but he meant to try."

"Isn't it dreadful? He can't leave his business to go with me, and we shall have to get Aunt Miranda to come and see to him and the boys while I'm gone, and the boys can't bear her strict, old-fashioned ways. I've got to go that long journey all alone and stay among strangers, and these heaps of fall work to do first, and it will cost an immense sum to send us, and I don't know what is to become of me."

Here Mrs. Bennet stopped for breath, and Mrs. Gay asked briskly, "What is the matter with you and the children?"

"Well, Baby is having a hard time with his teeth and is

croupy, Polly doesn't get over scarlet fever well, and I'm used up—no strength or appetite, pain in my side, and low spirits. Entire change of scene—milder climate and less work for me—is what we want, the doctor says. John is very anxious about us, and I feel regularly discouraged."

"I'll spend the day and cheer you up a bit. You just rest and get ready for a new start tomorrow; it is a saving of time to stop short now and then and see where to begin next. Bring me the most pressing job of work. I can sew and see to this little rascal at the same time."

As she spoke, off went Mrs. Gay's bonnet, and by the time her hostess returned with the overflowing workbasket, the energetic lady had put a match to the ready-laid fire on the hearth; rolled up a couch, table, and easy chair; planted Baby on the rug with a bunch of keys to play with; and sat blooming and smiling herself, as if work, worry, and November weather were not in existence.

"Tot's frocks and Polly's aprons are the things I'm most hurried about. They need so many, and I do like my children to look nice among strangers," began Mrs. Bennet, unrolling yards upon yards of ruffling for the white frocks and pinafores, with a glance of despair at the sewing machine whose click had grown detestable to her ear.

"Make 'em plain if you are in a hurry. Children don't need trimming up; they are prettiest in simple clothes. I can finish off that batch of aprons before dinner, if you will put that ruffling away. Come now, do—it will be a load off your mind, and Polly won't know the difference."

"I always do trim them, and everyone does," began Mrs. Bennet, who was wedded to her idols.

"When I was in London, I saw a duke's children dressed in plain brown linen pinafores, and I thought I'd never seen such splendid babies. Try it, and if people make remarks, bring in the English aristocracy, and it will be all right."

There was a twinkle in Mrs. Gay's eye that made her

friend ashamed to argue, so she laughed and gave up the point, acknowledging with a sigh that it was a relief.

"It is this mania for trimming everything which is wearing out so many women. Necessary sewing is enough; then drop your needle and read, rest, walk, or play with the children, and see how much you have lost heretofore by this everlasting stitching. You'd soon get rid of that pain in your side if you'd let the machine stand idle while you went out for an hour every day."

"Perhaps I should, but I can't leave the children—Biddy is so careless."

"Take them with you. Roll Baby up and down that nice, dry sidewalk and let Polly run before, and you'd be a different set of people in a month."

"Do you really think so?"

"Not only that, but if you'd change your way of living, I don't believe you'd need to think of going to Florida at all."

"Why, Mary Gay, what do you mean?" demanded Mrs. Bennet, sitting erect upon the couch in her surprise at this unexpected remark.

"I have often wanted to say this before, and now I will, though you will think I'm an interfering woman if I do. Never mind; if I can only save you further worry and expense and suffering, I won't mind if you are offended for a time. In the first place, you must move," and Mrs. Gay gave such a decided nod that the other lady could only ejaculate, "Why? Where? When?"

"Because you want more sun and space; into this room, because you will find both; and today, because I'm here to help you."

Mrs. Bennet gave a little gasp and looked about her in dismay at the bare idea of living in her cherished best parlor.

"But the back room does very well," she protested. "It is warm and small and handy to the kitchen, and we always live there."

"No, my dear, it does *not* do very well, for those very reasons. It is *too* warm and small and near the kitchen to make it a fit place to live in, especially for little children. Why don't you put your plants there if it is such a nice place?" asked Mrs. Gay, bent on making a clean sweep of her friend's delusions and prejudices.

"Why, they need more sun and air and room, so I keep them in here."

"Exactly! And your babies need sun and air and room more than your roses, geraniums, and callas. The plants would soon die in that close, hot, dark north room. Do you wonder your babies are pale and fretful and weak? Bring them in here and see how soon they will bloom if you give them a chance."

"I never thought of that. I'm sure I would do anything to see them well and hearty, but it does seem a pity to spoil my nice parlor. Wouldn't the best chamber overhead do as well?"

"I want that too, for your bedroom, and the little one at the side for the children. You use the back chamber now, and have the cribs there also, don't you?"

"Yes. My patience! Mary, would you have me turn my house upside down just for a little more sun?"

"Do you love your best rooms better than your children? Hadn't you rather see them spoiled by daily use than empty and neat because the little busy feet were gone, never to come back? I'm in earnest, Lizzie, and I know you will agree with me when you think it over. My own dear little boy was killed by my ignorance, and I have learned by sad experience that we mothers should make it the study of our lives to keep home healthy and happy for our boys and girls, no matter how much we sacrifice show and fashion. Come now, try it for a month, and see if you don't all feel the better for enjoying the best and sunniest side of life."

Mrs. Bennet's eye wandered around the pretty room and went from Polly singing to herself as she sat looking out of the pleasant window, to Baby contentedly playing bopeep through the bars of the fender with the yellow flames which were his delight, and then came back to her friend's kind, earnest face and seemed to wake with sudden energy and life and resolution.

"I'll try it!" she said, feeling that it was a heroic thing to give up all her cherished ideas and put her Sunday-best things into everyday wear. But Mrs. Gay's words touched and startled her, and with a self-reproachful pang she resolved that it should never be said she loved her plants more than her children, or that her house should ever miss the sweet clamor of baby voices if she had the power to keep that music there.

"Good! I knew you would, and I'm going to show you how easy it will be to change the climate you live in as well as the scene, and lighten your work, and benefit your health without going far away," cried Mrs. Gay, delighted with her success and eager to see her reform well carried out.

"What *will* John say?" and Mrs. Bennet felt inclined both to laugh and to cry at the thought of the coming revolution.

"He will approve. Men always like to have things bright and roomy and nice about them. I've been through it and I know, for when we kept in two rooms, we got careless and narrow and low-spirited. Now we live all over the house and keep everything as bright and pretty and nice as we can. George does not shut himself up in his untidy den, but stays with me; and people drop in, and we have a social, happy time of it, all enjoying our good things freely together and feeling the worth of them."

"How do we begin?" asked Mrs. Bennet, fired with the spirit of emulation now that the first shock was over; for John did shut himself up because the dining room was so full of an evening with two tumultuous boys, and the little woman wanted to see her husband during the only leisure hour she had out of the twenty-four.

"I should just move all the delicate things into the little library there, out of the way of the children. That room is rather bare, and they will make it more attractive. Leave the pictures. They are safe, and it is good to have pretty objects for young eyes to rest upon. Put the covers onto your furniture, a large drugget over your carpet, and take that other bay window for Polly and Baby's play corner. It is sunny and snug, and looking out always amuses them. And at night you can just drop the curtains before the recess and hide their little clutter without disturbing it. In the other window there is room for your table and chair, and close by the machine. There you can sit, as in a bower, with your flowers about you, a pleasant view outside, and everything cheerful, wholesome, and pretty—three very important things to a woman. Keep up the open fire—it is worth a dozen furnaces—and have a thermometer to be sure you don't get too warm. That takes all the strength out of you and makes taking cold easy."

"It wouldn't take long to make the change. John isn't coming home to dinner, so we can be all ready by night, if you really can stop and see me through the job. I declare I feel better already, for I *am* tired to death of that back room and don't wonder Polly is always teasing to 'go in parlor.' The boys will dance for joy to get full swing here. They never are allowed it except Sundays, and then they behave nicely and seem to enjoy the piano and pretty things, and so does John. Yes, I'll do it right away," and up jumped Mrs. Bennet, finding her most powerful impetus in the thought of pleasing "Father and the boys."

Working and talking busily together, the friends soon made the necessary changes below, to the great delight of Polly and the entire bewilderment of Baby, who fell asleep on the best sofa, as if bound to make the most of his comforts while they lasted.

A hasty lunch, and then, with Biddy to lug heavy articles, they rearranged the chambers, making a splendid nursery of the large one and a nice sleeping room of the smaller for the two children.

"Now, you see, you can undress them by this pleasant grate and then put them away in a cool, quiet place to sleep undisturbed by you older people. Only be sure the little mattresses and bedclothes get a good airing and sunning every day. You can shut the door and let them lie for hours, as you couldn't in the back room, and that is a great advantage," said Mrs. Gay, who was in high spirits at carrying everything before her in this fine style.

"It is lucky we seldom have guests to sleep in winter, for that north room isn't at all my ideal of a best chamber, though we have put some of my pretty things there. I feel like company myself in here, and John won't know what to do with so much space, I've kept him cramped so long. It does seem a shame to shut up this big room and not enjoy it. Mary, I have been a goose, and I'm glad you came and told me so."

Contented with that confession, Mrs. Gay kissed her convert, and leaving Biddy to finish off, she took her departure, with many last injunctions about "air, oatmeal, brown living, and sunshine."

When Mr. Bennet and the boys, who had been enjoying a holiday, came home to tea, amazement fell upon them at the sight of Mama and the babies waiting in the new sitting room with the announcement that there was not going to be any best parlor anymore.

When the events of the day had been explained and discussed, a sort of jubilee ensued; for all felt that a pleasant change in the domestic atmosphere had taken place, and all enjoyed it immensely. Mr. Bennet played and the boys and Polly danced and Papa frolicked with Baby, who forgot his teeth and crowed gleefully till bedtime.

Of course Mr. Bennet had his joke about women's notions and his doubts as to the success of the plan. But anything that cheered up his wife pleased him; for his heart sank at the thought of home without her, and Florida was a most distasteful idea to him. He expressed much satisfaction at his improved quarters, however, and that repaid Mrs. Bennet for the sacrifice she had made, though he, being a man, could never know how great a one it was.

It took some time to get fairly settled, but the sunny side of things grew more and more delightful as the change of scene and better influences did their quiet work. The children soon showed the effects of the daily sunshine, the well-aired chambers, simpler food, and cheerful play place allotted to them, for these little creatures show as quickly as flowers their susceptibility to natural laws. Polly was never tired of looking out of the window at the varying phases of street life, and her observations thereupon gave her mother many a hearty laugh.

Baby throve like a dandelion in spring, though infantile ills occasionally vexed his happy soul; for the mistaken training of months could not be rectified all at once, nor teething made easy.

Mrs. Bennet had her moments of regret as she saw the marks of little fingers on her paint and furniture, watched the fading of her carpet, and labored vainly to impress upon the boys that whittling, ball, and marbles had better be confined to the dining room. But the big, pleasant parlor was so inviting, with the open fire, the comfortable chairs, flowers, babies, work, and play, that no one could resist the charm, and tired Papa found it so attractive that he deserted the library set apart for him and spent his evenings in the bosom of his family, to his wife's great delight.

People got into the way of dropping in, not for a formal call in the prim best parlor, but a social visit with gossip and games, music, or whatever was going on, and soon it was generally agreed that the Bennets' house was the pleasantest in the neighborhood.

The doctor's standing joke was, "Well, ma'am, are you

ready for Florida?" and the answer, with ever-increasing decision, was, "I guess we can get on a little while longer without it."

It certainly seemed as if the chief invalid could, and now that the sewing machine had long rests and the ducal linen aprons needed only a bit of braid to finish them off, Mrs. Bennet found many a half hour to practice, read, walk with the children, and help the boys with lessons or play. In the evening it soon came to be a habit to clear up the parlor, get the babies cozily to bed, make herself neat and pretty, and be ready to show Papa a cheerful face when he came home. For, being no longer worn out with unnecessary stitching, languid for want of exercise, and nervous for the need of something to break the monotony of a busy housemother's life, she had spirits to enjoy a social hour, and found it very sweet to be the center of a happy little circle who looked to her for the sunshine of home.

"Some of us *must* go to Florida to get well, but a great many people might save their time and money and make a land of flowers for themselves out of the simplest materials, if they only knew how," said Mrs. Gay when the Bennets thanked her for the advice which did so much good, and everyone agreed with her.

JOHN MARLOW'S VICTORY

The Reverend John Marlow was preaching one of his most brilliant sermons, and his congregation listened with rapt attention. As is usual when the minister is a young and comely man, a large proportion of his hearers were women, and it is little wonder that he felt the inspiration of that array of sympathetic faces—as sensitive to varying emotions as a bed of flowers to the wind that sways them. A delightful yet dangerous excitement for a man like John Marlow—this weekly display of his unusual gifts, this weekly test of his power to move and win the devout and tender hearts that found religion wonderfully attractive as presented by their eloquent young pastor.

His own face was a study, to such as had the skill to read it, for it was one of those countenances which betray the divided nature of the man and irresistibly arouse the observer's curiosity as to which will ultimately win—good or evil. The upper part was very fine. A noble brow, a commanding eye, an expression of intellect and aspiration, courage and ardor, illuminated the whole face at times, betraying the splendid possibilities of this man. But when the high mood passed, one saw that the lips which uttered such spiritual truths were the pleasure-loving lips of one to whom it would be easier to preach than to practice holy living. The handsome chin was weak, and all the lines of the lower face lacked refinement. But there were few to understand the significance of this countenance; for the glow of emotion transformed it, the melodious voice called out its persuasive periods with effect, and it was impossible to watch the native grace and vigor of the man without yielding to the spell of temperament and talent.

Although his eye was not seen to dwell on any one face among the many upturned to his, there were two of which he never lost sight, and these two unconsciously represented the good and evil powers contending that day for John Marlow's soul.

Both were women's faces—both full of an undisguisable interest in the pastor and each other; both conscious of the covert observation of their neighbors, as if some peculiar tie bound the three. One was a woman of thirty, of the true New England type: slender, pale, and serious, with the broad brow, sincere eyes, firm mouth, and air of mingled strength and sweetness which mark the women who think as well as love, achieve as well as suffer. A little cold in manner and reserved in speech, but true as steel and capable of ardor, passion even, when the moment comes. Simply dressed, quiet and intent she sat, with a bright-faced boy on either side leaning against her, as if finding rest for their unrest in the patient motherliness which made a reposeful atmosphere about her.

The other woman's beauty seemed the more brilliant for the weeds she wore, since grief had left no trace and life was in its prime. A seductive, yet a heartless face, for there were hard lines underneath the bloom. Love of power was there, and love of ease; worldly wisdom and the wiles that bend all things to one selfish end. A keen eye, a restless mouth, and a devout air, belied by the sidelong glances shot now and then from under the demure lids, so often dropped in pensive thought.

"A splendid effort. A most gifted man, with a grand future before him," said an enthusiastic stranger, as the congregation slowly filtered out, as if loath to break the spell.

"If he does not ruin it by a false step at the outset," answered the gray-headed parishioner who was doing the honors of his church. "Too much adulation is the rock on which so many promising ministers go to wreck, and these dear, pious women are the Loreleis who lure them to destruction. John Marlow stands in a slippery place, and must look well to his steps, or he will fall—and he knows it."

"Hush! His wife is just behind us," whispered the lady on the speaker's arm, as she hastened her steps with a troubled air.

But the wife heard, and so did the handsome widow, waiting near to whisper her thanks and praises with eyes that said more than lips dared utter. The effect of that speech upon the two women was curiously diverse, for Mrs. Marlow's quiet face kindled with a sudden flush of mingled pain and pride, as if the words had touched some secret wound, while the widow's bloom paled a little as she dropped her veil to hide the conscious smile which betrayed her. Nor was that all, for Mrs. Marlow, instead of waiting, as she usually did, went to meet her husband, took his arm, and led him past the veiled figure, with no pause, no greeting but a bow.

John Marlow wondered at the gentle urgency of the hand upon his arm, but he instinctively obeyed it. His wife tried to believe that the brilliant eyes behind the veil flashed no warning or defiance in the glance she met; but she remembered it, and the pair walked down the aisle, with the pretty boys going hand in hand before them, the dark figure following, noiseless and somber as a shadow, and both were uncomfortably conscious of it.

"What are you thinking of, Mary?" asked the husband, suddenly seeming to remember her after a long silence, as they went home together through the gray November weather.

"Of something I heard coming out of church, which troubled me," she answered, with the gentle sincerity native to her; and she repeated the words which conveyed a warning she too often longed of late to utter.

John Marlow flushed and smiled, but did not meet his wife's eyes, and ended his reply with a weary sort of sigh.

"My good deacon need not be anxious about me. What he calls danger is only one form of the stimulant all brain work craves, and far less hurtful than that which some men use. Heaven knows I have worked long and hard for my success, and no one need grudge it to me now."

"No one does, dear, but the wise old man knows that sudden sunshine after darkness dazzles the eyes and makes the feet unsteady. You *have* earned your success, and for that reason those who love and honor you want it to be the most genuine and enduring sort. It will be if in our prosperity we hold fast the integrity that has kept us patient, brave, and happy all these hard years."

A little quiver in the earnest voice, a sudden dew in the tender eyes, was the only sign she gave of the keen anxiety which had haunted her of late. He heard, he saw, and the first pang of remorse showed him where he stood, for memory recalled all he owed the loyal, loving creature at his side and how poor a return he had made her. Instinctively his hand pressed the hand upon his arm, almost like one glad to cling to a sure anchor, conscious of some treacherous undercurrent ready to sweep even a strong swimmer away if once in its grasp.

"We will, Mary! This is not the first slippery road I've walked in safety, with you for my guide. Hold me up, and please God the success *shall* be worth having."

The look he gave her was a cordial to the wifely heart that

trusted even while it trembled, for she knew how strong a hold she had upon the nobler nature of her husband, a hold never threatened till the warmth of prosperity made the weeds that grow in the richest soil spring up luxuriantly.

Poverty and neglect, labor, and an all-sustaining love had fostered the best in him for years. Now wealth and popularity, ease and adulation, were testing the metal of the man and, by showing him how weak he was, taught him the humility which is real strength.

By yielding to many of the lesser temptations which surrounded him, he had paved the way to downfall; else, when the greater trial came, it would have been more manfully resisted. Only the old story, old as Samson and Delilah: a beautiful, unprincipled woman, to whom his duty as pastor led him in the first place, there to be held by every insidious spell such sirens use till sympathy, interest, and admiration ended in the blind infatuation which wrecks so many men. He had been growing conscious of this for some time and had struggled against it, trying to soothe the disquiet of the senses by redoubled mental efforts, which left him weak and weary when the false excitement was over. He knew that unless some manful resolution was taken and manfully kept, the fatal moment would come when he could no longer resist the impulse which all misled natures feel at times to break away from every restraint and, for an hour at least, taste entire freedom. He also knew that such liberty is not worth the price paid for it, such drafts of pleasure sure to leave bitterness upon the lips, and that only by curbing the strong passions can the soul sit secure, the life bear God's scrutiny.

Yet there was a singular and subtle charm about this dallying with danger, this testing of his own courage to face sin and resist, forgetting that one soon loses the power to say, "Get thee behind me," if one pauses to study Satan, in whatever shape he comes.

John Marlow thought that no one saw the perilous pastime in which he had been indulging for some months. But his parishioner's words, his wife's look, that day startled him wide awake, and he felt that the time had come when he must break the spell, whose dangerous power he never fully realized till he felt how much the effort cost him.

"I will see my friend this evening and prepare her delicately for the change which must be made. She will understand why it is best to silence the first breath of gossip, and I can gradually wean myself from the too delightful society of this charming woman before anyone's peace is disturbed."

A wise resolve. How did he keep it?

He went to see "the friend" that evening, as often before; for the beautiful woman had been passing through an experience of religious doubt and investigation, with her pastor for a guide, and he had flattered himself that she was receiving much help and comfort from his ministrations. But he knew now that it was all a sham, that he was learning more than he taught, and that, sweet as the lessons were, the price he must pay for them was his own peace of mind, unless they ended now.

The instant Mrs. Cary's eye fell on him that night, she knew that the crisis had come; but she had so often played her part in this sort of emotional drama that she was ready to finish the scene with its appropriate climax. Many motives led her to take unusual interest in this role; for she had seldom found a subject harder to subdue, more worth the subduing, and John Marlow was not a man to be lightly set aside when once the dormant fire was kindled. She could not resist the desire to try her power to the utmost; for she knew that another woman had a holier right to this heart, that anxious eyes watched her, that patient prayers went up against her as a true and tender soul struggled with her for the integrity of this man, and in the conflict she found excitement for an empty and embittered life. That reproachful glance, that decisive act in the church, seemed a mute defiance, and the words she overheard told her that it was time to end this episode by a prudent retreat before other tongues began to wag, or to complete her conquest by showing this deluded parish how poor an idol they had been devoutly worshiping.

Divining his purpose at a glance, she chose to take the first step herself and by an effective stroke break down the last barrier between them; for hitherto they had preserved the utmost decorum in word and act, while the subtle language of eye and tone, the silent magnetism of beauty and presence, made these interviews doubly dangerous and delightful. Before John Marlow could touch upon his delicate and distasteful errand, she destroyed his composure and filled him with dismay by the abrupt announcement:

"I am glad you come, for I am going away."

"Going! Where?"

"I scarcely know. The world is all before me where to choose."

"But why?" And he held his breath to hear the answer, which came with a look and tone that made it bittersweet.

"I go because I am tired of the narrow circle in which I could not have lived so long if it had not been for you. I can never pay my debt of gratitude, but I am trying to do it. And so I go away before your friendship costs too much."

"Who has dared?" began John Marlow with kindling eyes, then stopped, lest he should say too much.

"Do not feign ignorance, nor try to keep me. I can go and find happiness elsewhere; but you are tied here, and nothing must make your bondage more irksome. I understand you better than these good people, for I sympathize in the free spirit now so cramped by duty, position, and the prejudices of those you serve; and I will prove myself a true friend by leaving you to your work with an undivided mind, hard as I find the task."

These words, uttered rapidly, with appealing eyes, trembling lips, and a white hand laid upon his own, as if to check the poorly simulated indignation under which he tried to veil his dismay, made John Marlow's resolution waver, though he vainly endeavored to strengthen it by assuming a courage he did not possess.

"I should be very foolish to let you pay so high a price for the little it has been my happiness to do for you. I will not permit you to banish yourself for so poor a reason as this. Stay, to prove that a friendship like ours is too sincere to be frightened away by a breath of foolish gossip."

"It is not that alone. I must go. I shall be happier away, and you will find a safer friend—a truer one you can never have."

Her voice broke there, and she turned her face aside, lest it should betray too much. But the silence was more eloquent than words. The averted countenance touched and troubled the man's heart more dangerously than blushes, tears, or looks of tender anguish.

John Marlow felt the rush of a coming impulse and tried to stay it by a seeming assent to the separation this half-uttered avowal made imperative.

"Go, then. I will not try to keep you by a word. But tell me *where* you go, for I cannot bear to lose all knowledge of one in whom I have taken so sincere an interest and tried to serve in my poor way. I endeavored to console and teach you. If I have added another sorrow or proved a false guide, forgive me, and be sure I shall atone for it by greater pain and more lasting regret than any you can feel."

She looked up then and for an instant hesitated, while there was yet time; for in the agitated face before her, the vain attempt to do a hard duty manfully, she saw an unconscious appeal to her for help to be true and was half tempted to answer the appeal against herself. But that glance also showed her so much that women prize, she could not resist the desire to subjugate the power, peace, and freedom of one so richly gifted; for it needed but a word now to over-throw the last defense of a citadel already undermined.

With a magical change of the mobile face from softness to something like exultation, the gesture of one throwing off some irksome restraint, she said, in a tone that made her hearer's nerves thrill in response:

"You ask where I am going, and I will answer truly, though my frankness may disappoint and disgust you. I am not hypocrite enough to feign longer a sorrow I do not feel. My marriage was a loveless one, as you know. My year of mourning is over. I have sacrificed enough to custom and decorum. My long captivity makes freedom exquisitely sweet, and I will revel in it, for I have been defrauded of my youth. The pent-up energies of an ardent nature shall have vent at last. It may sound reckless, unwise, wicked even; but I am tired of the dull, pale, narrow life which satisfies most women, and I want to follow where my instincts lead me. Why not? Who will care? Who has the right to control me now? I am free at last, and I will enjoy life to the uttermost!"

She sprang up and walked fast through the room, as if to rest limbs cramped by fetters which had lately fallen off; and as she walked, she looked backward, with that new expression in her flushed and kindled face making it far more seductive than its former demure coquetry or appealing sadness. No lure she could have used would have been as effective as this unexpected confession, for it roused all the lawless impulses that lay dormant in the man; and by painting the life she chose, she made the life she left doubly distasteful by force of contrast. She was going, but he must stay, to find existence all the colder and more colorless for the romance which had lent enchantment to reality. By no word did she link her fate with his; but even as she went from him, her eye said "Come!" and Fancy, turning traitor, pictured a future that intoxicated for the moment. As she paused at the far end of the room, he took a step, as if to join her, then checked himself on the brink of a mad impulse, with doubt, desire, and despair all tugging at his heart.

"I am not disappointed. I am glad your bondage is over. I wish to God mine was also, or I dared to break away!"

She came slowly back, with a smile on her face, a smile full of the pity that stings pride; and there was a touch of contempt in her voice, which changed to a regretful softness, infinitely suggestive.

"You have chosen your career and fought hard to secure the success men covet. Rest content with it, if you can. I am a poor, weak woman, who values happiness more than fame and, being denied love, consoles herself with liberty. Now you know me as I am, and since our friendship is unsafe, be wise. Let me drift away a waif, as I came, and forget that we ever met."

"That is impossible."

She had offered her hand as she spoke. He held it fast and looked into her face, with no attempt to conceal the passion in his own, as she stood so still, so near that she could hear the loud beating of his heart. Only an instant—then, with a vain attempt to free the hand from his close grasp, she whispered in a broken voice:

"Now we must part. Good night, good-bye!"

"Not good-bye. I shall see you again?"

"I go tomorrow."

"Alone?"

"Alone."

A very strange and fateful pause ensued as they stood, mute and pale, eye to eye, while some purpose neither dared to utter shaped itself in silence. Then, in strong contrast to the intense emotion hidden under an unnatural quietude of manner, they parted, with no farewell but the whispered echo of their own words, uttered with ominous significance.

"I shall see you again?"

"Tomorrow."

II

The bell rang sharply as Mrs. Marlow sat at work in the early afternoon of Monday, and being in an anxious mood, she did not wait for the tardy maid, but answered it herself. A blue-coated telegraph boy handed her a yellow envelope, and her fingers closed on it with the thrill of mingled expectation and alarm which seldom fails to warn the receiver of bad news. Involuntarily she turned into her husband's study to give it to him. Then, remembering that he was out, she read the message, with eager eyes, the paper trembling in her hold.

"Merchants' Bank down. Cashier absconded. General smash. Come at once."

Bad news, but evidently not what she had expected; for the hand stopped trembling, and a long sigh of relief seemed to lift the weight of some great dread that had lain heavy on the woman's heart.

"Thank God it is no worse!" she said. "I must tell John and get him off at once. Where can he be?"

She paused on the threshold to bethink herself. Her eye roved around the room, finding in it an air of desolation that struck coldly on her; for that message seemed to have set in motion a more subtle electricity than its own, and every startled sense was doing its best to warn her of impending danger. Heart and brain worked fast as memory flashed a thousand hints along the wires and instinct deciphered them with sudden skill. The fire was out, but on the hearth lay a pile of burned papers; a drawer usually locked stood empty and ajar. John had shut himself up that morning to write his Thanksgiving sermon, but not a line marred the white sheets laid ready on the desk. Usually the gray dressing gown was flung across the easy chair; now it was put away, as if for the long absence of its wearer. Never before had he left her, even for an hour or two, without telling his errand; now he had gone without a word, when and how no one knew.

Perhaps he had received some hint of their loss and slipped quietly away to spare her anxiety and suspense. But as the thought brightened the face fast growing sharp and haggard with quick-coming doubts and fears, the eye that questioned all familiar objects, as if to wring the truth from them, fell upon an envelope lying in the wastepaper basket beside the desk. A delicately scented thing, with nothing on it but the pastor's name, in hurried feminine hand, and a broken seal, with the sentimental motto "I wait"; but a long shiver went through Mrs. Marlow as she read the date of that day, and the paper dropped from her fingers, as if it had burned them. For a moment she clasped her hands before her face to hide the despair in it even from herself. But when she looked up, it was white and calm, as if cut in marble; only in the steadfast eyes there beamed a fire never seen there before.

"I must find John," she said, and swiftly making ready, went away to look for him in the few places he was wont to haunt. He was in none of them, and to the discreet inquiries she made, the answers were always the same: "We have not seen him." She scarcely seemed surprised, but steadily went on, as if she had set herself a certain task and could not rest till it was accomplished.

"This is the last," she said low to herself, as she rang the bell of a fashionable boardinghouse, and held her breath to catch the answer to her question: "Is Mrs. Cary in?"

"She was, but very busy—"

The man got no further, for as the visitor stepped in, a pile of luggage confronted her, with the widow's name upon it.

"I shall detain her but a moment," and straight upstairs went the guest, waiting for no announcement, as if her errand was one of life or death.

It was to her, poor soul! But the heroic moment had come, and she played her part bravely; for nothing but her pallor betrayed the hidden anguish, and there was a smile on her lips as she went to meet her fate.

Startled by the unexpected call, Mrs. Cary could not at once conceal her surprise, though her reception was most gracious, in spite of the hurry and confusion of what was evidently a sudden departure.

"Pardon me for disturbing you, but a telegram requiring immediate attention has come for Mr. Marlow. And after I looked for him at several other places, it occurred to me that he might be here," began the wife, going straight to the point with her accustomed sincerity.

"I have not seen him today." And like an actress ready for her part, the widow drew a mask of amiable solicitude before her own face, while studying that other with covert scrutiny.

"I must look elsewhere, then." But despite her haste, Mrs. Marlow did not go, and, glancing at the confusion of the room, added with intention:

"You are leaving us unexpectedly. Have you too received bad news?"

Her look and air, as well as words, perplexed the widow, seemed to rouse curiosity, and put her off her guard a little; for she said, hastily yet with an irrepressible glimmer of malicious intelligence in her eyes, as she trifled with a folded bit of paper lying on the table before her:

"Yes, I am off, but no bad tidings call me away. I merely follow a whim of my own and, being tired of one place, go to seek another."

"I hope it will be more congenial than this quiet spot. You will have little to regret in leaving us—much to enjoy in the gay world which attracts you. Bon voyage."

Mary Marlow would have been more than a mortal woman if she could have kept a slight touch of contempt out of her voice, a very visible air of relief from her manner, as she bade adieu to one who had been a thorn in her flesh for months. Quick to see and retaliate, Anna Cary gave blow for blow in this woman's battle; and her strokes brought blood, for they were pitiless and pierced an already wounded heart. The malicious glimmer flashed into open defiance, and in her voice, exultation was barely veiled by assumed generosity and pain.

"I have much to regret, for I have enjoyed much, thanks to your husband's kindness. I am grateful for it, and so I go away as soon as the first breath of scandal shows me that my friendship may be harmful to him. I do this cheerfully, because I take with me the solace of knowing that I assure his happiness."

It was an audacious speech, and a cruel one, because of the truth it uttered and the falsehood it concealed. The wife shrank involuntarily, and for an instant the hot color burned in her cheek, as if a blow had smitten it. But the native courage and candor of the woman taught her how to answer the truth and shame the falsehood by ignoring neither.

"You are wise, and I thank you. Self-denial is good for us all, and John will be the happier for practicing it. Perhaps the great loss which has come to us may make all lesser ones easier to bear. For his sake I hope so."

"For his sake let me ask, what loss?" A quick shadow seemed to fall upon the widow's brilliant face, her eyes grew keen, her voice a little hard, as she put the question which sprang to her lips.

To no one else had Mary Marlow told the bad news, but now, obeying the instinct which led her to use every weapon in her power, she answered briefly:

"We have lost all we possess by the failure of the bank, which is ruined by one man's dishonesty."

"All?" echoed the widow sharply, and a frown knit her smooth forehead, for this stroke left her a poor as well as a remorseful lover.

"All but John's salary."

"What a misfortune! How will Mr. Marlow bear it?"

"It *is* a misfortune, and I feel it; but while husband and children are spared to me, I am not troubled. John will bear it bravely. He knows what poverty is, and neither of us fear it, if we can meet it *together*."

As if to gain time for her own swift-working thoughts, the widow said again, with something like real compassion in her tone, for money was her idol:

"But it is terrible to lose one's all by such knavery. It must be a sad blow to you."

"It would be a far sadder one if I were the wife of the unhappy man who has brought such trouble upon many, such disgrace upon himself. My children's fortune is their father's good name, and no man can steal that from him, thank God!"

"But a woman might."

It seemed as if a disappointed devil uttered that sneer, and as if a pitying angel answered, in a voice full of the sweet belief in the divine spark which is salvation for the most degraded.

"No woman would who valued her soul's peace, for such theft is the basest the world knows."

How still the room was for an instant as those two looked at one another. All had been said now, and the next word was to make or mar the future of three lives. One waited with pathetic patience in the eyes that pleaded mutely for the treasure not yet wholly lost. The other, yielding reluctant submission to a nobility she could not imitate, said within herself:

"The game is not worth the candle, since the toy has lost its gilding. I have proved my power over both the woman I respect and the man I despise. Why not be content with this and leave at least one friend behind me?"

As if afraid that the good impulse might desert her as suddenly as it came, Mrs. Cary opened the bit of paper she had been playing with, and offered it to her guest, with an irrepressible smile of triumph, though her voice betrayed the discontent and weariness of those who find forbidden fruit bitter to the taste.

"I wrote today to say farewell. This is the answer I received. It will help you to find your husband, and it may not be too late to save something from the ruin."

Mixed motives prompted the act, a double meaning lurked in the words, and by the light of that day's events Mary Marlow read the true significance of the four lines her eyes devoured at a glance.

Dear Friend,
    Business takes me to L——; but as your train stops there at 3:30, I shall have a moment to see you on your way East.
                                    In haste, J. M.

That was all the little note contained. But the innocent and friendly-seeming words were heavier news than the other message brought her, and the look the wife gave the beautiful woman watching her was such as she might have lifted from the dead body of her husband to the creature who had murdered him. Such love and anguish made that passing fancy show so weak and wicked that it seemed to perish in the fire of a great grief as the note shriveled to ashes in the blaze, where it was flung with a gesture of detestation and despair.

The clock struck three, and as if roused to something like genuine remorse, the widow cried impulsively:

"Go! Go at once, or you will be too late!"

"It will *never* be too late for me to find and save my husband."

The answer rang through the room full of the indomitable courage, the passionate devotion that inspired the wife; and as if the words struck her to the heart, finding there something true and womanly enough to make her shrink from the deed she would have done, the widow stretched her hand to avert the righteous indignation that confronted her, saying brokenly:

"Forgive me! He is safe. Go in peace."

"But you?"

"I leave by the express, which goes at four and does not stop."

Question and answer passed swiftly as breath could shape them. And as the last words were uttered, Mary Marlow caught the hand that gave her back a hope, whispered fervently, "Heaven bless you!" and was gone.

III

John Marlow sat in the waiting room of the station, seeking, in the confusion of the place, distraction from the thoughts that had harassed him all day, in spite of the reckless purpose which was driving him to the worst sort of suicide—self-abandonment. He knew it, but could not control himself, for he had got into the swift current now and was drifting to destruction, unless some arm stronger than his own rescued him. He knew that remorse, disgrace, despair, awaited him when the delirious dream was over, but till then he shut his eyes. He would not look beyond the moment when he should join that fair, false friend and with her rush away into the wide world, leaving honor, happiness, home, Heaven itself, perhaps, behind him. He was not a systematic villain who coolly planned and calmly enjoyed each downward step. He was for the time a monomaniac, who felt himself at the mercy of an evil passion yet had neither will nor sanity enough to free himself from its fatal power.

As he sat in the noisy, crowded place, with his hat over his eyes, seldom stirring except to glance at the great clock, as if longing for yet dreading the moment when the decisive step must be taken, one thought, one memory, haunted him like a beseeching ghost, which would not be exorcised. The thought of his wife, the memory of all she had been to him, from the hour when, a girl, she had given him her heart to that very day, when, as he stole like a thief from his own doors, he caught a last glimpse of her at work for him, with hands that loved their labor and an anxious shadow on the face that always wore a smile when it met his eyes. All the patient, hopeful years through which she had cheered him with brave words, helped him with her own hard earnings, and sustained him with unfaltering love came back and pleaded for her now. Every sorrow and privation sweetly borne, every care banished, burden lightened, joy increased, and good gift cherished for his sake rose again like reproachful spirits and confronted him. All the dear domestic confidence and comfort, the tender ties and daily sacrifices, that make life lovely grew very precious as he gave them up. Children's arms seemed to cling so close that it was hard to put them away forever; and the faithful bosom which had pillowed his sins and sorrows, ambitions and anxieties, so long seemed to lie before him, stabbed to the heart by the premeditated wrong which already cast its hateful shadow over all the happy past.

He sprang to his feet and, hurrying out, paced the platform restlessly, feeling that perhaps it would be better to fling himself under one of the fiery monsters panting in and out, and so end the miserable struggle at once. A shrill-voiced newsboy arrested him with the cry: "Latest edition! Failure Merchants' Bank! Cashier absconded!" Brought back from a world of inward conflict to external trials, Marlow bought a paper and read the news of a misfortune which seemed to wake him with the shock of a sleepwalker plunging into a river from a dream of safe and sunny meadows.

It was curious how the lesser loss outweighed the greater in the man's mind for a moment and how he involuntarily paused to plan relief for the physical privations of those whom he was about to desert, forgetting that his own act would make their bread bitter, their pillows thorny forevermore.

"What will she do?" he asked himself, returning to the dusty seat to ponder this new complication, for a sense of the horrible meanness of leaving Mary to bear the loss of their earthly all alone cut him to the soul. It was *her* money, a legacy coming late but welcome, and at her desire invested in his name, to be used for his advancement. He had planned to take a part of it for this mad expedition, well knowing that the liberty he sought must be paid for with gold as well as honor. Now a peculiar baseness seemed to attach to this act, making it a theft to blush for, since he left his family poverty as well as disgrace.

"She gave me all, and I meant to rob as well as to desert her. God forgive me! How low I am already fallen!" And to hide the hot flush of shame that burned in his face, John Marlow lifted the paper, to read again the brief, disgraceful story of trust betrayed.

Too common a story in these times to need many words in the telling, but every one stung the reader like the strokes of a whip, for he knew that another day might see a still more shameful tale given to the public, with himself for its hero. As his eyes glanced over the phrases of contempt for the defaulter, pity for his unhappy family, and detestation for the breach of faith which wrought such widespread misery, he felt a sudden horror of himself—a desperate longing to escape like ignominy, if it were not too late. Was it too late? The fatal step was not yet taken and there was time to retreat. He had given no promise, written no compromising word, made no confidant. His brief absence could be explained by the pretext of business, and he might slip back into his safe and honored place, with no stain on his name.

The sigh of relief that came with this thought changed to an inward groan, for inexorable conscience told him that the stain *was* on his soul till penitential prayers and tears effaced it. No word had been spoken, but a look confessed the secret. No crime had been committed; but the premeditated sin had left its blight behind, and though no human voice should accuse him, no human eye reproach or hand punish, he knew himself to be a traitor, who never again could look his fellowmen in the face with the proud consciousness of unblemished honor.

An unspeakably bitter moment for John Marlow, but a memorable one; for with this utter self-abasement came the self-knowledge that was salvation. The shock that startled had saved him, and every penny of the little fortune was well lost, since, in pausing to resent another man's treachery, he saw how much greater his own would have been. But in spite of the revulsion which had taken place within him, the better self struggling to escape from the temptation that ensnared it, the chain he had forged still hampered him, and the weight of a dead perfidy seemed to burden him like a corpse, which he could neither hide nor carry. He felt spent and shaken by the conflict which he hoped was ended. But even while awakened conscience cried, "Turn and flee while there is time!" his eye was on the clock, and he was saying to himself, "This news gives me an excuse for going on. I can explain it all when I come back."

Would he come back? Dare he trust himself in the charmed circle again and risk even one hour with the beautiful temptation which had brought him to this pass?

There was no time to answer; for the half hour struck, the moment had come, and the train rolled in that brought his fate. Scarcely knowing how he got there, John Marlow found himself in the midst of the crowd without, conscious of but one idea as his eyes swept along the line of windows, each framing a face. No white signal arrested his glance, no hand moved its welcome, no eye met his full of dangerous suggestion, and he stood hesitating as disappointment and relief contended for the mastery.

"John!"

"Anna!"

He turned with a start, a flush, as the name escaped his lips, then fell back a step, looking as if he had seen a ghost. And well he might, for his wife stood beside him.

"In heaven's name, what brought you here, Mary?" he stammered, putting out his hand, as if to keep her off.

"Bad news."

"You know it, then?"

"I know it."

Alas! Poor soul, she knew the worst now. There was no need of words to tell her that her fear was true; for in the half-averted face, that involuntary gesture that betrayed both doubt and dread, she read the loss of the old faith, dearer than a dozen fortunes. But with the loyalty of a true woman she hid the bitter knowledge with a smile more pathetic than a rain of tears, and taking the outstretched hand in hers, as if to prop up the fallen man, she said, with the accustomed tenderness, all the deeper for the grief and pity that it hid:

"I know, and I am come to help you bear it."

Like one half bewildered by the turmoil of his own emotions, he seemed about to follow; then, as a warning bell rang, he paused, looked back, and said irresolutely:

"Ought I not to go? It may not be too late. Something may be saved."

But Mary clutched his arm, as if to hold a drowning man, and answered, with a look that made her words a passionate appeal:

"Stay with me, John, and let the money go! All I care for *is* saved if I keep you."

He did not see where she led, but followed blindly; for that cry smote him to the heart, and he longed to fall down at her feet and pray for pardon.

The waiting room was empty now, and in a shadowy corner they sat, side by side, unconsciously adding another to the list of comic and tragic episodes such places know. Neither spoke for a moment. Then, seeing how his white lips worked, the wife brought a draft of water, saying, in a quiet tone that hurt her husband more than the bitterest reproach:

"Dear, drink this and rest while I tell you how I came here. We cannot go yet."

He drank without a word and, leaning his head upon his hand, listened while she spoke, with now and then a tender touch, as if to soften the hard truth and assure him of the nearness of his faithful comforter. If she had accused, reproached, lamented, it might have roused him to deny, resent, defend. But her generous silence regarding her own suspicions, sufferings, and loss was even more bitter to bear than the knowledge of the worthlessness of the idol for whom he had been about to sacrifice so much. The man's pride bled, and wrathful shame was hot within him at finding himself so easily thrown aside. The glamour vanished and the horrible reality stared him in the face, as he contrasted the woman who deserted him at the first hint of misfortune with her who "came to help him bear it" and tried to screen him from his own remorse, only making it the sharper for the loving subterfuge which left him bowed and broken by a contrition too deep for words.

Feeling that this was not the time or place for a confession like this, he turned with relief to the safe subject of their altered fortunes; and conscious of intense gratitude for all that was still left them, neither felt nor expressed much regret for what was gone, as they tried to speak cheerfully of the future. Why both rose simultaneously and silently went out when it was time for the express to pass, just before their own homeward-bound train was due, neither explained, but stood arm in arm, mute, pale, and intent, as the distant sound drew near. There was no pause as, with a shriek, a fiery rush, a cloud of dust, the train swept by, leaving a breathless sort of pause behind it for a moment. To other eyes it was only a splendid specimen of power, speed, and ingenuity. To the silent pair it seemed like the departing flash and roar of a storm which had threatened destruction but, passing by, left them spent and shaken, but clinging the closer for the whirlwind.

The flutter of a white flag of truce, the glimpse of a blooming face which bent to watch for them, proved that the fair defaulter had kept one promise, at least; and the quick move of a hand in answer to the signal showed that she did in truth leave one friend behind who thanked her for it.

"Now, John, come home, and let us comfort one another."

"Home!" he echoed, with a sob in his throat, remembering how nearly he had lost that dear right forever, feeling how much he needed that safe shelter now.

"Yes, dear, this still remains to us—poorer than before, but neither dishonored nor deserted, thank God!"

"And you, Mary!"

Very little was seen of the Reverend John Marlow for several days, and the stream of sympathizing parishioners who called to condole with him were surprised to find neither the pastor's wife, who received most of them, nor the pastor's self at all overwhelmed by their misfortune, but full of a calm and cheerful resignation, which much impressed their visitors. Still more impressed was the parish when John Marlow stood up in his pulpit on Thanksgiving Day, for both the minister and his sermon were utterly unlike anything they had been accustomed to see and hear.

It was evident that the man had passed through some deep experience, which left its marks behind—an experience that seemed to have added years to his age, yet ennobled him with a new manliness infinitely better than the glow and gloss of the departed youth. Serious, pale, and a little bowed, as if trouble had taught him humility, he scarcely lifted up his eyes at first, and had read with an entire absence of the usual air of conscious power, the forceful gestures, and sonorous tones which were wont to make that hour dramatic. And never before had he preached such a sermon, for now there were no flowing periods, no brilliant bits of word painting, none of the daring speculations that stimulate the intellect but do not feed the soul. An almost stern simplicity and sincerity marked his words, but an undercurrent of deep earnestness and emotion gave power as well as pathos to his speech and made it both eloquent and memorable. It seemed as if he had gathered up his highest thought and holiest feeling as a thanks offering for that day; and as they listened with glad surprise, his people saw that they had never known their pastor at his best before, and gave the revelation a quick recognition, a grateful welcome.

There were wet eyes, full hearts, and glances of affectionate admiration when, in summing up the mercies for which to return thanks, he mentioned sorrow, misfortune, humiliation, poverty, and pain as blessings in disguise, sent to prove men's souls by the sweet uses of adversity. A slight stir went through the crowded pews as he said, looking down with a singular glance, which seemed to pierce every breast and read its secret sin by the light of his own transgression: "When we read the story of yesterday's defaulter fleeing today, an exile and an outcast, or sitting gloomily behind his prison bars, it is not with an angel's innocent wonder what a sin like his can mean. It is with the understanding of men who have felt the same temptation to which the poor wretch has yielded that we deplore his fate. The worst of men stirs, by the sight of his human sin, some sense of what human power of sinfulness we too possess." But the touch that went straight to the hearts of all and made them one by the tender thrill of sympathy was when he thanked God with a broken voice for "the love which is our earthly providence, our refuge, solace, and salvation"; for one woman's face was hidden in her hands and silent tears were her thanksgiving.

As if those tears had washed the sin away and won a higher pardon than her own, a mellow ray of sunlight shot athwart the gloom to lay its benediction on the preacher's head as he reverently bent it, saying, "Let us pray."

The sunshine seemed to follow the husband and the wife as they went down the aisle together, the little golden heads going before them, with no shadow of shame or sorrow to dim their brightness; and behind them came the wise old man, softly saying to his companion:

"That was a grand sermon, for John Marlow has learned the secret of true eloquence. Misfortune has made a man of him, and he may well thank God for it."

VICTORIA

A WOMAN'S STATUE

CLAY

The man sat painting with a stern absorption which betrayed the hard-won power of fettering rebellious thoughts by the enforced industry of a skillful hand. A weird, sad picture grew beneath his brush. A wreck upon the rocks, a sea subsiding after storm, and through the heavy clouds one ray of moonlight shone on a fair, dead figure washed ashore.

John Stanhope always painted in that style, and people found a curious charm in his melancholy work, for there was always a touch of human suffering to give pathetic interest to these fine studies of Nature in her darker moods. A silent, solitary man, shunning society, careless of praise, without ambition, living solely for his art, yet seeming to find little satisfaction in it beyond the occupation of his lonely years, and the money which flowed in from generous patrons, for his pictures sold before they left the easel. What became of the sums thus earned no one knew, for he lived like an anchorite in his studio, in one of the quietest suburbs of London.

One luxury he permitted himself, a lovely model; for in

nearly all his pictures the same face and figure appeared, and his admirers had learned to watch for it with a certain romantic interest, wondering in what new guise the soft eyes, dark hair, and perfect curves of this young creature would next appear. There was a mysterious charm about this face which wore so many tragic expressions, this form which told in every line the varying emotions of desolation, despair, or death; for long practice and stern teaching had rendered it easy to feign moods which made youth and beauty terrible or touching.

This model was before him now, stretched upon the platform with every limb relaxed, as if life had left them. Dark drapery, close-clinging, as if drenched by the salt sea, swept across her, leaving only the round arms, the pallid face, and upturned throat visible through the veil of hair that lay dark against their whiteness. So motionless was the figure, so entire was the abandon of the pose, so full of death's pathetic peace was the beautiful countenance, that the sight would have touched the heart of any observer unused to such displays of artistic skill.

But John Stanhope glanced at it with a coldly critical eye as his brush touched here and there a shadow in the folds, a gleam of light on the pale brow, a strand of hair, or the wave-washed feet that left no trace upon the sand. Suddenly he threw down the brush, pushed back the easel, and said in a regretful tone:

"The light is gone. Go, child, and rest; you have done well today."

At the word the dead figure woke to life with a shudder and, gathering itself up, became a tired girl of eighteen, who opened a pair of brilliant dark eyes, stretched her fine arms, and, wrapping the drapery about her, sat a moment in a moody attitude, looking out into the spring twilight through the cloud of hair that rippled to her knees.

"If I have done well, I should be rewarded. You know what

kind of rest I like best, Father," she said after a moment's silence, with a smile that woke and warmed her whole face like sudden sunshine.

"So soon again? Better come out for a quiet stroll in the park. Theaters are no places for either of us, Victoria," answered Stanhope, now walking to and fro with restless steps, as if, bereft of work, he was a prey to ennui.

"It is three months. I long so for a little change that I count the hours and days between the few pleasures you give me. The park is dreary at this hour. I love the light, the music, the splendor of the theater, and only seem to live when there, for that is the only glimpse of the world I get. Are you ashamed of me, Father, that you so dislike to have me seen?"

The girl looked up at him with a tender sort of trouble in her eyes, as if she vaguely felt that her youthful beauty was not a source of either pride or pleasure to her father. A strange expression passed across his face as he shot a quick glance at this fair daughter, who lived for him alone, jealously hidden from the world.

"Ashamed? Not yet," he answered, low to himself. Then, feeling a keener reproach in her words than she could know, he added, with a sudden softening of his austere face:

"It *is* dull for you, poor child. I forget that you are growing up, and I am selfish in my love. There is no need for *you* to suffer and renounce."

"Then I may go. Say yes, and see how well I will pose tomorrow, after one happy evening. I am so tired of being dead! Do let me live a little now and then—live and be gay like other girls."

She had sprung up as she spoke, and stood in an attitude of glad expectancy, waiting for a word to set her free from the solitary slavery which daily grew more irksome to an ardent nature seeking pleasure as naturally as flowers seek the sun.

"Go, then, and make ready. You shall live tonight for the

sake of tomorrow's work." Then, as the girl vanished with joyful haste, he added bitterly, "Her shipwreck has not come yet. May I never live to see it." And locking his hands above a head too early gray, he paused before the easel, looking at his work with eyes that saw in it the tragedy of his own life.

Half an hour later, as he leaned from the window watching the May dusk deepen quietly, a sudden light shone out behind him, a gay voice called, "I am ready, Father," and a lovely apparition looked at him from between the dark curtains that framed it like a pretty picture.

Holding a candle in either hand, Victoria, with unconscious art, illuminated a sweeter, brighter study than was often seen in that solitary atelier. The love of color, luxury, and light, as native to her as her beauty, tried to find vent in the gayest costumes her girlish wardrobe allowed, and warm-hued muslins flowed about her like a rosy cloud. There were flowers in her dark hair, a little ornament glittered on her white neck, and a dainty fan swung from one wrist as, lifting the candles above her head, she swept a stately curtsy, looking up with eyes so lustrous, lips so smiling, and an air of such artless coquetry, it seemed impossible for any man to resist the charm of this blooming girl.

But Stanhope regarded her with a startled look, which deepened to something almost like terror as he exclaimed, in a tone of mingled pain, aversion, and surprise:

"Good God, child, how like her you are!"

"Whom, Father?" and Victoria hastily put down the lights to run and take him about the neck, half pleased, half troubled by the impression her toilet had produced.

He shrank a little as the soft arms touched him, and held her off to look down into the wistful face, with an expression which bewildered her, as he answered briefly, his own face hardening as he spoke:

"A woman I once knew."

"And loved, Father?"

"No, hated."

"Is she dead?"

"I hope so!" and he put the girl away, as if the sight of her made some old wound ache anew.

Accustomed to his moods, she said no more and, when he left the room, amused herself till his return by attitudinizing before the mirror with the naive delight of a child in its holiday dress.

The drive was a silent one, but once in her box at the theater, Victoria forgot everything but her own keen enjoyment, while her father sat behind her in the shadow, wrapped in his own thoughts; for the charm was gone to him, and he saw only tinsel, paint, and melodrama where she found beauty, splendor, and romance.

He watched his daughter tonight as if he saw another woman in her place and found a painful interest in the likeness. Excited by the gay scene about her, Victoria unconsciously increased this resemblance by the change which came over her. She was no longer the quiet, docile pupil who led a secluded, colorless life year after year without complaint. She seemed suddenly to bloom into an eager, pleasure-loving woman, conscious of the admiration her fresh beauty won, brightening visibly in the artificial glare, and looking about her with the proud, glad air of one who finds and takes her place at last.

Presently the play absorbed her, and she forgot herself in following the mimic loves and woes of actors who played their parts so well that colder hearts than hers confessed their power. Victoria was wrought upon as only such susceptible natures can be, and when the curtain fell on the second act, she turned to her father, full of enthusiasm, exclaiming eagerly:

"Papa, let me be an actress! That is the life I long for. Let me try it."

"I would rather lay you in your grave with my own hands."

The answer daunted her less by its stern brevity than by the undertone of bitter passion which checked the entreaties crowding to her lips. She drew back, saying, as she dried the tears from her flushed cheeks, as if ashamed of them:

"I am so tired of modeling cold clay and posing for melancholy pictures! I want life and warmth—to see and to enjoy the world as others do. Must we always live as we are living now?"

"Always, while I am here to watch over you. When I go, may God have mercy on you."

His words, his face, warned her to ask no more, and turning away, she tried to forget them in watching the crowd about her. Glancing from box to box, her own eyes were arrested by the gaze of another pair so pertinaciously fixed upon her that she could not escape them.

Just opposite, a lady sat alone, unless some companion lurked in the soft gloom behind her. The wreck of a once lovely woman, gaily dressed, skillfully painted, gracefully self-possessed, smiling without mirth, listening without pleasure, looking out upon her fellow beings with bold, bright eyes, which seemed to have both entreaty and defiance in them, for the lace that drooped between her and them was a barrier she could not pass to take her place among the blameless women who pitifully eyed her askance or proudly ignored her presence.

With the quick intuition of a sensitive girl, Victoria felt, rather than understood, the truth and hastily averted the candid eyes that could not hide their innocent dismay at the encounter. Had she looked a moment longer, she would have seen the woman shrink and lift her fan, as if that glance had hurt her, then lean and look again, like one yielding to an irresistible impulse.

A smothered exclamation made the girl turn to see her father looking where she had looked, with an expression of despair fixed upon his face, as if the shock of that recognition had frozen it there. Mute with wonder, Victoria watched the two for one breathless instant; then the man covered up his eyes, as if to shut out some detested object, and the light curtain fell before the woman's face.

"Who is that? It frightens me to see you look so pale," whispered the girl, involuntarily stretching out her arms to protect and sustain him.

Stanhope took both hands into his own, saying, with a look and tone that stamped the words upon her memory forever:

"That was an actress once, as beautiful and young as you. See what she is now, and what you surely will become if you step beyond the safe, small circle I have drawn about you. Am I not right in saying that I had rather see you dead than live to be a thing like that?"

"Yes, keep me safe, Father. I will be contented. I will not ask to come again. It is not good for me—I feel it now—and I will go back to the quiet life you choose for me," whispered the girl, with a shudder.

"I have some hold upon you, then? I was afraid the poison was at work and I should see you drift away from me. I could not bear the old misery again. Hush, now, enjoy the play. We will talk more at home."

But the play was spoiled for Victoria. A glimpse of real tragedy, the saddest life can show a woman, had swept the glamour from her eyes; and though she looked again, the love and sorrow now seemed pale and cold, the actors only lay figures posing well, the romance quite gone, since she had heard the accents of a real passion.

"Come away, Father. I long for darkness and fresh air. These crowds of people weary me," she said impatiently, as, hanging on his arm, she went out into the throng slowly ebbing down the wide stairs when the play ended.

Another flight was opposite, another crowd descending, and from the wall of faces one stood out distinctly as the girl's eyes rested there. The same woman in her brilliant dress, but as she drew nearer, a strange, yearning expression came into her face—tender, sweet, yet infinitely sad—the look a soul shut out from Paradise might wear, remembering all it had lost. Victoria saw it, glanced at her father's set, white countenance, and thrilled with a vague yet ominous fear, feeling as if with each step she drew nearer to some great sorrow that had come to meet her.

So, eye to eye, the three went slowly down to meet and mingle in the denser throng below, but just as the stairway turned, a great mirror confronted them, and in it Victoria seemed to see a young, fresh image of the woman whom she dared not name even in her thoughts. The likeness was terrible, for the same brilliant eyes, dark hair, and lips whose shape was a smile were there; the same warmth of coloring and grace of carriage; even the dress seemed alike, for the elder woman's costume was airy, gay, and youthful; and as if the fatal resemblance must be complete, she leaned on the arm of a tall, gray-haired man, who, like Stanhope, looked straight before him, smileless, grim, and silent.

"Who is it?" asked Victoria, recoiling from her own reflection and turning involuntarily to meet again the desperate longing of those other eyes as a perception of the truth pierced her heart before a broken voice whispered it in her ear.

"I am your mother!"

There was no time for any answer. Her father caught her back, the crowd swept between them, and the girl felt herself sinking into a sea of sorrow from which no hand could save her.

She woke on her own little bed, with one lamp burning dimly and a sense of having lived years since she left her room.

Her father sat beside her with a face paler than her own, but no longer stern. Never had she seen such tenderness in his sad eyes as now, never heard such quiet resignation in his voice, or felt more deeply how strong was the love he bore her, the one treasure saved from the wreck when his happiness was lost forever.

"I know—I guess—you need not tell me, Father," she whispered, trying, womanlike, to spare him the pain of putting the bitter truth into words.

"I tried to save you from the knowledge of the trouble that made me what I am, but it was to be, and we must bear it together now," he answered wearily, as a pressure of the hand thanked her for her thought of him.

"It is the old, old story and needs no telling. I gave up art, ambition, everything for her, but she left you a year-old baby and went back to the life she loved. I tried to be both father and mother to you, my poor deserted child, and for seventeen years you have been my only consolation," he added, with his hand upon her head, as if he feared to lose his one comfort.

"She will not come? She has no power over me? I am all yours, Father?" cried Victoria, clinging to him as a sudden fear came over her, remembering the intense yearning of the face that so strongly attracted and repelled her.

"She dare not come while I live. Her right is forfeited, yet she *has* power over you, and against that I have been guarding you all these years. My girl, your mother gave you not only her beauty but the still more fatal gift of an unstable, pleasure-loving temperament. I feared it was so. I watched for it, labored to check its growth by a life free from excitement, full of study, work, and the cultivation of the higher nature, the nobler talents given you. Child, I cannot keep you long. Let me at least have the consolation of knowing that I leave you safer and stronger for these years of jealous care."

He spoke slowly, with the pale, pinched look Victoria had seen before and always dreaded, but so imploring was the expression of his face, the pressure of his hand, that they would have won her consent to anything.

With her arms about him, she answered fervently:

"You must not leave me, Father. I know now what you

fear for me; I feel my need of you; I bless you for your care of me. Stay with me till I am wise and strong; make me what you would have me; save me from the worser self that already begins to tempt and trouble me. I will be all yours; I will help you to forget and be happy; I will be a true and tender daughter and bring you honor and peace instead of shame and sorrow."

He held her close, kissed her fondly, and said, looking deep into the earnest eyes fixed on him, full of love and reverence: "Be a good woman; I ask nothing more. Cling to your art, for such devotion ennobles the poorest life. Work is your salvation, as it has been mine. By your virtue and genius, efface the stain upon my name, and make me proud of my brave and gifted girl."

"I will, Father!" she cried, and sealed the promise with a kiss which she never forgot.

He returned it and left her, saying with a smile, a gesture both sweet and solemn:

"I never shall leave you. Here or there, I will watch over you. Good night, and God bless you, my darling."

All night Victoria lay waking, weeping, suffering with the passionate abandon of youth, rebellious against its first sorrow. But something of her father's patient courage seemed to spring up within her, dominating the weaker part of her nature and showing her not only new griefs and duties but also reserves of strength with which to bear them bravely. A very bitter hour, but it made a woman of the girl, stamping on the impressionable clay lines of power and beauty to be wrought out in after years, with the skill suffering and experience bring, till the spirit of the creature was ready for the marble which is a type of immortality.

In the gray dawn she rose, a pale shadow of the blooming girl who used to haunt the room, for that night's vigil had added years to her life. Tearing off the gay dress, forgotten until now, she crushed it out of sight with the dead flowers, the little ornaments so happily put on; and yielding to an intense desire to destroy the likeness which afflicted her like a visible brand of infamy, she cut away the luxuriant hair that had been her pride. Then, gathering up the long locks that curled beseechingly about her fingers, she spread them like a pall over the relics of her innocent youth, locked the lid upon them, and hung the key about her neck, a talisman to remind her of the promise given that night.

A girlish act, yet wonderfully characteristic of the dramatic instincts sleeping in her. So was the toilet that followed; for, having bathed vigorously, as if to wash away some stain, Victoria put on a gray gown, like a nun's, brushed the short curls back with a relentless hand, and then leaned to look into the mirror, as if to detect any lingering trace of the bright, carefree girl who died last night. She seemed satisfied, for her father's face, softened by youth, looked back at her—broad-browed, clear-eyed, with the firm lips, the strength, the genius, the sorrow all there, as if the fire of pain had brought out characters unseen before.

"Nothing to remind him of *her* now. I will forget I am a woman, and be a son to him; then he will trust me and be happy," she said, with a faint smile at the boyish reflection of herself and a stifled sigh for the beauty she had sacrificed so that it might not be a temptation to herself or others.

There was no sound in her father's room, and for several hours she waited, hoping that he slept. Then, growing anxious, she went to look for him, sadly wondering how the new life would begin, for a word, a look, had changed all the world to her and laid the weight of the father's burden on the daughter's shoulders.

He was not in his chamber, and hastening to the studio, she found him there, already seated before his easel, as if instinctively he sought the old solace for despair. He had evidently worked for hours, and seemed to have fallen asleep with his head upon his arms, wearied out at last. Fearing to wake him, Victoria stood silently looking at the picture, for it was changed and to her startled eyes seemed a message or a prophecy for her.

A few strokes of the magic brush had changed the pale moonlight to a ray of sunshine, the rift of clouds now showed a rosy dawn instead of melancholy dusk, and on the silvery sands beside the drowned woman there seemed to stand a spirit with a face like hers, but full of blessed hope, peace, and aspiration as the tender eyes looked down and one shadowy hand pointed upward, while the other was outstretched to lift the fallen creature to the light that bathed the sad ocean in its glow.

"Am I to be the angel of salvation to my poor lost mother? Or is it a symbol of the better self he hopes will rise from the ruin of my happy youth? Oh, Father, teach me, help me. I am ready for whatever task you give me."

She spoke aloud and turned toward him with eyes too dim for seeing. But he did not lift his head to answer, and the cheek against which she laid her own was cold as ice. He had spoken his last word, given his last caress, put the last touch to his picture; and sat there dead, with a smile on his lips, as if glad to be released from the long anguish that had worn his life away till the weary heart could bear no more.

II
PLASTER

"Where has the old fellow hidden himself? Among the clouds to study sunsets, I fancy," said a young man, as he sprang up the long flight of stone stairs in one of the tall houses where artists congregate in Rome. Door after door he scrutinized, but none bore the name he wanted; and growing impatient, he knocked loudly at one which stood ajar, with a modest card nailed to it bearing the name "V. Stanhope."

A clear voice answered, "Good morning, neighbor," and stepping in, Max Albany found himself face to face with a beautiful woman standing in a flood of sunshine that glorified all it touched.

Hastily uncovering, he added, with surprise and admiration very visible upon his comely countenance:

"Pardon my abruptness. I am looking for Owen Hurst, and I cannot find him. Has he left Rome?"

"His studio is at the end of the corridor, but he is not there yet. Gone to meet a friend, I think," answered the lady, in a voice which made one long to hear it again.

"I am the friend. I will wait for him, lest we miss one another. Is it permitted to look and admire, mademoiselle?" asked Albany, glancing about the large room, rich only in casts, statuettes, and medallions.

A gracious gesture gave the required permission, and the artist returned to her work, like one accustomed to such requests and loath to waste time in listening to compliments.

Full of interest and curiosity, Albany looked at the groups of childish figures, the female heads, and graceful studies of vines and flowers all about the room, for these seemed to be the chosen work of this fair artist and a fitting task for the slender hands that so skillfully molded the ductile clay.

But the loveliest face there was the living one, and this alone satisfied Albany's beauty-loving eye. While affecting to examine the work, which he found wonderfully good, he was covertly studying this woman, who seemed to be unconscious of her own charms, indifferent to praise, and careless of the impression she could not fail to make upon whoever saw her for the first time.

As if disdainful of all feminine arts to enhance her beauty, she wore her hair clustering in dark rings about her head, tried vainly to conceal the symmetry of her figure under an artistic blouse of gray linen, and kept her studio as bare of all color and ornament as a nun's cell, except the pure marble faces and innocent images of little children.

There was something wonderfully attractive in this blooming woman, so free from any touch of coquetry, so austerely simple in her surroundings, so utterly wrapped up in her chosen work, leading a high and lonely life with all Rome and its allurements waiting to welcome her below there. To Albany it was pathetic; for the sculptor's trained eye could read years of effort in the work before him, and the fact that so many of these exquisite studies still lingered there hinted at disappointment, or a rare patience in their maker, the modesty of true genius which can bide its time and never tire of striving after perfection.

Why had he never heard of her as woman or artist? Why had Hurst never written of his fair neighbor, for the studio bore signs of long occupancy and his friend had been in Rome for years? Who was "V. Stanhope," hidden away here, unknown, unsought, unwon? Such beauty and talent could not be long concealed. Was he to be the finder of the treasure, the happy patron to give the world another artist worthy of the name? He was rich, a worshiper of art, and had made his own mark, young as he was; generous and enthusiastic, as successful men should be; and just returned from several years of solitary travel in the East, he eagerly welcomed any touch of romance to give color to the life which seemed tame after the wild splendors he had been enjoying.

Resolved to wake the statue to a knowledge of his admiration, he soon turned from the finished works to that she was so intent upon and, pausing beside her, said warmly, after a moment of silent regard:

"This is your best. A noble head, and very like."

"Whom?" she asked, with a quick look and a bright color in cheeks before as pale as if she lived too secluded and absorbed a life.

"Yourself. One cannot help recognizing the arch of the brow, the large-lidded eyes, the firm mouth, and softly molded outlines, even in this poor clay," he answered, longing to caress the curves that enchanted the sculptor's eye.

"As I hope to be, not as I am," she said as if to herself, and with the yearning look Goethe's Mignon wore when she sang:

Oh, let me seem until I be!

Struck with the tone, the look, Albany forgot the compliment upon his lips and answered with the grave sincerity of one who understood her mood and meaning:

"It would be well for all of us to put our ideals into shape, if only to show how far we fall short in our efforts to attain them. I have tried it, and I know the help it is."

Such frank sympathy seemed to touch Victoria to a fuller confidence. She looked at her guest with the calm scrutiny of one used to reading character, and a sudden smile warmed her whole face as she turned to a curtained alcove, saying, with a half-eager, half-timid look very flattering to the young sculptor:

"You are the friend Hurst has often spoken of. You take a kind interest in beginners, and your criticism would be valuable. May I show you my most ambitious work, and will you honestly tell me if it has any merit?"

"If you will honor me so much. Let me help you," and Albany held the curtain while Victoria slowly drew a light veil from her model, showing him the statue of a woman standing in the soft gloom of the red-lined alcove.

It was only plaster, but it shone white and fair against the warm background, draped from throat to ankle, with loosely folded hands, looking straight before her with a singular expression of mingled strength and sweetness in the finely molded face. Involuntarily Albany fell back a step, surprised at the magnificent proportions of the creature, for she was life-sized and as full of power as of beauty.

One look suggested its meaning to the quick fancy of a man who understood the language of lines, for it was the attitude, the look of so many women who stand awaiting what fate shall bring them—with the same expectancy in the wistful eyes, tenderness in the sweet mouth; on the forehead a gentle pride; and in every feature a hint of lovely possibilities biding their time to bloom and bless, or wither under the blight of sorrow, pain, or sin.

Unconsciously Victoria had fallen into the same pose, and looked up at her work with the same glance, as if asking fate for some success greater than art could ever bring her. Glancing at her, Albany saw this, and marked also the difference in the live model and her counterpart, for the statue proved how beautiful the woman could be when she chose and how sternly she hid the charms most women would have gloried in.

It almost seemed as if the work betrayed how much the sacrifice had cost her; for she had dwelt with loving fidelity upon the graceful outlines of limbs hidden jealously under the gray blouse, had lengthened the short locks to rich masses on the shoulders, let the serious lips relax into an enchanting smile, lifted the large eyes with a look of passionate aspiration, softened the straight dark brows, and folded the delicate hands together with a soft naturalness that made one long to touch and feel them cling. Even the drapery, simple as were the large, loose folds, had a hint of an innate love of ornament; for the hems were embroidered, a deeply wrought girdle bound the waist, and at the feet lay a crown, a rose garland, a pen, and a brush, as if waiting for her to stoop and choose among these symbols of a woman's different kingdoms.

Victoria stood mute, and Albany looked in silence till he was satisfied. Then, turning to her, he offered his hand, saying heartily:

"Welcome, comrade! This is brave work and will bring you honor. Why is it here unknown?"

She pressed the generous hand gratefully, but shook her head as she said, looking at the clay upon her stand:

"It has waited five years, and must wait still longer, for it is not perfect yet. I am in no haste to show it, and I think it never will be done, because I live my studies for it and am never tired of trying to find in myself the image of the woman I hope to create. A foolish fancy, perhaps. But I work so slowly and poorly there is little danger of its engrossing me too much, and these simple things keep me busy with happy, humble models, as you see."

"Have you no ambition to be known and honored, as the rest of us have? These lovely creations need only to be seen to give you a high place in our world of art. Why are they here unknown?" asked Albany, finding the interview grow more interesting with each moment.

"I have a very high ambition, so high that I cannot hope to satisfy it for years to come. My father was an artist and bequeathed his name and fame to me. I must do honor to them both by adding my own success to his. That is what I work for; and when I have anything worthy of him, will gladly show it to the world."

There was no doubt of her assertion; for as she spoke, her eyes kindled, her face glowed, and she looked up at the one picture the room contained with the brave, bright expression of one born to achieve success in spite of all obstacles.

"You are right, that head *is* better than this; but it still lacks the expression you desire to give it. I see it now and wish I could catch and preserve it for you," said Albany, recognizing a spirit as ambitious as his own and finding a new charm in this awakened face.

"You cannot. It is fugitive, and will vanish with the momentary emotion that brings it. I want to make that woman's face *after* the battle has been fought, the victory won, the courage tried and proved, the life a success in spite of fate, the soul safe above temptation, at whatever cost of happiness and hope."

Victoria's voice and countenance were almost tragic with

the intensity of her desire, and Albany was hesitating how to reply when quick steps approached and Hurst appeared, eager to greet his friend, though evidently surprised to find him there. With a few words of thanks for her hospitality, the men departed, leaving the woman to veil her statue, draw the curtain before it, and return to her work with new energy born of that unexpected interview.

"Who is that fine creature?" was Albany's first question when they were alone.

"The bravest woman in Rome, and the most inaccessible," answered Hurst gruffly.

"I did not find her so." And the other related his visit with satisfaction, adding, as if anxious to know more:

"Is she poor?"

"No, rich."

"Yet lives alone here and works with a terrible sort of ardor, to judge by what she has done. Has she no friends, no family?"

"No family, and few friends, because she does not care for them. Ten years ago her father died—you remember him?— and this girl, eighteen then, came here to live for her art. She has done so with a devotion that puts us drones to shame. She might be known, admired, and adored, if she would. But she will not, and lives here like a nun, with a few good women for her friends and me for her watchdog."

Albany laughed at Hurst's grim look and evident desire to keep his fair neighbor to himself. But the younger man felt that he had already crossed the threshold of the enchanted castle, and was conscious of a strong desire to wake this sleeping beauty into life, since he had caught a glimpse of the real woman in an unguarded moment.

"Wait till the right Pygmalion comes; then see how readily the marble Galatea will step down from her pedestal and turn into a lover of the tenderest type. Well for us that these feminine geniuses value love more than fame. We should have to look to our laurels if their hearts did not conquer pride and ambition."

"Do not disturb her peace, Max. She has known sorrow, but is happy now. Let her rest and dream and work till her hour comes, as I have done."

Hurst spoke earnestly, and his friend saw something in his rugged face that bade him respect the loyal love which could live silent and faithful all those years.

"I will," he answered heartily, and asked no more. But his love of beauty and the irresistible desire to seek whatever is forbidden half unconsciously influenced both acts and words from that day forth.

He had come to Rome for the winter, and naturally took a studio under the same roof with his friend. His presence was like a fresh breeze in that dim and dusty place, where the others had worked so long, saying little, feeling much, and leading the inward life which is too apt to foster melancholy and unfit the dreamer for the wholesome duties that keep brain and heart sane and steadfast. This newcomer, with his cheerful voice, fine face, rich gifts, and all the romance of adventure still fresh about him, was irresistibly charming not only to serious Hurst but to solitary Victoria, who could not forget him even when she tried to shut him out of both studio and mind.

She heard him singing as he worked, and paused to listen; caught a gay word as he passed her door, and found herself smiling after he had gone. When he was silent, she wondered what absorbed him; when he left flowers on her threshold, she could not let them lie and wither there as other offerings did; and when he ventured to knock at her door, it was opened to him with ever-increasing willingness, she knew not why.

Sympathy did its subtle work without the need of many words, and very soon Hurst knew why Max lingered there, why Victoria forgot the old friend for the new, leaving him to a sadder solitude than before.

"The statue is waking at last, though not for me," poor Hurst said to himself, trying to face the truth manfully after a visit which plainly proved that his fears were well founded.

Dust lay thick on Victoria's marbles, the clay was dry on her molding stand, no new work had left her hand, and she was sitting idly at her high window in the attitude of one who waits and watches for a desired guest. Hurst's jealous eye also marked several slight changes which were full of meaning. The ugly blouse was replaced by a silvery-gray dress that flowed about her in soft folds. A little scarf of lace was drawn over the dark hair, as if to hide the short curls; the hands that used to be so busy now played with a splendid rose; and the eyes, once so seldom lifted from their task, looked out at the purple sunset, as if they saw some lovely castle in the air and longed to inhabit it. The wonder-working breath of love had blown over her, and ten years of lonely sacrifice and struggle were effaced. A new ambition possessed her; the woman had found her fate, and waited to enter into her kingdom. Hurst saw it, and without a word went away to bury the hope he had cherished so patiently and long.

Albany had spoken, and Victoria had asked for a day to look into her own heart before she answered him. She had looked, and the reply had come too swiftly and sweetly for her to doubt its truth. With the morning he would return to hear it, and she sat wrapped in the blissful dream that comes but once in any life.

"This is safe and happy, and I do not lose my art, but gain a constant inspiration in such companionship. Father would have loved and trusted Max as I do, and I may venture at last to be a woman as well as an artist. Ah, how could I live so long without him!"

The words were on her lips when a low tap at the door roused her, and with a quick flutter of the expectant heart she half rose to greet her lover, who could not wait until tomorrow. In answer to her call the door slowly opened, and on the threshold stood a woman, closely veiled and dressed in faded weeds. An old woman she seemed; for the hands trembled, the step was feeble, and behind the veil a worn white face was dimly visible.

Anxious not to betray her disappointment, Victoria was about to hasten toward her unknown guest when she was startled by a half-articulate cry, as the woman fell upon her knees, thrust back the veil, and showed her the face she saw ten years ago, awfully aged by suffering and time.

"Hear me before you turn from me!" besought the unhappy woman in a voice of passionate entreaty, as she stretched her wasted hands to the daughter who stood regarding her as if turned to stone.

"I have come a weary way to find you, for I am dying and I have no friend on earth but you, my child," went on the piteous voice, choked with tears and full of a despairing humility which would have wrung the coldest heart. "I could not die till I had seen you, asked for pardon, and heard you call me 'Mother' once. I have searched for you so long! Hoped and waited, prayed Heaven to grant me this one boon, and kept alive in spite of suffering, poverty, and the bitterest remorse, that I might fall down before my daughter and let my heart break in telling her how great my love is, how terrible my penance."

The words ended in a rain of tears, and the gray head was bowed into the hands, as if to hide its dishonor from the clear, cold eyes that seemed to have no pity in them. The room was very still, and from without came the soft chime of bells ringing the Angelus, as if to remind these troubled souls that to all earthly anguish rest comes at last.

Victoria stood motionless, trying to recover from the shock of that swift and sudden fall from perfect happiness to unspeakable despair. In one clear sentence, written as if with fire, she saw the answer she must give her lover—the future that now lay before her, the darker for the brightness out of which she stepped. This terrible burden must be accepted, yet could not be shared, for she would not bring her shame to the man whom she most desired to honor. She had long believed this mother dead and had shrunk from even confiding her story to Max till love made it right for her to speak and possible for him to forgive. Death brings pardon and oblivion for all sin, but the living sinner, working out his inevitable punishment, is the saddest ghost that haunts the world. Could she bring such a shadow into the proud and honorable home she hoped to share? Could she bear to let him help her turn the last pathetic pages of this tragedy, the memory of which would always stand between them in spite of pity, love, and time? Involuntarily Victoria looked about her for some hope to sustain, some sign to guide her in this sore strait, and there before her hung the picture that had never left her since she found her father dead beside it. There was her answer, and reading it, her soul seemed to grow calm and strong. Her promise upheld her, and the memory of his suffering softened her heart toward this suppliant who should have been so near and dear, yet was so distant and so dreaded.

Looking down at the bowed figure, worn and wasted, gray and feeble, homeless, friendless, and abased, a sudden dew filled the daughter's eyes; the ice melted from her face; and the voice that simply said, "My poor mother!" was as tender as the arms that lifted the gray head and laid it on an innocent bosom as its last refuge.

No one ever knew what passed between those two women; but when morning came at last, bringing Albany to learn his fate, no sign of that night's storm was visible except in Victoria's colorless face, sad eyes, and steady lips.

"I love you, but I will not marry you because of a great shame and sorrow in my life and a new duty which you cannot share with me. A time may come when I can hope for happiness and be worthier of it after I have earned it. Do not try to turn or change me. Say farewell, and let me go my way alone. Forget me and forgive me, since fate parts us and I can only submit."

This was his answer, and all day he vainly tried to win a different one. She told him enough of the truth to see how it afflicted him, and wise in her love, she resolved to spare him further struggle, herself further temptation, by flight.

In the silence of the night she vanished with the pale shadow which henceforth was to be always hovering near her; and when morning came, the door was locked, the studio deserted, and only the unfinished statue left to haunt the place Victoria fled from to live the hardest chapter of her life.

For more than a year she lived alone with her dying mother in a small Italian village by the sea, shut away from friends, art, love, and hope. The brave soul lived for duty only; for all that could make her task sweet was wanting, and the poor creature whose ruined life left only bitterness and despair was a mother but in name. There was a peculiar anguish in this companionship, for in the once brilliant, beautiful woman, Victoria saw and recognized the traits she had inherited—traits which but for her father's warning might have led her by the same primrose path to an end as sad as this. A stern lesson, to watch the slow wasting of what seemed her worser self, but a salutary one; and when it ended, she felt as if the earth had closed over the sin and shame of her life, leaving only a great pity and sympathy for all human weakness in her heart.

"My hard duty is done. Now I may hope for happiness and feel that I have earned it," she said, as she turned her face toward Rome, leaving a quiet grave and bitter grief behind her.

Hurst alone knew where she had hidden herself, and he had written now and then a word of cheer, but few tidings, for Albany had gone to solace his impatience elsewhere and never wrote. Victoria was too proud to recall him, yet in spite of an instinctive fear that he would find it impossible to accept and share the stain on her name, she still hoped; and as she climbed the stairs to her old studio, her heart beat fast and she listened for the beloved voice to welcome her. No one came, not even Hurst, who knew she was to arrive. But her door stood open, the sunlight shone warm across her floor, no dust lay on her lovely images, and a great sheaf of lilies stood before the alcove where her veiled statue waited. Her modeling tools were ready, and a mass of clay upon the stand invited her longing hands to the labor they loved. A letter lay beside the tools, and opening it, she read, with all the eager color fading out of her face and lips that closed as if to shut in the cry of a broken heart:

My Friend,
There is no way to spare you the hard truth, and it is best to learn it from one who loves you. Max is married. He was not brave enough to share your burden, nor patient enough to wait till you were free. Forget him and live for your art, as I try to do. I know you will prefer to suffer the first grief alone, but I am near to live and die for you. Remember me,
Hurst

How Victoria lived through that night no words ever told, but when her anxious neighbor ventured to tap at her door next day, he was startled to hear the same clear voice bid him enter, to see the woman he loved turn from her work with a smile sadder than tears, and to hear her say, in a voice the more pathetic for its struggle to be cheery:

"Welcome, old friend! See, I obey you and try to find consolation in work, as you do. Say nothing of the past, but help me to bear the present. It is so hard—the future so hopeless!"

She stretched her hands to him, as if there was no other refuge left her, and he took her tenderly in his strong arms, blessing the sorrow that gave him the bliss of comforting her.

"I hoped so much—love was so sweet—life looked so rich and full. How shall I bear to live when all my beautiful dreams are gone, my happiness destroyed?" she cried, clinging to him, with a rain of tears that washed the bloom of youth away forever.

"Build stronger, look higher, and live down despair. Love is not all, nor happiness, my child. Wring the sweet out of the bitter, and grow strong through suffering. Great souls are made so, and you are too noble to be weak. Give me your hand, brave comrade, and let us face this hard world together. I will never fail you, and ask nothing but the right to be your friend."

There was such an inspiring ring in Hurst's voice, such courage in his face, where the last year of patient waiting had left deep lines, such utter self-forgetfulness in his words and tender devotion in the spirit that looked out of his honest eyes, that Victoria felt her heavy heart answer as to stirring music; and standing erect, she swept away her tears and answered heroically:

"Lead me; I will follow. It is not necessary to be happy—it is necessary to be brave and true."

III
MARBLE

It was a charming place, full of homelike ease and comfort and the sweet influences some women diffuse as unconsciously as a flower its perfume. In one room a substantial supper table was surrounded by hungry-looking gentlemen, whose picturesque shabbiness stamped them all as artists. The salon, full of rich, quaint, or beautiful objects, was still further adorned by groups of women, young and old, plainly dressed, but with the earnest look of persons doing and daring much to carry out some chosen purpose—a look which beautifies the plainest face, for earnest living always ennobles.

The third room was a studio, the walls of which were lined with such a variety of paintings that it was evident no single hand had produced them. Many pieces of statuary stood about, none bearing the unmistakable marks of genius, however, except one statue standing apart in an alcove and one picture hanging over it.

Two men were looking at this fine figure, with the ideally beautiful face hinted rather than carved, for the head was still unfinished.

"Why does she delay, when it needs so little to make this splendid piece of work perfect?" asked the younger man, with genuine admiration and irrepressible envy in his face, distinguished sculptor though he was.

"Because Victoria values love and gratitude more than fame and fortune. She is so busy helping others win small successes that she has no time to secure the great ones waiting for her," answered the other man, in a tone that made the hearer wince, as if conscious that his own ambitions suffered by comparison with hers.

"That is very noble! Tell me more about her before we meet again. Your letters are so brief they never tell me half enough. Yet I have no right to demand more," and Albany sighed, remembering the English wife who had chained him to her side so long.

Hurst pitied him and, dropping the satirical undertone that wounded his friend, generously told what he alone could tell, unconsciously betraying how proud and happy this task made him.

"You know how faithfully she did her hard duty, how patiently she waited for your return as her reward, how bravely she bore the bitter disappointment; for contempt killed love and pride made her strong. What you do not know is the life she has led for the last ten years. I could not let her pine in solitude there in Rome, but persuaded her to come to Paris, where one is forced to work and finds it impossible to resist the charms of society."

"Beautiful and brilliant as she was, it must have been a dangerous experiment for you, old friend," said Albany with a smile, as he glanced at the gray head and plain face beside him.

"I did not think of myself, but of her," he answered simply, with a look that made the other redden. "I was not disappointed in my hope, but surprised at the task she gave herself to. Shunning the gay world, as if for her it had too dangerous a charm, she worked at her art till she attracted to her the best of our guild, making a little world of her own. Her benevolence unconsciously widened it till it embraced the poor, the young, the unfortunate, the aspiring who come to suffer, hope, strive, and despair, or succeed here in this city of tragedy and comedy. If these faulty pictures and statues could speak, they would tell an eloquent story of effort encouraged, virtue cherished, poverty lightened, and talent kindly fostered, without hope of reward or thought of praise."

As Hurst paused, he pointed from the walls of the studio to the salon beyond, where these weary, homeless artists gathered for rest, good cheer, and the social influences so many of them suffered for in the lonely studios of Paris.

"Such a life would be impossible for any but a very noble woman. And you are happy to have been allowed to share it with her," said Albany, trying to speak heartily, yet bitterly envying the loyal heart whose faithfulness had made friendship almost as sweet as love.

"I am happy, and still hope to be supremely so," answered Hurst, with a glow that transfigured his rugged face. "She *is* noble. Look and see if that is not a creature to love and trust and honor like a patron saint, as these young people do," he added, as the group fell apart, leaving visible the person who had attracted them all about her like a household fire.

A woman of forty, very simply dressed in black, with no ornament but the nosegay of odorous violets some loving soul had brought her, stood there bidding a guest good night. Youth was gone, but in its place was the imperishable charm experience brings to those who discover the true significance of life—the wise, sweet look of one who has learned to suffer and submit; the repose of a spirit strong yet humble, glad to live because it knows how to make life happy, fit to die because the faith that sustains it is immortal. Silver threads shone in the dark hair, lines were on the serene forehead, and the shadow of pain or weariness sometimes dimmed for a moment the brave, bright expression this face always wore. But Victoria at forty was more beautiful than in her prime, for the stern yet salutary lessons the last ten years had brought her had refined both countenance and heart, till the one was pure as marble, the other tender as a mother's for all the sins and sorrows of this weary world.

Both men looked long and in silence.

"If I had only waited and been true!" thought the man who had loved and left her, with a regretful pang.

"I have not waited in vain if that smile is for me," said the other to himself, as his eyes met a glance from Victoria, full of affectionate confidence and respect.

"The expression she desired for her statue is on her own face now. A lovely look, and yet it troubles me, it is so like the peace one sees only on faces when they wait for death and are not afraid," said Albany half aloud, for his trained eye was quick to see lines of suffering which had escaped Hurst, familiar as he was with that beloved face.

"Only a fancy—she is tired—they ask too much of her, and she forgets herself. Wait a little, they are going; then she will come to us and rest."

Hurst spoke quickly and shrank as if the words his friend spoke touched some hidden fear of his own. Then they stood for a few moments watching their hostess as her guests took leave, and as he looked, Albany saw her give a smile to each so cordial that it was like sunshine. He heard her speak to them so wisely, so kindly, that each felt the balm of sympathy.

He recognized her power over these ardent young men and aspiring women and learned how much she had done for them; for Hurst, in rapid, graphic sentences, poured into his ear the history of many of those who lingered beside this beautiful woman with the maternal face, the generous hand, the beneficent heart.

She came to them at last, as calm and frank in manner as when she greeted Albany on his arrival, and even jealous Hurst could see no trace of pain or regret as she welcomed again this old lover after years of absence.

"I am reproaching you for not finishing this fine work and letting the world admire it as I do," said Albany, taking refuge in the safe subject of the statue, as he was ill at ease in the presence of these two.

"I am tired of marble and have been trying to work in a more precious material," answered Victoria with a tranquil smile, adding, as her face grew serious and a gesture explained her words: "These are my statues, and I find the task of helping to mold and perfect them so absorbing that any other form of art seems selfish, poor, and cold beside it."

She spoke humbly, but if Albany had any doubt of her success, he would have been beautifully answered by the grateful and affectionate faces that turned to look their last at her with glances that softened and brightened each like a flash of sunshine.

"I know, I have heard of this, and I feel how much nobler your art is than mine, how much greater the genius that shapes human lives than the talent that only molds clay and chisels stone," and Albany bowed to her as to a master, while admiration, love, and reverence met and mingled in the look he gave her.

"Nearly two years spent in watching the slow and painful liberation of a penitent soul from a suffering body was too deep an experience to be forgotten, and when my duty was done, I found art would not satisfy my hungry heart nor fill my empty arms, so I took in these needy comrades and learned to be happy serving them. Owen helped me, and I am content, though I have given no great work to the world."

There was something sweet yet solemn in Victoria's expression as she spoke and laid her hand on Hurst's arm, as if accustomed to lean on this support which never failed her.

"I was less patient, wise, and strong. And now, though the world applauds me and I seem successful, I know that I am a failure, and each year find life more wearisome. I blindly left the friend who would have been my guide and inspiration. Now it is too late to go back and undo my folly."

Intense regret sounded sharp and bitter in Albany's words, and he turned away to hide the pain he could not control. But Hurst held the slender hand fast, as if eager to claim it and prouder of its touch than if it made a knight of him.

Victoria saw the look, felt the remorse, and, following a sudden impulse, resolved to say now what she had thought to keep secret a little longer. The pain of one friend would be diverted from past wrong to present pity, and the hope of the other would no longer be fed in vain.

"I have something to tell and to ask of you both. Come and listen, for we may never be together again as in the old times, when we were comrades in Rome," she said cheerfully, leading the way to a group of seats close by and beckoning them to places beside her.

They followed, and sat looking at her, vaguely feeling that some crisis was at hand, but glad to look and listen in the still, bright room, with the beautiful marble face smiling down at them, as if the woman who spoke were already transfigured there.

"I meant to tell this only to Owen, and not so soon, so abruptly. But I am not as strong as I thought myself, and the sight of these familiar faces makes me long for sympathy and find it hard to keep silent." She began with a slight tremor in her voice as she looked with eyes suddenly grown dim from one friend to the other.

"Tell us, what shall we do for you?" cried both, involuntarily leaning nearer, as if to protect her from some unknown harm.

"Help me to die bravely, for my days are numbered and life is very sweet," she answered, with a hand outstretched to each and a wistful yet submissive look that made their hearts stand still with fear and pity.

She gave them no time to question, but in a few rapid words told the hard truth, seeming to find courage as she shared the burden that oppressed her.

"My father bequeathed me this malady as well as his talent, and I have known it for a year. But I hoped to work on and accomplish more before the summons came. I want to finish one statue and leave one evidence behind me of my skill, not for my own honor but for his. Seeing you, Max, seems to rouse the old ambition, and I shall try to put these last touches to my woman. If I cannot, will you promise me to do it? No one can so well, and for my sake I think you will find time in your busy, brilliant life for this little labor of love."

"I will, so gladly, so proudly, if I must, but you will be here to finish it, I know. This is not true—we cannot let you die," cried Albany in despair, for he felt what he tried not to believe.

Hurst sat dumb, his face grown years older in a moment, for in losing Victoria he lost all.

"I am not mistaken. I have seen the wisest men, and they have told me the truth. A few months more are left me, and I have much to do. Keep my secret for a little while, and help me to be ready for the end."

"We will!" they answered solemnly. Then Albany bowed his head upon his hands, unmanned for the moment. But Hurst forgot himself, and when she turned to him, the brave face looked back at her steady, strong, and tender, in spite of the despair at his heart.

"Faithful friend, you never fail me!" she said, holding fast the hand that was ready to sustain her even through the valley of the shadow.

For an hour they talked together as men and women talk when confronted with the stern realities of life—those rare and memorable moments when strong emotion loosens the tongue, unbars the heart, and sets human beings face-to-face without disguise. Albany needed comfort most, for he had no store of sweet memories to console and strengthen him; and Victoria forgot to pity herself in compassion for him. Hurst was like a man who suddenly sees an end to a long-cherished hope and accepts the inevitable with dignity and courage.

When they went at last, both looked back for a parting glance, as the others had done, at the beloved mistress of this home for the homeless, and saw her standing in the soft glow of the lamps serene again, smiling at them so cheerfully that it was impossible to believe that such a life must end so soon.

But it did end sooner than they thought; for Victoria had lived so long for others she could not leave any duty undone, and hastened to set her house in order without delay. When all else was done, she finished her statue, working with the old ardor while her strength lasted and refusing to give over in spite of Hurst's entreaties and Albany's desire to have a hand in this masterly work.

"You may name it for me and say a good word for it if Hurst chooses to let others see it. I give it to him, a very poor return for all these years of tender friendship," she said, as she laid down her tools and folded the hands now grown too weak to wield them.

"He asked for love and you gave him a stone. Poor Hurst!" answered Albany, with a sympathetic glance at Owen, who was carefully blowing away the fine dust from the waves of hair upon the marble forehead.

"No, happy Hurst, for instead of a feeble, faulty woman, he has an imperishable image of a far-finer creature than I can ever be. I finished it for him and put my heart into the work. It is well there was so little to do, because the old fever came back, the old dreams haunted me, and I felt as I used to feel when an ambitious girl."

Victoria spoke as if to herself, leaning back upon her couch weary yet happy, looking like one glad to rest after a long and arduous pilgrimage.

"A great artist was spoiled when you gave up your dreams and laid down your chisel. Did the sacrifice cost you nothing?" asked Albany, feeling how impossible it was for him to do likewise, much as he admired her devotion.

"It cost me twelve years and the love of my life. But I do not regret the loss, for though the artist is spoiled, the woman is saved. That statue is all I leave behind to do me honor. But in the hearts of those who love me is a memory I value more than the world's praise. So I am content, and when I meet my father, I can truly say, 'I have done my best to keep the promise I made you.'"

She looked up at the picture which always hung before her as she worked, and an expression brighter than a smile passed over her face, as if some voice inaudible to other ears answered her with words of tender commendation. Seeing how wan and weary she was, Hurst softly laid a cushion underneath her head, begging her to rest. Like a docile child, she thanked him and obeyed, giving Albany her hand as he said good-bye. But as he lingered at the door, loath to go, he saw her draw Hurst's rough head down and kiss him with a silent tenderness more eloquent than the sweetest words.

"Come in an hour and wake me. I shall be rested then, and I love to be with you while I can," she said, laying her cheek upon the pillow he had smoothed for her.

"I will come. Sleep, my dearest, nothing shall disturb you."

Hurst's voice was soft and steady. But as he left the room, he groped like a blind man, with eyes too dim for seeing, and his friend had no words of comfort for the grief he saw in that haggard face.

Victoria rested well after twenty years of patient pain and effort, so well that when her lover went to call her, he found her lying there beautiful and white, and cold as the pale statue looking down upon the rapture of repose which makes dead faces lovely when the end is peace. Her work was done, her probation over, her hard-won reward bestowed; for those who loved her felt the inspiration of her life even while they mourned her death. And for years, in many striving, aspiring souls, her memory was a talisman against temptation, a consolation in hours of trial.

This was the success she chose, and this was hers; for the beauty that might have been a snare made virtue lovely, the talent that might have rendered the womanly heart hard and selfish was sacrificed to a higher art, and the life that was full of effort, disappointment, solitude, and pain for her was help, sunshine, courage, and devotion for others.

As she lay dead in the home that had been the refuge for so many, those who came to look their last found that some hand had carved a name upon the pedestal of the statue at whose feet she rested. The word "Victoria" made it seem the beautiful symbol of its creator, for the dead face now wore the same high and holy look, carved there by the Great Sculptor who alone can stamp upon perishable clay the immortal longings of a human soul.

MRS. GAY'S HINT,
AND HOW IT WAS TAKEN

"My dear Mrs. Merril, what's the matter? Is the baby sick?" asked a pleasant voice, as a neighborly face appeared at the door of the dull, disorderly room where a tired woman sat crying in the twilight.

"The children are all well and asleep, thank heaven, but I'm so anxious and discouraged that I couldn't help having a good cry," answered Mrs. Merril, wiping her eyes, as if already comforted by the arrival of a friend.

"Tell me about it," said Mrs. Gay, the newcomer, as she poked up the fire till a little blaze brightened the whole room.

"I wouldn't tell anyone but you, and I'm afraid I'm partly to blame in some way, yet I don't see how," began Mrs. Merril, leaning back with a sigh of relief at the prospect of a chance to tell her troubles and receive sympathy, if not advice.

"If the babies are all well, you cannot have any very heavy grief, dear. But I know that the small trials are often the hardest to bear. So confide in me, and we will see if we can't make the burden lighter," said Mrs. Gay, patting the hand that held the handkerchief, with such a cheery face that her neighbor opened her heart freely.

"I'm worrying about John, and you will see that I have cause to do it when I tell you that for the last month he doesn't come home to his supper half the time, but spends the evenings at the tavern. He comes in late, and so cross and beery that I can't be glad to see him. If it goes on much longer, he will take to something stronger than lager, and I shall be a drunkard's wife."

Here the poor little woman fell to sobbing again as if her heart was broken. But Mrs. Gay's kind arms were around her, and the friendly voice said hopefully:

"It will be your own fault if you are, my dear, for John Merril is too good a man to do anything of that kind unless he is driven to it."

"What will drive him? Not poverty or trouble, for we are doing well and haven't a debt in the world," said Mrs. Merril, with an air of honest pride.

"The want of a comfortable home will do it for him, as for many another man."

"What do you mean? I'm sure this is a nice house, and I do my best to keep it so," cried the well-to-do mechanic's wife, surprised and a little offended.

"Forgive me, my dear, but I want to help you and can only do so by giving you some pain. Look around this room, and tell me frankly if it is the sort of home a tired man likes to come to."

A long pause followed this bold speech as Mrs. Merril looked at the scene before her with eyes that seemed to see the clearer for the tears so lately shed. The room was comfortably furnished but in the state of disorder which three lively children would produce during the day. Toys lay about the floor, chairs stood here and there, work was heaped upon the sofa, and supper was spread on the table in a corner. Not a tempting meal: an untidy joint of cold meat, heavy-looking bread, a lump of butter, and cold tea. The cloth was rumpled, the lamp unlit, the fire untrimmed, and the wife sat red-eyed and despondent in her wrapper, with her hair half down, waiting to receive her husband with tears and reproaches.

For the first time she seemed to see herself in a new light, and after that long look she gave a great sigh as she said humbly:

"I see what you mean. It *is* hard on John, but I get so tired and he doesn't seem to care. I've lost my pride in things and got shiftless. How can I do better?"

"I'll show you. Practice is better than preaching. Go up and make yourself nice, and tell me when you come back if things are not improved," answered Mrs. Gay, with a nod and a smile that seemed to lift the other woman out of her Slough of Despond like magic.

"I'm ashamed to let you, but I will for John's sake. If he will only come!" and Mrs. Merril ran away to hide the trouble in her face as she thought of her John driven from home by her ignorance and neglect.

She did not hurry, for she was tired, and stopped to kiss her rosy children and cry a little more before she came slowly down in a neat woolen dress, white collar and apron, smooth hair, and a hopeful smile on her face.

It changed to a laugh of pleasure and surprise as she opened the door and stood surveying the cheerful change Mrs. Gay had wrought so quickly.

The room was in order, the lamps were lighted, the table drawn to the hearth, where a cheerful fire blazed and a pair of slippers lay warming cozily. A well-worn dressing gown hung over the back of the easy chair, and the evening paper lay invitingly nearby. A red geranium with a green leaf or two stood in a glass in the middle of the table and gave quite an air of elegance to the clean cloth, the dish of nicely sliced cold meat, tidy plate of butter, and the pie Mrs. Merril had forgotten.

The fragrance of hot tea and toast was in the air, and Mrs. Gay was singing as she flew about the little kitchen.

When she heard the laugh, she came in to receive the much improved hostess with the words:

"There! Isn't that better? I couldn't do much at short notice, but it just gives a hint of what I mean. I don't think a tired man will want to leave a warm hearth, a comfortable supper, and a pretty wife for beer, smoke, and cards, do you?"

"No! Indeed I don't! How nice it all is. I used to keep it so till I got discouraged and careless. I hope John will come soon and enjoy it all."

"Put the lamp in the window, and run to meet him when he does come. I shall slip away, and I advise you not to tell him your plan. Just say you want to have things nicer, and be your pleasantest self. He will be surprised and pleased, and fall into the trap we have set for him. Keep it always ready, and show a happy face, no matter how tired you are—that is a man's best welcome home."

"How can I thank you? Tell me something more that I can do to attract John. Shall I have beer for him? He depends on it now, and will miss it, I'm afraid," said Mrs. Merril, holding her good neighbor fast, eager for more helpful hints.

"Give him plenty of well-cooked wholesome food, with a cheerful wife to serve it, and he will soon cease to care for beer, I think. Try good coffee, tea, and milk for drinks. Give up pies and such stuff. Things of that sort create a bad state of the stomach, and dyspepsia brings morbid taste for stimulants. Have your bread good and serve up simple inviting meals every day, and John will soon enjoy them too much to want anything poorer," answered Mrs. Gay, hood in hand.

"I will try my best. I never thought that food made any difference. I *can* cook, and I'll feed John as you advise, nicely and wisely."

"My dear, half the drunkards we see are led to their bad ways by poor food, uncomfortable homes, and wives who, through ignorance, selfishness, or neglect, leave their husbands open to temptation. The poor men want rest, comfort, and cheerful society when the day's work is done; home is the safest place to find them in. See that your John is not driven away by any failure on your part. Then, if trouble comes, remorse won't add its bitterness to your share of the sorrow. I hear the gate creak—good night and God bless you!" cried Mrs. Gay, cutting her lecture short and vanishing out at the back door as Mr. Merril came in at the front.

His wife was so anxious to play her part well that she could only express her thanks by a hasty handshake, and then turned to greet her husband with a smile he had not seen for weeks.

"Hullo, how smart and cozy we are! Is it anybody's birthday?" he exclaimed, pausing to look about with a face that rapidly changed from weary indifference to pleased surprise.

Mrs. Merril meant to obey her friend and say nothing of the fear which led to this happy change, but her heart was so full it would overflow in spite of her; and running to her husband, she held him fast, saying with a voice that trembled with love and hope and self-reproach:

"I wanted to make home look pleasant to you, John. I've been a selfish, careless wife, and don't wonder you like other places better, but I'm going to try to do my duty and make you to love to here more than to the tavern, before it is too late. Forgive me, dear, and help me to keep Father safe, for the babies' sake and mine."

There she broke down and hid her face in John's waistcoat. But her tears said what she dared only hint, and Merril found it hard to keep his own voice steady for a minute.

He understood better than she knew what danger menaced him, and blessed her for opening this refuge from the temptation which was just beginning to make its power felt.

"I will, please God!" he said manfully, as he laid his hand on the earnest little woman's bent head. "Don't blame yourself, Kitty, when you have the hardest part to do. I hope I'm man enough to keep steady and not disgrace my children. I'll quit my bad ways and stay with you, for I'm sick of them. I was tired of finding things in a muddle here—crying children, worried wife, and all the rest of it—but I ought to have lent a hand and not run away."

"No, it was my fault. Don't say a word more, but come and have tea. It's all ready, thanks to Mrs. Gay, who came and cheered me up and told me what to do," said Mrs. Merril, wisely leading her husband to his easy chair and bustling about to bring in supper and prove her penitence by deeds rather than by words.

"Ah, this is comfort! Beer be hanged. Here's to Mrs. Gay's health, and long life to her!" cried Merril, holding up his first good cup of tea, with a nod and a smile to his wife.

They drank the toast and kept the pledge they silently made that night, helping one another to stand fast against the mutual temptations and doing their best to make home a safe and happy place for both parents and children.

STORIES FOR CHILDREN

MILLY'S MESSENGER

"Look! De Rebels is comin'! Run and tell yer ma, but don't be scart, missy. We'll 'fend yer," whispered old Jake to little Milly, as he came hurrying in from the field, with an anxious face, one afternoon during the dreadful war times, which are over now.

"Oh, where? What will they do? How will you save us?" cried Milly, dropping her flowers and looking frightened.

Milly's father was a loyal Southerner, doing his duty in our army; her mother lay ill, and the lonely house on the great plantation was but poorly guarded, by the few faithful servants who remained when Mr. Conway freed his slaves; so that Milly might well look alarmed; for though no one had molested them yet, it was known that the family was loyal, and the Rebels might choose to make them pay the price of their loyalty. Milly knew this, but she was a brave child by nature, and hearing much of the courage of the men fighting all about her made her long to do something to prove she was no coward.

"Hush! Don't wake Mama; she is just asleep. Maybe they will pass and not do any harm. If they do stop, don't make them angry. Father said they wouldn't hurt us if we were civil. Remember that, Jake, and give them what they want," said Milly, after thinking a minute and collecting her wits.

"Yes, missy. Dey'll want food and drink, mos' likely, and we's got enough for dem. Dey may be ugly, and rob and swar, and make a heap ob trubble, but we'll be cibel and git rid ob 'em as soon as possible. Don't 'sturb yer ma, if dey's quiet. You be de missis, and p'raps dey'll behabe."

Old Jake shuffled away to tell the other servants, and Milly stood at the door, watching for the Rebels with a beating heart but a steady face, determined to save her mother from alarm if she could, and try to be as brave as her father would like to have her. Presently she saw the graycoats come riding up the avenue, a large party of them, evidently on a scouting expedition. Milly looked hard at the leader and, child as she was, saw at a glance that he was a gentleman. She drew a long breath, and though her face was pale and her hands trembled, she stood her ground, watching them quietly as they rode up, looking half surprised and half amused at the sight of the little figure in the doorway, with its steady blue eyes fixed on their faces.

The leader, a young, good-looking man, swung himself off his horse and touched his cap with a smile as he said, coming up the steps: "Is this Major Conway's?"

"Yes, sir, but Father is away," answered Milly, never stirring, though the tall man stood close to her.

"We shouldn't be here if he wasn't," laughed the young captain, adding quickly, "Who's at home, child?"

"No one but Mama and me and the people."

"Good! Stable your horses, boys, and come in to supper." As he gave the order, he took a step forward and put out his hand, as if to move the child out of the way. But Milly caught his hand, saying earnestly, as she forgot fear for herself in anxiety for her mother: "Oh, please, tell them to be quiet, sir, for poor Mama is very ill! She's just got to sleep, and a fright might kill her. I'll give you anything you want, if you won't hurt her—indeed I will! I'm not afraid—I'm the mistress now, and I'll take good care of you if you'll only be kind to dear Mama."

As she spoke, with her eager, innocent little face lifted up to him, the young man stopped, listened good-naturedly, and, looking over his shoulder, said, with a smile, "Behave yourselves, boys, and little madam here will take good care of us."

The men obeyed him and went off to make themselves comfortable as quietly as possible, for the young captain's orders were seldom disobeyed. "Now, Miss Conway, as I'm hungry, thirsty, and tired, I'll trouble you to let me in," said the captain.

"You promise to be good, sir?"

"On my honor, as a gentleman."

"Then you shall have a nice supper and Papa's best wine. Come and rest, while I tell Hepsy to be quick," said Milly, with a relieved air, for she had seen much company in her life and was full of Southern hospitality. Striding after her, the captain took a survey of the premises and then threw himself down on a sofa, as if worn out. His men put up their horses, and while some kept guard against a surprise, the others refreshed themselves in the kitchen, to the great wrath of old Hepsy, who scowled at them but dared not say a word as her larder was rapidly emptied. Milly crept to her mother's door, told Nurse Rose what had happened, and begged her to keep the news from her mother if possible. Then the child ran down to attend to her guest, anxious to keep her part of the bargain. She found him half asleep, but quite ready for supper, over which she presided with a childish dignity that amused him very much. He watched her as he ate, and thought to himself, "She is an intelligent little thing, and evidently much trusted, so I daresay I can get some news out of her which may be useful."

"Where's your father now, my dear?" he asked suddenly,

after winning her confidence by behaving very well and chatting pleasantly for some time.

Milly opened her lips to answer promptly, for the abrupt question threw her off her guard. But she remembered just in time that she was not talking to a friend, and turned quite red with alarm at her sudden escape as she stammered out, "Please don't ask me, for I mustn't tell."

"Then you *do* know?"

Milly made no answer, and the captain put down his glass with a frown, for it was very necessary to the success of his expedition that he should learn all he could about the movements of the enemy. "You'll tell me if I give you this, I'm sure," and he offered Milly his watch, with a most friendly air.

She looked at it—such a fine gold watch, with a heavy chain and some charming little ornaments dangling from it. Milly would have liked it so much, but she could not tell what she had promised to keep secret, for her father was only twenty miles away and hoped to be at home in a few days. She shut her eyes as the captain waved the glittering chain temptingly before her, and shook her head as she said resolutely, "I can't tell you because I promised I wouldn't."

"Never mind your promise," began the captain eagerly, but Milly looked at him with an air of innocent surprise, saying gravely, "Don't you mind your promises? I thought gentlemen always did."

The captain bit his lip, put his watch in his pocket, and finished his supper in silence, annoyed at the child's unconscious rebuke, yet resolved to discover the secret from the servants if possible. He failed, however, for the old people were faithful; and after a long time, spent in coaxing, threatening, and bribing, he lounged back to the parlor, much out of temper, and lay down for a brief rest after a sleepless night and fatiguing march.

Milly, meanwhile, had been laying plans with old Jake; for a bright idea had come into her little head, and she determined to try it, though Jake had not much faith in its success. It was evident that the captain suspected Major Conway's whereabouts and hoped to intercept him, for the Major's regiment was acting as guard to a train of army supplies, which the Rebels wanted. Milly knew that her father would pass near them on his way from one post to another, and she feared that the captain and his men would surprise him unless he was warned. Who should go to put the Major on his guard? Milly was too young, Jake too old, the other servants too stupid, and Mrs. Conway too ill to advise or help. While the little girl sat pondering over the trouble and wondering how she should conquer it, a friend unexpectedly appeared. A white dove came tripping down the walk, for Milly and Jake had gone to the garden to talk, leaving the men resting in house and barn. As the pretty bird came toward them, Milly clapped her hands and ran to meet it, for it was her favorite pet and dearly loved its mistress.

"Oh Jake! Downy will go for us! I never thought of him, but he's just the one to help us!" cried Milly, returning to the old man with the bird in her hands.

"Bress de chile! He's fergot his ole ways by dis time, I 'spec', and won't find de way to de Major ef we tries it," said Jake, shaking his head.

"Yes, he will, won't you, Downy?" and the dove turned its bright eye on the child with a soft coo, as if it understood and answered her. "Now, Jake, you go and keep watch while I send off my message. I'll get paper and a pencil and string, and creep up to my little room, where no one will see me, and Downy and I will help dear Papa."

Away ran Milly, wrote a tiny note warning her father, and then, tying it under the dove's wing, bade him go straight to his old home in the town, twenty miles off, where friends lived who would see that the Major got it at once. "Fly fast, dear, and don't forget what I tell you. Good-bye! Good-bye!" and with a kiss on its white bosom Milly tossed her carrier dove into the air, watching it soar away till the silvery speck vanished behind the hills.

In the twilight the captain ordered up his men and took leave, saying, as he shook Milly's little hand: "I've kept my promise, and you've kept yours. Now, suppose we kiss and be friends."

"No, I thank you, sir. I don't like Rebels," and Milly drew back with such a funny little air of dignity that the captain laughed outright, and rode away, saying he'd call again another day. He never expected to do so, but he did, for Downy performed his errand well. And thanks to the warning, Major Conway not only saved his army stores but captured the captain and some of his men.

Two days after Downy returned without the letter, Milly saw her father come riding home, and with him a man in gray, who had pulled his cap so low over his forehead that she could not see his face. "Mama is better, and, oh, we are so glad to see you, all safe and well, Papa!" cried Milly, running to welcome him. "Why, that's my captain! Why did he come back?" she added, catching a glimpse of the gray-coated man's face as he dismounted.

"Because he couldn't help it, little madam," answered the captain, lifting his cap, with the good-natured smile. But there was a look in his face that touched Milly's kind heart, and with a childish impulse, full of generosity and pity, she offered her little hand and put up her lips, saying softly, "I'll kiss and be friends now, sir, because you didn't beat."

UNCLE SMILEY'S BOYS

"What's the matter, Bob?" asked the kind old gentleman, as my brother came in, looking both angry and ashamed.

"Got whipped at school, and I don't like it," growled Bob, rubbing his right hand, the palm of which was still red and tingling.

"I'm sorry, but I guess you deserved it," said Uncle soberly.

"Don't care if I did. It's a mean shame—ought not to be allowed," answered Bob indignantly.

"I don't like it, either, and when I kept school, I never tried it but once."

"Tell about that, Uncle. I like to hear your stories," said Bob, brightening up a little.

"Well, I was a young man, and I took a country school to begin with. It was wintertime, and a good many big boys came. You know I'm a mild man naturally. I was very mild then, and the boys thought they could do as they liked with the new master.

"I bore their tricks and disrespect as long as I could, hoping to conquer by kindness. But they didn't understand that sort of discipline, and I soon found that the order of the whole school would be destroyed if I did not assert my authority and subdue these fellows.

"So I made up my mind to punish the worst boy of the set, as an example to the rest. I didn't like the task, and put it off as long as I could. But this boy soon gave me a chance which I could not pass by, and I whipped him.

"He was almost as large as myself and resisted stoutly, so we had a regular tussle; for when I once began, I was bent on finishing the job. I did finish it, and the boy went home entirely subdued.

"The others appeared to be deeply impressed, and treated me with more respect after I conquered the biggest and worst boy in the school.

"It seemed to have a good effect, but I was not satisfied with myself. I felt ashamed when I recalled that scene and saw myself fighting with the boy. It wasn't dignified and, worse still, it wasn't kind. Something must be wanting in me if I couldn't sway the lad by gentler means but had to set an example of brute force and unlovely anger.

"Well, I turned the matter over in my mind and resolved to try some other way if I was called upon to punish any more of my pupils.

"For some time they behaved very well, and I hoped there never would be any need of another scene. But one day two of the middling-sized boys behaved very badly, so badly that I could not let it pass, and decided to try my new punishment.

"So I bade all the scholars put down their books and listen to me. The two unruly lads were called up, and looking at them as kindly and sorrowfully as I felt, I said:

"'Boys, I've tried to be patient with you, tried to remind you of the rules and help you keep them. But you *won't* be good, and I can't let you disturb the whole school, so I must punish you. I can't bear to whip you. It hurts me more than it does you, and I've thought it might help you to remember better if you feruled me instead of my feruling you.'

"There was a dead silence as I paused, then a stir of excitement all through the room. The girls looked half scared, half indignant, for they all loved me and did their best to be good. Most of the boys looked sober, all very much surprised, and a few rather amused.

"Bill, the older culprit, laughed, as if he thought it would be a good joke to whip the master. Charley, the younger, a boy who was naughty from thoughtlessness more than from love of evil, looked much distressed and seemed covered with shame at the idea.

"Handing the rule to Bill, I said gravely, as I held out my hand:

"'Give me half a dozen strokes, and if it pains you to do it to me as it does me to do it to you, I think you will try not to forget the rules again.'

"Bill was a poor, neglected lad, who had never had home care and love, and so was bad because he thought no one cared what he did. He took the rule, struck three blows, then paused suddenly and glanced around the room as a sob was heard. Several girls were crying, and all the boys looked ashamed of him.

"'Go on,' I said, and he hurriedly added three much lighter strokes, then dropped the rule as if it burned him, and thrust both hands into his pockets, trying to look unconcerned.

"'Now, Charley,' I said, still kindly and sorrowfully.

"The poor little fellow looked from my reddened palm to my face several times, but couldn't do it, and throwing the rule away from him, he caught my hand in both his, saying, with tears running down his cheeks:

"'Oh sir, I can't hit you! Don't ask me to! I deserve a whipping, and I'd rather have two than strike you once.'

"Good for Charley, he was a regular trump!" cried Bob, much excited.

Uncle smiled at his forgetfulness of his own tingling palm and went on.

"Well, that touched us all, of course. It was just what I wanted, and it did more good than a dozen whippings.

"I just took both the lads by the hand and said:

"'My dear boys, I think this is punishment enough, so let us forgive and try to do better for the future. Only remember one thing: I don't want to be nothing but a *master* to you; I want to be a *friend,* to help you, and make not only good scholars but good and happy boys. Come, shake hands, and promise me you will try.'

"I got two hearty squeezes, two muttered 'thanky, sirs,' and the boys went back to their seats perfectly subdued and very penitent. Charley never gave me any more trouble, and Bill tried his very best. I knew how much he had to fight against, so I did my best to make things easy for him, and interested the scholars in him by telling them how rich they were compared to him and how much they could do for the poor fellow.

"They all had kind hearts, and all lent a hand, to Bill's great surprise and gratitude, and by spring he was a different boy."

"I wish I'd been to your school," sighed Bob, suddenly remembering his wrongs. "Tell some more about it."

"Go and play now, and I'll think up some interesting things to tell you this evening," said Uncle, and he kept his word.

II

"Fire away, please, Uncle," said Bob, as he settled himself on the rug when the evening lamp was lighted.

"How have you got on at school this afternoon?" asked the old gentleman, looking down at the boy with the sympathizing expression which always made its way.

"First-rate, sir," answered Bob. "And what do you think?" he added eagerly; "I was telling your story to some of the fellows, and all of a sudden there was Mr. Hale himself listening. I had just got through and stopped short when I saw him, for I was saying, 'That's the way to bring chaps round, not thrash 'em like—' 'Old Hale,' I was going to say, when Ned Tracy punched me, and I saw the master. He knew what name was 'most out, but he only laughed and walked off, saying, 'I'll try that plan next time, if you like it so well.'

"I just wish he would. Guess some of the boys would give his hand a rousing knock."

Uncle smiled at Bob's earnestness and said, in his placid way:

"I guess you'd all be too manly to think of paying off old scores at such a time. But the little story may do him good and set him to thinking."

"Now for the new one, Uncle. I'm all ready," broke in Bob, who didn't care to have any moralizing.

"Well, let me see, what was I going to tell you? Oh, I remember, about the medals.

"At another school which I kept some years after, a city school, with many pupils, we tried to do without corporal punishment. It was hard work at first, but it succeeded in the end, and everyone agreed that it was the better way.

"I didn't like the old fashion of medals, and I got up a new plan. It was to have a medal for each school, and the class that had been most perfect in lessons and good behavior for a week had the medal, and that class were to choose among themselves who should be the medal bearer.

"This made each pupil eager to do honor to his class, and there was much generosity and good feeling shown in the choice of the bearer.

"In one of these classes, numbering twenty-five or thirty pupils, there was one boy who was very hard to manage—a lively, harum-scarum lad, always in motion and always in mischief. I was at my wit's end sometimes to know how to govern him without returning to the old fashion of whipping.

"When the new medal plan began, he was fired with a

desire to keep from disgracing his class, and he really tried very hard.

"I watched him with a good deal of interest and was glad to see how faithful he was, in spite of old habits and the many temptations that beset a boy like him.

"Well, his class got the medal, and to the great surprise of the whole school, they chose this Sam to be the medal bearer. He was not the best scholar, and he had not the highest marks for good behavior. But they said they gave it to him because *he had tried the hardest,* and they thought he deserved some reward for that hard work.

"I was charmed with this beautiful spirit of sympathy and encouragement, and poor Sam was completely overcome by the unexpected honor so generously bestowed.

"When I put the medal around his neck, he colored up and stammered out:

"'I don't deserve it, sir, but I will! I truly will.' And when he reached his seat, he put down his head and cried, he was so touched by this token of kind feeling from his mates.

"That little thing was the making of Sam. He was so grateful that he worked early and late to be a credit to his fellows. He learned self-control and went through school with very few relapses into his old ways."

"I'll advise old Hale to have a medal like that, and you see if I don't get it," cried Bob, as Uncle paused.

"One of the bad habits Sam cured was speaking disrespectfully of his teacher," observed Uncle, as if addressing the fire.

Bob looked as if he was hit, and changed the subject by saying, very politely:

"If you have any more stories, sir, I should like to hear them very much."

"I once taught a while in a reform school and had a very interesting time of it. I remember one of the first things I did was to put on a gray suit just like the uniform the boys wore.

They didn't like their 'prison toggery,' as they called it; for everyone knew where they came from, and the outside boys jeered at them sometimes.

"There had been a good deal of trouble about this. Some tore and burned their clothes out of spite, others kept up a continual worry about it, and all found fault with the neat gray clothes.

"They soon took a fancy to me and thought whatever I did all right. I don't know why they should, but the little folks are always very friendly to me wherever I go, and I'm very grateful for their confidence."

"I'd like to see 'em help being fond of you," burst out Bob, laying his brown hand on Uncle's knee, with a face full of affection.

"Thanky, my lad. Well, I just put on a suit like theirs, and I wish you could have seen them stare when I went into the playground.

"'What have you got the prison rig on for?' they asked, crowding around me.

"'It's a good, neat, warm dress, and I like folks to know that I belong to the school,' I said very coolly.

"They understood it in a minute and gave me a hearty cheer, adding, with as hearty a laugh, when they got their breath:

"'Now you can't "flash" any more than we can.'

"'Flash' is their slang word for running away, and it tickled them to think that I should be known everywhere as a *reform schooler* and easily identified by my clothes if I cut any capers.

"We heard no more complaints about the clothes from that day, and I never enjoyed a suit more."

"You are a Christian, anyway, and I wish I could do things just like you," said Bob, privately resolving to take Uncle for his model.

"I had another little experience while there which confirmed my belief that kindness is *always* the best and surest way of governing and helping bad people.

"We had one very wicked boy, and we despaired of curing him, for he didn't seem to have any heart to touch, or any moral sense to appeal to.

"We had tried all sorts of things, but nothing did any good. And at last we put him in the solitary confinement room, and kept him there for several days. The teachers went in now and then to see if they could soften him. But he was as hard and sullen as ever, and they left him, much discouraged.

"I had not had much to do with him, but my heart was full of pity for the poor fellow; and when I went to bed the third night of his confinement, I couldn't sleep for thinking of him, all alone down there, feeling shut out from human society, and very likely full of hard, bitter feelings against us all.

"Perhaps he *did* have good minutes sometimes. Perhaps he *was* tired of being vicious, and longed to repent, if anyone could only know just the instant to take him.

"I thought so much of this that I could get no rest. And remembering how my dear mother used to come and talk to me at night, when solitude and silence made the still, small voice of conscience audible, and how glad I was to tell her my troubles, to be comforted and helped to begin again, I said to myself:

"'I'll go down to speak to poor Nat. This may be the very time to find his heart open, and if I can once get in there, I'll save him in spite of everything.'

"Up I got, and went down, feeling a strong attraction toward that hard, unlovable young rascal. He was awake, and looked up, startled, as I went in. That motion showed me wet cheeks and a softer look than I had ever seen before in those bold black eyes. In a minute he put on the old defiant expression and asked roughly:

"'What do you want?'

"I went up to him and, putting my hand on his hot head, told him what had sent me there.

"He looked up for an instant, as if he hardly understood, but I stooped down and kissed him on the cheek, where tears still shone, and said heartily:

"'My poor Nat, let me help you. I'm so full of pity and goodwill I can't rest. You have no mother to come and talk to you. Play I'm your older brother, and don't shut your heart against me.'

"That upset him entirely. He was taken by surprise. The soft mood was on him, and he hadn't time to harden himself. His boy's heart was longing for a little sympathy, and when it came, he couldn't resist it.

"As I spoke, he hid his face in the pillow and sobbed like a girl.

"I knew then that I'd got him, and I sat down and talked to him for an hour. He made a clean breast of it, told all his troubles, sins, and temptations, and humbly promised to try to mend if I'd stand by him.

"I promised I would, and I did, for the simple fact of my coming to him, when he thought he was forgotten and despised by everyone, had a strange influence over him.

"He behaved better, but was always a silent, moody fellow who wouldn't show his soft side to anyone but me.

"He never made a saint, and he was lost on the first voyage he took, for he became a sailor after he left us. But I know a little seed was planted that night, that a desire to do better woke up in the poor, neglected lad, and the feeling that one human being cared for him was the beginning of a new life."

Uncle's benign face was full of fatherly sorrow as he gave a tender thought to the poor boy, whose heart he had won when it was shut against everyone else.

MOTHER'S TRIAL

"If I never had to do anything I didn't like, I should be good without any talking-to," muttered Will, slamming down the armful of wood he had been asked to bring.

"So should I. When I'm a woman, I'll never do anything I hate, and then I shall always be good and happy," added Kitty, jerking her needle through the patchwork which should have been done in the afternoon and not left till evening.

"I'm afraid you'd be neither, my dear," said Mama, patiently putting the tangled work to rights and saying nothing of the slam which made her head ache worse than before.

"I'd like to try it, anyhow. It's so disagreeable to be always doing stupid things when you want to enjoy yourself," answered Kitty, scowling over her work.

"I'd just like to do what I pleased for a day and see how it seemed. Wouldn't you, Kit?" asked Will.

"Wouldn't I, though! What fun we'd have, and how good we'd be, if we weren't being bothered with lessons and useful things all the time!"

"How would it be if other people did the same?" said Mama.

"Well, that would be all fair. I don't want people to be

plagued as I am. I can take care of myself, I hope," said Will, standing before the fire with his hands in his pockets, in what he thought a manly attitude.

"It's time for bed now, and you can get yourselves to sleep thinking what you'd do if you could have your own way about everything," said Mama.

"There, that's just the way! As soon as ever the work is all done and the fun begins, we have to pack off and leave the nice fire, and light, and books, and games for that stupid old bed. Won't I sit up late when I'm a man?"

"And won't I fling my patchwork in the fire and read fairy books all the time when I'm a woman?"

As they made these speeches, the children kissed their mother and went grumbling upstairs, to talk and dream of the joys of doing what they liked.

They were awakened next morning by the sun staring in their faces.

"Hello!" said Will. "It must be late. I guess we didn't hear Mother call. I say, Kit, are you up?"

"No, but I'm so hungry I'm going to get up right away," answered his sister, from her little room next his. "I shouldn't wonder if Mama was ill today. She had a headache last night, and she don't come to braid my hair, as she generally does," added Kitty, bundling her thick locks into a net and putting on her clothes any way, being in a hurry.

"Let's go and see what's the matter," said Will, when both were ready.

Down they went, to find no fire anywhere, no breakfast, no Betty, no Mama.

"Deary me, something must have happened," cried Kitty, and they ran up to their mother's room. She was in bed, and when they softly asked if she was ill, she answered drowsily:

"No, I'm tired and don't want to get up."

"But where is Betty? We can't find her, and nothing is done downstairs," said the children.

"She's gone out for the day, I suppose. She doesn't like

work as well as play, and I told her we were all going to do what we pleased today, so she is off to enjoy herself, I fancy."

The children looked at one another and clapped their hands, exclaiming, "Won't it be fun? But, Mama, what shall we do about breakfast?"

"I don't know. Don't bother me," and Mama settled herself comfortably for another nap.

Never had she spoken so to them before, and they looked rather sober as they walked away. Downstairs it was cold and dull, and everything looked strange. They could find nothing but bread and milk and gingersnaps, for the storeroom was locked; and they didn't know how to cook anything.

"Betty might have left us a fire and something warm to eat, I think. She had tea and toast and eggs, and let the fire go out before she went," said Kitty, poking about the kitchen with a hungry air, for cold bread and milk on a chilly autumn morning weren't so nice as the warm meals Mama always had ready for them.

"She's a selfish pig. No matter, we can make a fire and cook something, can't we?" asked Will, rubbing his cold hands.

"No, I can't, but we can get warm," answered Kitty.

So they tried, but Will had not split any kindlings. And when he tried, he cut his finger, and Kitty was frightened and wanted to call Mama. But Will said:

"No, she has left us to ourselves, and we must do the best we can."

It was just what he had asked for, but now he had his wish, he wasn't as contented as he thought he should be, and privately considered Mama rather selfish to lie abed and leave them to do as they could. The finger was tied up, and they worked hard to make a fire. But it wouldn't burn, so they went out to play, hoping to get warm. It was rather dull, however; for somehow the day didn't seem to have been begun right, and they couldn't feel merry and well as usual. Suddenly Will had an idea.

"Kit, let's go and spend our dollar. We can do what we like, you know, and with that money we can get lots of candy and cake and nice things. Let's, will you?"

"Why, you know we meant to buy something for Mama with that."

"I don't care. I'd rather have some fun with it now. She don't mind what we do, so we needn't care about her. Come on, I know where they have jolly pies."

Kitty went rather reluctantly. But the sight of the good things made her forget her kind little plan, and she munched cake and candy for half an hour, as she and Will sat on the steps with their goodies between them.

Rather cheered by their feast, they amused themselves with all kinds of mischief. Will climbed trees and shook down apples enough to fill their pockets and keep them supplied all day. Kitty let out the hens, because she didn't want to feed them and they could get grasshoppers for themselves. They climbed forbidden ladders in the barn and played in the meal bins till they looked like little millers. They went to look for nuts and got dreadfully tired without finding any. And coming home, Will lost his pet knife and Kitty fell into a ditch. So both arrived hungry, dirty, cross, and wet at dinnertime.

No dinner was ready, however, and they were in despair. They found Mama in her room, before a nice fire, reading, with a tray of good things beside her, looking very comfortable. She didn't take much notice of them, and they very quietly sat down to warm themselves, eyeing the hot oysters longingly and sniffing at the coffee as Mama read and ate and lounged in her big chair.

"Is that what you like to do?" asked Kitty meekly.

"Sometimes, but I *don't* like to answer questions," and Mama turned her page with the air of a person who wished to be let alone.

"Dear me, what lots we ask every day! And how kindly

she always answers them!" said Kitty to Will, with a sudden recollection of the patience that never had failed till now.

"Mama, shall I take away the dishes for you?" she said, as her mother pushed back her cup.

"If you like. I don't care," was the answer. But as the children both went out, Mama's eye followed them, and she looked half anxious and half amused as she said to herself:

"There are oysters enough for them both, and a little hot coffee will do them good. Poor dears, I long to pet them, but I'll hold off till night, else the lesson will do no good."

"My heart! Ain't they good, though?" cried Will, eating out of the dish and enjoying his first good meal, with a relish.

"I don't feel very well," said Kitty, trying to enjoy the coffee, which she often longed for but was seldom allowed to have.

"Too many apples," said Will, with his mouth full. "Take some peppermint and lie down."

"It's my head. It aches dreadfully, and I'm so tired I can hardly stand."

"You just go put on a dry gown and boots, and we'll play horse. That'll cure your head, ma'am."

"Oh, I couldn't! I'm going to lie down and rest. Can't you read to me in our new books? That would be nice," said poor Kitty, as she crept upstairs.

"I could, but I guess I won't, for I don't *like* to read loud, very well," answered Will, anxious to enjoy his freedom while it lasted.

Kitty cuddled down in her bed and lay thinking a good many thoughts about doing things for others, and forgetting oneself, till she dropped asleep. Will read the new books in the sunny window till he was tired of being quiet and wanted his sister to hear something funny. But she was asleep, and he felt very lonely.

"I never saw such a selfish girl as Kit is, always doing what I don't want to. She might wake up and be jolly and not leave me all alone in the dark," growled Will, as the sun set and twilight began to gather.

Sitting in the dusk, he began to think how much his comfort and pleasure depended on Mama and Kitty and how strange it seemed to be without them. He had a kind heart of his own—boys almost always have—and Will was sorry he had been cross. He didn't say anything about it. But he made a fire in the nursery, and that was the best atonement he could think of, for if there was anything he especially hated, it was making fires.

To his surprise it burned readily, and he wondered if it was because he was kindly doing it for another. Then he got some milk, and boiled it, and crumbled bread in it, and had it all ready in her china bowl, as she liked it, when Kitty woke up. She was much pleased and ate it all, though the milk was scorched and the bread crusty. But she didn't speak of these things, for Will had tried to please her and she was grateful. Somehow things went better after this, for a little bit of the true home spirit had appeared and both felt its influence.

Sitting by the pleasant fire, they talked, and played, and roasted apples, and were very happy, till they began to quarrel. They were playing shipwreck on the old sofa, and Kitty wanted to row the lifeboat in which they escaped. The boat was a long bathtub, and the oars were the hearth brush and a cane. Will wouldn't take his turn at the tiller, and Kitty teased till her patience gave out.

"I will row," she said, seizing the brush.

"You shan't. It's my place," cried Will. "Let go."

"I won't."

"I'll put you overboard if you don't."

"I'll slap you if you don't let me."

"Pooh! Who's afraid—" Will got no further, for up went Kitty's hand, and gave him a box on the ear.

She was over the side of the boat in a minute, and it was well for both that the sea was of carpet, not water; for Will went, too, and for a minute there was a sad sight to be seen as this little brother and sister struggled angrily for an old brush.

The noise brought Mama up, and the first they knew, she was looking in at them, saying gravely:

"Is this the way you are good and happy?"

"I don't care. Kitty is a regular crosspatch," said Will, turning, with a red face and fists all ready for another pound.

"You're another!" screamed Kitty in a passion, as she put her hair out of her eyes and showed a bruised arm.

"You don't catch me fixing nice bread and milk for you again, miss."

"It wasn't nice—it was horrid. The milk was all burned and the bread knobby."

"Then you told a fib, for you said it was good."

"I was only polite, but I'll never be anymore, to you."

"You won't have a chance. I don't like slapping girls."

"I hate pounding boys."

"Mama, I wish you'd put her to bed. She's a—a nuisance," and Will looked as if the long word was a finisher for Kitty.

"Mama won't send me to bed, because we can do as we like, and I don't want to go—so now."

"I certainly don't like to have anything to do with such children," and without another word Mama went away.

Both were much ashamed, but neither would own it. Will sat down and began to whittle; Kitty sat down and began to undress her dolly; and each affected to entirely forget the other. The clock struck nine, and both gaped involuntarily.

"You'd better go to bed," said Kitty, with an aggravating little sniff.

"I shan't go for hours yet, but it's time little chits were in bed," answered Will coolly.

"Hold your tongue," returned Kitty snappishly.

"See if I don't," and not another word would Will say.

There they sat, the two silly children, tired to death and

longing for bed, but too stubborn to go. The clock ticked, the fire burned low, the heavy heads nodded, and the sleepy lids wouldn't stay up.

"The fire is going out," said Kitty, picking her doll out of the ashes, where it had fallen during one of her naps.

No answer.

"I shan't get any wood."

Not a word in reply.

"It is getting very cold here."

A snore was all the sound she heard.

The clock struck ten, and Kitty began to feel afraid. For she'd never been up so late before, and it was very dismal in the great, lonely nursery, with one dim lamp and the pleasant firelight dying away.

"If Will would kiss and be friends, I would," said Kitty, hoping he would hear.

He did, but thought a little fright would do her good, so he appeared to sleep on and made no reply. Kitty sat a while, then went and peeped over the baluster, hoping Mama was up. But there was no light under her door, and everything was very still.

"There ain't any ghosts, but what should I do if one came?" thought Kitty, creeping back.

The lamp flickered, as if going out, and in a great panic lest she should be left in the dark, Kitty hurried into bed, cold and sad and sick; for the cake and apples and the tumble had made her very poorly.

As soon as she was gone, Will whisked into his bed, being almost as much afraid of the ghosts as Kitty.

The lamp went out, the fire died, the room was dark and still and cold, and everyone seemed asleep, when Will heard a little sob from Kitty's bed, then the sound of bare feet pattering across the carpet; and in a minute a cold, small hand touched his, a wet cheek came beside his own, and with quite a shower of tears Kitty whispered softly:

"Will, dear, please forgive me, 'cause I can't sleep till you do."

"Of course I will, Kit. I ain't such a pig as I seem. I'm sorry I was cross, and I won't again. There, don't cry, but kiss and go bylow."

Will sat up and put his arm around her, for he wasn't afraid of this little ghost. He didn't cry. Oh dear, no, that would never do for a boy, he thought, but he hemmed once or twice and sniffed a little, as if he could have done it if he'd chosen.

"Hasn't it been a dreadful day, without Mama, or lessons, or meals, or anything nice and cozy?" sighed Kitty, as Will tried to warm her little cold feet and wiped her tears away.

"Yes, I don't think my plan goes good. Somehow it seems pleasanter to do things we don't like, after all. I guess being selfish doesn't make folks happy," answered Will, folding the blankets around Kitty and smoothing the poor little head that ached.

"I hope Mama has had a nicer day than we have. She's slept, and read, and played songs, and walked out, and done all she likes, and see how different this day is from the ones she spends working for us! Will, don't let's fret and be lazy anymore. Let's be like her, and then maybe we'll be as good and as happy."

As Kitty spoke, a pair of soft arms came about the two little figures sitting there in the dark, and the voice that was dearest in all the world to them said tenderly, as Mama gathered them close to her motherly bosom:

"My darlings, Mama has spent a miserable day without you, for the pleasure of my life is to love and care for you. But I am satisfied if you have learned how much happier it makes us, old and young, to bear and forbear, to deny ourselves for others and make duty pleasant by a willing heart. Good night, you will sleep now, and wake tomorrow all the better for Mother's trial."

BONFIRES

It was a wild, wet evening, the wind blowing a gale, and torrents of rain falling at intervals, dark and dreary everywhere, and especially so up there in the narrow valley among the mountains.

Little Phebe stood at the door looking anxiously out into the gloom, wondering why Father did not come, and listening to the rush and roar of the river that came tumbling down the rocky ravine from the hills beyond.

It sounded so loud that Phebe threw on an old shawl and ran down to the bridge to look at it, for she loved to watch the wild stream fret and foam between its prison walls.

Her mother lay asleep after a sick day, and longing for a breath of fresh air, the child slipped away into the stormy twilight, for she was a hardy little mountaineer and feared neither wind nor rain.

The house stood alone on the slope of a great hill, with the forest all around it and no sign of civilization but a small garden patch and the railroad that wound through the valley. A steep footpath led to a town some miles away, and not a neighbor was in sight.

Phebe's father was a charcoal burner and was often away for days together with his men at their camp, piling and burning the trees they felled.

Little Phebe led a very lonely but a happy life, with no playmates but the wood creatures around her, no books but earth and sky, no friends but father and mother, and few glimpses of the world beyond the hills.

One of her favorite amusements was to sit on the bank near the bridge that spanned the noisy river, and watch the long trains that swept swiftly around the curve, thundered over the little bridge, and vanished in the woods beyond.

All sorts of sights amused and interested the curious child. Sometimes the cars were loaded with stone or lumber, coal or cattle, and she loved to see the great loads rumble by, especially the cattle trains, with sheep bleating plaintively, patient cows peering through the bars, or wild-eyed horses tossing their beautiful heads as they rolled swiftly by.

But the passenger trains were best of all, and gave her glimpses of things that seemed as lovely and strange as any fairy tale. Sometimes pretty children nodded and smiled at her, coming from or going to enjoy happy holidays among the healthful hills. Fine ladies, looking like queens to the country child, amazed and delighted her with passing views of gay hats and wonderful heads of hair. Gentlemen audibly admired the lovely scenery as they passed, and friendly engineers sometimes tossed out a paper for her father, or some odd trifle to please the child so often to be seen peering down with round blue eyes and little freckled face full of interest and delight.

It had rained for several days, and the river had risen higher than Phebe ever remembered seeing it, except during a spring freshet. Now it raged, and roared, and beat against the piers of the bridge, as if it longed to tear it down. Fallen trees dashed by, timbers from broken fences, and once a dead sheep swept past, making the child's heart ache with pity for the poor lost thing.

"I wish Father would come. It's so stormy and dismal, with Mother sick and me all alone," she said to herself, holding fast to a birch as the wind rudely ruffled its green petticoat and blew Phebe's hair all over her face.

But Father was far away finishing up his week's work, knowing nothing of Mother's illness and little dreaming how bravely his small daughter was to fill his place that night.

As Phebe turned to go in, she was startled by a sound like distant thunder, far up the valley. Then, with a wild rush, a great torrent of water came pouring down the ravine, sweeping all before it. Trees snapped, earth caved in, rocks fell, and with a crash the little railroad bridge was swept away like a handful of chips.

Terrified half out of her wits, Phebe clung to her tree far up on the green bank, too startled for a moment to think of anything but the wild sight before her.

"The dam must have broke up by the mill. I hope no one is hurt. We are all safe, but it's awful down there," said the child to herself, as the first tumult subsided and she looked down on the ruin it had made.

All of a sudden she began to tremble and clasped her hands together, saying aloud, with a face full of dismay:

"Oh, the train—the train! The folks won't know about the bridge, and they'll all be killed!"

Sure enough, the late express train would come rushing by at half past eight, and who was to warn the engineer of the danger?

"Oh, if Father would *only* come!" cried Phebe, feeling how helpless she was.

But she had not lived all the twelve years of her life in the woods without learning courage, self-reliance, and many helpful things that stood her in good stead now.

There was no time to run to town for help and no neighbor within two miles, unless the draggle-tailed squirrel scolding in the hemlock might be called one, and he was of no use.

It would not do to wait for Father, for he was often late on

Saturday night. Mother was threatened with a fever, and the doctor said she must be kept perfectly quiet. Yet something should be done at once, for it was eight o'clock now. The storm had shortened the summer twilight, and it would soon be dark, so it was of no use to stand and wave a red flannel petticoat at the train. The wind would drown her childish voice if she tried to call and warn them. There was no station near, no break, no anything to stop the doomed train but one lonely little girl.

So many thoughts rushed through her head for a few minutes that she felt quite dizzy and at first could see no way out of the trouble. Then, as her eyes turned toward the house, as if for help, and saw the ruddy shimmer of a fire dancing on the windowpanes, a bright idea flashed into her mind, and clapping her hands, she cried out so suddenly that Bunny gave a skip and dived into his hole.

"A bonfire! A bonfire! I'll make a big one by the road, and they'll see it and stop!"

Away she ran and, finding Mother still asleep, got matches, chips, and paper in a basket, as many sticks as she could carry, and the old lantern. Fortunately the train would approach on her side of the river. So, choosing the most sheltered place she could find beside the railroad, Phebe laid her fire as her father had taught her; then lighted it and screened the little blaze with her hands and dress till it caught the dry wood and flamed up through the deepening dusk.

It took both time and patience, but as if they knew what charitable work the child was about, the rain ceased to fall and the wind seemed to try to help her with gentler gusts. At last it blazed up finely, that bonfire at the foot of the rock, and beside stood Phebe, hot and tired, wet and torn, for she had struggled stoutly with the elements and won the victory in the end.

"It's 'most time for them to come. They can't help seeing my fire, and I'll shout and wave my bonnet and make 'em stop," she said to herself, getting the faded little cape bonnet all ready to swing briskly.

Just then a new fear came into her head. The train was a fast one, and might come around the curve at a speed that could not be checked in time. She had forgotten that and had built her fire too near the broken bridge.

"I must make another. Oh dear, I'm afraid I can't be quick enough!" and catching up two brands and some chips, she ran off as fast as her tired legs would carry her. Around the curve she went, and there made another fire with infinite trouble. The wind blew the smoke in her face, the brands wouldn't burn, a little shower nearly put it out, and many times did the patient child run to and fro, feeding her fires, watching and waiting with her little heart full of anxiety and fear.

The train was late, delayed by an accident, and the far-off clocks struck nine before any sign of it appeared. Phebe usually went to bed with the birds, and this seemed like the middle of the night to her, so lonely, dark, and wild out there, with only the fire to bear her company. When the wind roared in the pines and the mad river thundered by, when the sky lowered blacker and blacker and the lights died out from the village on the hill, little Phebe was afraid and hid her face, longing for Father to come as she had never longed before.

She said her prayers and thought of all the pleasant things she could recall. She imagined the little children in the cars coming nearer and nearer and how glad they would be to have her save them from a dreadful fall into the gulf just around the corner. This was such a comfortable thought that she forgot her fears, and having fed her fires till the red blaze rose clear and strong, she went back to sit on a wet stone, and wait, and watch, and cheer herself with the little songs her mother taught her.

So tired was poor Phebe that her head began to nod, and

right in the middle of "Cherries Are Ripe," she dropped asleep and dreamed that she was a runaway engine.

How long she slept she did not know, but she was just trying to tell her playmate Bunny to clear the track when a shrill whistle made her spring up wide awake, to hear the rumbling of the approaching train and to see its red eye gleaming through the darkness.

Stirring up her fire till the sparks rose in a glittering shower, she began to dance up and down in the light, waving her arms, pointing toward the bridge, and shouting with all her might:

"Stop! Stop! Stop!"

The other accident had made the engineer cautious. He was not going at full speed, and the fire in that lonely place at once suggested danger. He remembered the bridge, guessed what had happened, and stopped in time, halfway between the two bonfires.

Out popped heads from all the windows. Off leaped engineer and conductor, and everyone asked wildly, "What's the matter?" "Anything broken?" "Where's the danger?"

Nothing could be seen but two big fires burning splendidly and one small, chubby girl with a pale face, who stood in the midst of the excited crowd, saying in a happy little voice:

"The bridge got swept away. There was no one but me to tell you in time, so I tried to do it, and I'm so glad—so glad!"

The story flew from mouth to mouth, and Phebe found herself kissed by grateful mothers, hugged by old ladies, patted and praised by gentlemen of all sorts, and, best of all, coddled by many boys and girls, who regarded her as a strange and wonderful creature who beat their storybook pets out-and-out.

People shuddered and said, "Thank God for the child's warning!" as they looked into the dark ravine, where the swollen river foamed among the jagged rocks, as if angry at being disappointed of its prey.

"She's a brave child. What shall we do for her?" said one fatherly gentleman, holding his own rosy little daughter close and thinking what might have happened but for Phebe.

"I guess she's poor; her gown's all torn, and she's barefooted. Give her lots of money, Papa," whispered back little Maud, and set the example by pulling off her new locket to throw it around Phebe's neck, with a hearty kiss, as she said in her sweet child way:

"You must keep it to 'member me by. It was so good of you to save us from being smashed, with your nice bonfires."

Others followed, and like one in a dream, Phebe let all sorts of treasures fall into her torn apron, only saying, with a grateful, tired face:

"Thanky, ma'am. I'm obliged, sir. I didn't want no reward; I liked to do it, please."

There was no going on that night. So, with warm goodbyes, the people swarmed into the cars again and were backed away to town, where they could take another train an hour later by a different road.

Dozens of handkerchiefs were waved from the windows as the train went slowly off. Many little voices cried:

"Good-bye, Phebe." "Come and see me someday." "I won't forget you, Phebe." And the dirty-faced fireman led off three rousing cheers for "Little Phebe and her bonfires!"

A LITTLE CINDERELLA

Phoebe sat by the kitchen fire, watching the pot and wishing with all her heart that she could go to the party, for she was sixteen, was pretty, and so tired of her daily work it seemed sometimes as if she must run away.

Her life was very dull and hard; for her father and mother were dead, and she lived with an aunt who felt her a burden, but took care that she should know it. Poor little Phoebe did her best to be patient, diligent, and cheerful, but she could not help feeling that she did not get her fair share of the good times which are so precious and delightful to the young.

Aunt Myra took boarders in the summertime; for the mountain hotel was always overflowing, and strangers were glad to find refuge in the old farmhouse. This gave Phoebe glimpses of the gay world, the memory of which cheered the long, cold winters up among the hills. It was a great pleasure, but also a great pain; for the poor girl could take no part in the merrymaking, only run and serve, and grub away behind the scenes, with no thanks, no reward, but the food and shelter Aunt Myra grudgingly gave her.

So it was no wonder that her heart was full of loneliness and longing as she sat there that bright summer day, watching the pot and dreaming dreams, as Cinderella did.

But help and happiness were on their way to her, if she had only known it, as though some fairy godmother was preparing joyful surprises at that very moment.

Upstairs in the big back chamber a bright-eyed girl and her mother were talking about this famous party as they sat at work among clouds of tarlatan and rainbows of ribbon.

"I'm quite sure I shall not be able to sing a note tomorrow night, Mama, for my throat isn't a bit better and I'm as hoarse as a crow," said Rose in a tone of despair, as she put down her work to cough and sneeze.

"I'm so sorry, dear, both for your sake and my own, because I wanted our little charity concert to be a grand success, and you were my prima donna. I agree with you that we must give up your song and find someone to take your place," answered the mother, with a face full of sympathy.

"But who can we find? You know I should not have appeared if anyone else had been here. The Glee Club will do their part splendidly, and the girls will play as much as you like. But not one will sing except Emma Houghton, and her voice is worse than mine now. I am *so* disappointed, for I wanted to show that I was in earnest about our charity plan, and set the example of singing ballads that everyone loves instead of opera music that only few care for."

"I think *I* can find a substitute, if you will help me a little," began Mrs. Heath, with a smile.

"Where? How? Who?" cried Rose, in great surprise.

Pointing downward, Mama answered in one word:

"Cinderella."

Rose stared a moment, with her blue eyes full of wonder, then clapped her hands and cried delightedly:

"Oh Mama, I do believe it could be done! How clever of you to remember the Phoebe-bird, as Mr. Lennox calls her. Do you think she will? Perhaps Aunt Myra won't let her. What will the girls say to it?"

"Go and ask the child. I will settle it with the aunt, and if the girls object, they can drop the affair. We suggested it, and we are the ones to decide."

"Mama, you are just the best mother in the world. I'll go and do my part at once," and away flew Rose, glowing with pleasure and goodwill.

This blooming, becoming face shone on Phoebe like the sun, and the hoarse voice sounded like the sweetest music to her ears as it said rapidly, while Rose stood smiling at her like a good fairy newly risen on the hearth:

"Please, Phoebe, will you be a dear and take my place in our little concert tomorrow night? You know we want to make some money for poor Widow Mills and her babies, and so Mama suggested a sing and a pleasant time afterwards. There are so many rich and lazy people up here just now, who like to be amused and will give more in this way than if we took up a contribution without any fun. Ah, Mama is a wise woman! Our tickets are all gone, and everyone is eager to help. I must give up my part, unfortunately, but if you will take my place, all will go nicely."

Phoebe sat speechless with surprise and delight, for such glory as this coming in one delicious burst almost took her breath away.

"Oh, Miss Rose, how kind you are! But how *could* I take your place? I can't sing well, for I only know common, old songs; and I ain't anybody," she stammered, clasping her hands and growing rosy with the innocent pride and pleasure swelling her heart.

"You can do one thing that I cannot, with all my years of teaching, and you do it so well I wonder no one ever carried you off and made a singer of you. I mean your bird song. It's the merriest, sweetest, most wonderful thing I ever heard, and that is what I want you to do," said Rose.

"But that is only mocking the birds, and it isn't real music," began Phoebe, quite unconscious of her gift.

"Ah, but the birds taught you their secret, and it *is* far truer music than any great composer ever wrote. Mama knows, and she says it is a wonderful imitation, and she often speaks of the time she first heard you do it, picking peas in the garden and answering the bobolinks, till she could not tell which was bird and which girl. Come now, don't be shy, there's a dear. Help me out of my trouble, and I'll prove I'm not ungrateful."

"Dear Miss Rose, I'll do anything in the world for you, and be glad and proud to do it. I don't know about my song, but if you say it is good and folks won't laugh at me, I'd love dearly to try it. I did so want to see the fun, and it would be extra nice to think I was helping poor Mrs. Mills."

"Then it's all settled. Mama will get your aunt's leave, and as soon as your work is done, you come into the parlors and I'll make a little accompaniment to the song. For I'd like to have a share in the best piece of the evening, and perhaps it will give you courage to have me near."

It was all so beautiful, and flattering, and kind, and un-expected, that Phoebe's full heart overflowed; and when she tried to say "Thank you," nothing but two bright tears would come as she pressed in both her little brown hands the soft white one Rose offered in settling the agreement with the new prima donna.

Then Rose ran back to tell her mother the good news, while Phoebe startled the old cat, two gray hens picking about the door, and an inquisitive robin perched on the windowsill by dancing around the kitchen as gaily as if all her troubles were gone and her heart was as light as her feet.

Suddenly she stopped. A cloud came over her happy face, and she dropped into a chair, saying, with a gesture of despair:

"I can't go—I've got nothing fit to wear!"

For a moment she sat disconsolate, then looked up with a resolute air and said softly:

"No matter if I do look like a fright in my faded dress, I won't disappoint Miss Rose, she is so good to me. I'd love to look pretty and be a credit to her, but I can't do it, so I won't mind myself. I'll sing my best and please her. The shabby gown can't hurt my voice—that's lucky," and the smile came back as she began to practice the song which she had just discovered was so wonderful.

That evening Rose composed a simple accompaniment to the bird song, adding much to its effect by a sweet chord here and there and giving Phoebe many hints as to the management of her voice. As they parted for the night, Rose said kindly:

"What shall you wear? Can I help you in any way?"

"Oh, thank you. I have a light muslin that will do well enough for me, and I can put some pansies in my hair, as I haven't any ribbons. I'll make myself as nice as I can, so you won't be ashamed of me," Phoebe answered bravely, being too grateful to ask more of one who had already been so kind.

Rose thought no more of the matter till she went up to dress the next evening. Phoebe was washing dishes, for Aunt Myra did not spare her one task and only allowed her this night's pleasure as a special favor to her most profitable boarder.

Rose peeped into the little bedroom under the eaves as she went upstairs, feeling a girlish desire to see what Phoebe was to wear.

On the bed was the "light muslin," carefully mended and done up, but still limp, old-fashioned, and so faded the once blue flowers were pale yellow now. No gloves, no ribbons, no trinkets, lay on the table; only a plain, clean handkerchief, with a fresh bergamot leaf folded in it, and a bunch of pansies stood ready in a mug without a handle.

Something about this poor little toilet brought the tears to Rose's eyes as she contrasted it with the blooming girl who was to wear it, and she said warmly:

"I'll lend her my blue ribbons and a locket for her pretty neck. She mustn't feel shabby and poor; for she is handsomer than any of us, and I won't have the girls sniff at her."

But when Rose came to her own room and saw the fresh white tarlatan piled like a snowy cloud on the bed, the dainty gloves and slippers, the knots of fresh roses, and the plumy fan, she stood a moment with a troubled look in her eyes.

"What is it, dear? Does not your dress please you? I like it simple for a young girl, but if you prefer a more elegant one, you can wear the white silk," said Mrs. Heath, anxious that her Rose should be the fairest flower in the bright bouquet of girls who were to grace her little festival.

"It has only one fault, and that is, it is so much prettier than Phoebe's. I can't bear to wear it and see her in such a poor old gown, when she is the best singer among us all. Mama dear, would you mind if I lent her this dress and wore my plain muslin?" asked Rose, with such a wistful look that her mother read her thought and loved her for it.

"I should think the plain muslin the most becoming dress you ever wore, for it would cover a heart without girlish vanity and full of generous feeling. Give Phoebe the pretty suit, and let this evening be quite perfect in its happiness, for the poor child may not have another soon." Mrs. Heath kissed her daughter, with a look that well repaid the small sacrifice, and Rose wrought a pleasant miracle in the little back chamber. For when Phoebe came up to dress in a hurry, she found the snow pile on *her* bed, with a pale green sash beside it, and on her table gloves, fan, and a wreath of delicate ferns all ready for her bright hair.

She could have cried for joy, but it wouldn't do to make her eyes red, so she made herself pretty with all speed and then went to thank the good fairy who had changed her rags to beauty, and made it possible for Cinderella to go to the festival ball.

It was a little thing, but it worked wonders, for Phoebe no longer felt shabby or insignificant, with poverty stamped all over her, asking pity even for her gift of song. No, she was like the others now—well dressed, looking her best, and able to take her place beside Rose with a sense of power unfelt before.

All girls know this feeling and how much it adds to one's enjoyment, so they can well imagine Phoebe's rapturous state of mind as she stood blushing and beaming, with eyes full of gratitude and a face aglow with girlish happiness, before Mrs. Heath and Rose, who surveyed her with infinite satisfaction.

"Isn't she sweet, Mama? I'm so proud of my Phoebe-bird I feel like clucking like an old hen," said Rose, prancing around the airy figure and giving a touch here and there.

"How are you going to transport your bird to the concert? She cannot fly, and I much fear that long skirt will be spoiled by the dust and dew."

"Now, Mama, don't croak! I do that and cannot allow anyone else to interfere. I thought of the trains, and I have arranged a carriage to take us down to the hotel without crumpling a frill or wetting a skirt. Behold!" and leaning from the window, Rose pointed to a farm cart in which two stools stood upon an old carpet, while Ben, the farm boy, in his best suit, sat on the seat grinning from ear to ear.

There was Cinderella's coach, to be sure, and into it she got, laughing as only a happy girl can laugh. Each white pyramid perched on a stool, and away they went, looking in the dusk like pretty ghosts out for a drive.

The big hotel was all astir that night, for everyone was interested in the charity concert and bound to help poor Mrs. Mills, whose house had been burned.

A dozen collegians on a mountain tramp had volunteered to sing their glees, several young ladies were to play, and then a "sociable" was to finish up this impromptu merrymaking.

All went well, and great was the applause from the good-natured audience that packed the parlors and piazzas. The boys sang their student songs and thundered out their Greek choruses in grand style, and the girls performed their pieces prettily and retired, blushing with modest pride as they bore away the flowers cast at their feet by the gallant listeners.

Mrs. Heath's fan began to flutter nervously as the moment approached when the bird song was to be given. There had been some surprise at the change of program, and prophecies of all sorts had been uttered as to the success of the new-comer. The elder ladies raised their brows and said to one another, "Dear Mrs. Heath has such odd notions, but then she can afford these whims, you know," for Mrs. Heath possessed rank and wealth as well as a kind heart and a wise head.

The young ladies, however, were not very well pleased at the introduction of Aunt Myra's niece, and some openly turned up their noses at the idea. But Rose carried her point, and when the girls saw Phoebe, they felt reassured on one point, for she was not a dowdy, and that was such a comfort.

"Now, Phoebe, don't be frightened. Just sing away as if you were in the garden picking peas, with no one to hear you but Ben and the bobolinks. Mama will be so disappointed if we fail."

"We won't fail, Miss Rose," answered Phoebe, catching her breath and setting her teeth with a resolute air, for she was bound to succeed, for their sake more than for her own.

"Come!" said Rose, and with a fluttering heart led in her protégée.

Bonny Rose was the belle of the little company that summer, and was greeted with smiles as she appeared, looking more like a rose than ever; for excitement made her cheeks glow, and the purpose that warmed her heart lent its loveliness to her girlish face.

Few knew the singer, and glasses went up as the slender white figure, with its green crown above the bright hair and shy eyes underneath, stood waiting to begin. Phoebe was very pale. Her breath came fast, her lips were dry, and she felt as if she never *could* do it. But just as the needful moment came, her eye caught an anxious face in the crowd, a sweet, motherly face that smiled at her and seemed to say cheerily:

"Take courage, dear. I am waiting to hear you and be proud of your success."

That look seemed to give the poor little prima donna sudden courage. All other faces faded away, and she saw only the kind one that said so much. All other ears were of no account just then, and Phoebe sang for friend alone as she began the soft twitter of a blackbird singing to himself on a blithe June day.

Rose was right. The birds had taught the girl their own music, and it rang true, for the pupil loved her little masters, finding in them teachers, playmates, friends.

People smiled at first, then listened more intently; and some shut their eyes, that the illusion might be perfect, for when the blackbird had gone over each different twitter, chirp, trill, and warble, it seemed to burst into a musical frenzy, pouring out a flood of mocking merriment, as if all the birds were holding high carnival in some meadow.

It was so sweet, so gay, so excellent and unexpected, that it took the hearers by surprise, and when the song died away with the faint, far-off echo of a lark among the clouds, there was that momentary hush which is more flattering than applause.

But Phoebe got that also, and plenty of it, for the listeners were well pleased and asked for more, to Rose's great delight.

"Come back and sing a song to show them that you are not quite a bird. I'll play for you and be proud to do it," she cried, tumbling down the bouquets Phoebe had been too modest to pick up.

"I can sing *anything* now," she answered readily, feeling equal to a whole opera, if she had known one.

It was a very different face that reappeared when Rose led

her back, flushed and kindled with her little triumph, and in her eyes an artless look of gratitude that touched the hearts of those who listened to the sweet old ballad the fresh voice sang to them.

"Who is the little wood nymph?" was the question of the evening when the concert was over.

"Only Aunt Myra's table girl," was Miss Houghton's reply, as she settled the diamond locket on her neck and cast an envious look at Phoebe, who was chatting gaily with the leader of the Greek choruses.

"A little friend of mine," was Miss Heath's answer to the same question, and her good word had such weight that nothing marred Phoebe's joy that night.

She did not even lose her slipper, and that, perhaps, accounts for the nonappearance of the prince. But she found something better than a kingdom: a helpful friend, who made life brighter for her all that summer and in the autumn took her away to reap the harvest she deserved.

Phoebe never became a famous singer, but lived with Miss Rose for years, the happiest little maid who ever loved and served a gentle, generous mistress; and the blithest song she sang about her willing tasks was the one she gave the night her good fairy took Cinderella to the ball.

NUMBER ELEVEN

"I wonder if I darst?" said Johnny Sullivan to himself, as he stared wistfully in at the window of a great store where hung a card with these words on it: "Cash Boy Wanted."

Poor Johnny was in an anxious state of mind; for times were hard, winter was coming on, Mother could not get work enough to make them all comfortable, and Johnny longed to help, because Father was dead and the little lad considered himself the man of the family now.

He had tried several things, but could not make much at any of them, and was sadly discouraged. A boy whom he knew told him that cash boys got three dollars a week; and though he rather doubted the story, he thought if it *was* true, that three dollars a week would be a fortune to him and a great help to poor tired Mother.

He had passed the sign two or three times that day, almost hoping to find it gone, and then his dreadful uncertainty would be over. But no; there it hung, and suddenly plucking up courage, he gave his shabby clothes a shake, pulled off his old cap, and walked boldly in.

It was a big, bustling place, and he had not the least idea where to go or whom to address. So he stood about with an anxious, irresolute air till a busy, gray-headed man, who seemed to be some sort of overseer, asked him what he wanted.

"To see about being a cash boy, please, sir," answered Johnny, brightening up.

"All right; come and see Mr. Clarke. He'll attend to it," said the busy man, hustling Johnny into an office and leaving him to his fate.

It evidently *was* "all right," and Mr. Clarke did "attend to it." For, after various questions and instructions, Johnny was engaged on trial for a week, and the three dollars proved to be a delightful fact.

How he raced home and burst in on his mother, wearily sewing slopwork, and told her the glad news! How she praised him and rejoiced, and fell to smartening him up for next day; and what splendid dreams the boy had that night, thinking of all the rich merchants he had heard of who started in life with pockets as empty as his own.

He was off bright and early next morning, and had a busy day of it, learning his new duties and trying to keep his wits through all the confusion about him. He was one of the boys at the ribbon counter, Number Eleven, and he nearly ran his legs off trying to keep up with the constant calls of "Cash Elevun!" as Mr. Perkins, the shop man, pronounced it.

Very few moments of rest did Johnny get, but when they came, he employed them staring at Mr. Perkins, who was a very elegant being, in his own and Johnny's eyes, at least.

The little lad got many a rap on the head with a yardstick as he stood gazing at the rapid evolutions of this gentleman, admiring his brilliant watch chain, his large seal ring, and his well-oiled hair; for Johnny thought the height of human bliss would be attained if he could look, act, and dress like Mr. Perkins.

The keen eyes of the little cash boy observed that this imposing gentleman's manners varied according to the dress of his customers; for he was very short and sharp with the plain people and extremely bland and obliging to the ladies in silk and velvet.

"I must do that way when I'm a clerk," thought Johnny, and just then Mr. Perkins's book hit him over the knuckles, and his loud voice said, "Now, then, Elevun, look alive there!" and that was the end of dreaming for that time.

How he ever lived through the first day Johnny never knew, and when he went home at night, he was so tired he fell asleep in the middle of a sentence.

But he soon got used to it, and trotted steadily from morning till night, getting a minute now and then for a "lark" with the other boys and holding his own among them very well. A happy little lad he was when he took his first week's earnings to his mother and told her he was to stay; for he felt as if his fortune was made.

Before the month was out, however, he found that he was sadly mistaken; for a great trouble came and all his fine dreams ended in smoke.

His admiration for Mr. Perkins had much diminished by this time, for he had an uncomfortable suspicion that Mr. Perkins sometimes cheated his customers. How it was done Johnny did not understand, for the change came back from the desk all right; that he knew. But once or twice an ignorant Irish girl had complained that the ribbon cost more than she thought, or a dim-eyed old lady had been deceived about the money obligingly whisked into her purse while she fumbled for her glasses and was pushed out of her place by the crowd.

Johnny was a quick-witted fellow, and he was sure something was wrong, though he could not prove it. And when he hinted the fact to his friend and crony, Bob White, Bob told him to look out and keep still, or he'd lose his place.

So Johnny "kept still"; he also "looked out," and one day saw something which did cost him his place.

A pretty young lady had been buying ribbons and neckties, and Johnny had just returned with her change when she exclaimed that she had lost her purse. Mr. Perkins made a great stir about it, and everyone was interested in searching for the little pearl porte-monnaie with twenty dollars in it.

Johnny got down on the dusty floor to search for it and crept half under the counter, feeling among the curls of paper and ribbon blocks, hoping to discover it. As he squirmed about there, he saw a hand with a large ring on it slip something small and white onto the little shelf under the counter where the cashbooks and pincushion lay.

He was very sure he knew the hand; for there was but one clerk at that side of the counter, and the big ring was perfectly familiar. Johnny was rather startled, and tried to get entirely under. But someone outside tumbled over his legs, and he scrambled out very red and dirty, saying in an excited tone:

"I think I saw the purse in there, but I can't get it."

"Where, sir?" demanded Mr. Perkins in an awful tone, as he also got very red and went on tossing the ribbons about, as if bent on finding the porte-monnaie.

"It's on the little shelf. I saw it, and *you* know I did," cried Johnny stoutly.

"Come around here and find it, then," said Mr. Perkins, giving him a shove toward the opening further down, for the counter was too full of goods for him to get over that way.

Johnny went as fast as he could, but when he got there, nothing remained upon the little shelf but the fat pincushion and some bits of paper.

"Now, then, hand it over. I thought you weren't sneaking about down there for nothing. Those that hide can find," said Mr. Perkins in a scornful tone, as Johnny stood staring blankly about him.

"I don't care! I *did* see it—I know I did!" he protested angrily, as people began to laugh and whisper; and just then Mr. Walker came bustling up to investigate matters.

He heard Johnny's story and ordered both shop man and cash boy to a private room to be searched, while the young lady, much disturbed at the affair, gave her address and went away as fast as possible.

Johnny was searched first and sent back to his work after having told all he knew and suspected about Mr. Perkins, whom he left in an agitated state of mind, for Mr. Walker evidently had other sins to convict him of.

No one seemed much surprised when Mr. Perkins did not return to his post, and it was whispered about that he had been discharged. The purse had not been found. But nobody doubted that he had it, and Johnny felt quite elated that he had been the means of convicting the evildoer.

Another clerk took his place, and everything went on smoothly, though there was a good deal of talk about Perkins which caused Johnny to see that fine clothes did not make a man.

As they were closing the store that night, Johnny swept up a lot of papers from under the counter and crammed them into his handkerchief, for he used them to write on first and then kindled the fire with them.

When he got home, he was so busy telling his mother about the events of the day that he did not touch his papers till he went to bed. Then he shook them out and began to smooth them away in his drawer for further use.

All of a sudden he dropped those he held as if he had touched a hot coal; for there, tangled up by its silver chain with the curly strips, was the white porte-monnaie!

No wonder it vanished easily, for it was a silly little thing to keep money in, but just one of the dainty trifles girls like to carry hung on one finger, all ready to be lost.

Johnny stood and looked at it for several minutes, while a great many thoughts flashed through his mind and his heart beat so that he could hear it. Then he took it up and opened it. Yes, there were the twenty dollars, folded neatly, and several car tickets. Johnny put them back and wished he had not looked at them, for somehow the sight of those crisp green bills had brought a dreadful temptation.

It seemed as if a sly little voice said to him, "Keep it. No one will suspect *you;* for Perkins has been proved to be a thief, and you know he meant to take this if you had not caught him. Keep the money. Throw away the purse, or smash it up—that will be the safest—and say nothing till New Year. Then give your mother a part of the money and tell her it was a present. Use the rest for yourself, and you can have many a good time out of it. Don't be afraid; it's all right. The lady is rich and don't need it, and you can help your mother in many ways. Think of that and hold your tongue."

It really did seem as if somebody planned it all out for him, and Johnny answered to this tempting voice, "I'll see about it," and tried to go to sleep.

But he had a restless night, and the next day seemed the longest he had ever known, for he carried a heavy secret and it spoiled everything.

He kept saying, "I'm only thinking about it." But the thinking worried him so that when he went home, he made up his mind that he would stop thinking and do something; for Johnny was honest at heart, and the temptation did not get the better of him long.

Next morning he told his mother, and she said things to him that made him both humble and brave, for he took the purse to Mr. Clarke, told the story, and begged to be forgiven.

Now, in the story style, Mr. Clarke ought to have embraced him, said, "My noble boy, henceforth you are my son," and have immediately made his fortune. Not being the hero of a series of remarkable tales, poor Johnny had no such good luck; for Mr. Clarke not only gave him a sound scolding, but discharged him without a character, for he did not believe his story.

It *was* hard, and Johnny's freckled cheeks were wet with

tears as he went sadly home with his direful tale to tell. Hardest of all was the sight of his mother's face as she said patiently:

"Well, dear, it will be a lesson which I hope you will never forget. Now try for something else and do better."

Johnny did try, and after many failures and several weeks of idleness, he saw another card with "Boy Wanted" on it. This time it was in the window of a doctor's office, and doubting very much if he would suit at all, Johnny went in.

Dr. Brown rather liked the appearance of this little fellow who looked up at him with honest blue eyes and answered all his questions with respectful frankness till he said:

"What did you leave the store for?"

"Because I was tired of being a cash boy," suggested the same little voice that had spoken to him before. For a minute Johnny hesitated. It seemed so easy to say that, and if he told the truth, he would probably lose the place. Then he remembered what bad advice this same sly voice had given him before, and he turned his ear resolutely to the whisper of his conscience, for that said clearly:

"Tell the truth and take the consequences."

It all passed in a flash, while the color rose in Johnny's face and the honest eyes fell. The doctor saw it, guessed that something was amiss, and was glad when the boy lifted his face, took a long breath, and told the little story of his temptation straight out.

"I like that!" said the doctor, holding out his hand when it was done.

Johnny was much surprised at the hearty shake he got, and said wistfully, as he fumbled with his cap:

"Of course you don't—want—me after that, sir, but I thought I'd feel better if I told."

"I think I do want you," began the doctor, reading the boy's face like an open book and trusting it more than his words. As he spoke, his eye was arrested by the figure eleven tattooed on the back of the small hand he held, and he said, smiling:

"What does that mean? Secret societies, hey?"

"No, sir, I got a sailor fellow I know to do it, so I might remember what I've been telling you," answered Johnny, looking rather ashamed yet very earnest. "You see, we poor folks get tempted dreadfully, and it's hard to keep from taking things when we need 'em so much, 'specially for our mothers. Now, you see, I never can put out this hand to steal without being reminded how near I came to it once and how glad I was that I kept honest, though I lost my place."

"This is the sort of hand I want to work for me. You've learned your lesson, and got a place that I think you'll keep, my boy," said the doctor warmly.

And his confidence never was betrayed; for Johnny was a faithful servant to him many years, and that marked right hand earned honestly a comfortable living for the mother and a good name for the son.

GRANDMAMA'S PEARLS

My dear Granddaughters,

Before you go to meet the little trials and temptations of the coming week, I want to make a proposition. I am old-fashioned, and I do not like to see young girls in so public a place as the café of a great fair. Your mothers differ with me, and I have no right to dissuade you. But I have asked leave to try and keep the young heads from being quite turned and the young hearts from forgetting the sweet old virtues—modesty, obedience, and self-denial. So I write to say that I intend to give the set of pearls you all so much admire to the one who behaves best during the week. Like the fairy godmother in the story, I shall know what happens and which of you deserves the reward. Laugh, if you will, but keep our little secret and try to please

Grandmama

This was the letter read aloud by one of three young girls who sat together in the pretty, old-time dresses they were to wear while serving as attendants in the refreshment saloon at the fair. A very select and fashionable fair, you may be sure, or Kitty, Kate, and Catherine St. John would not be allowed to play waiter girls in these dainty costumes of muslin, silk, and lace.

"That is just one of Grandma's queer ideas. I don't mind trying, but I know I shan't get the pearls, because I'm always doing something dreadful," said Kitty, the merry member of the Kit Kat Club, as the three cousins were called.

"I'd do anything to get them, for they are perfectly lovely, and just what I want," cried Kate, dropping the letter to give the kitten in her lap a joyful squeeze.

"I suppose she will find out how we spend the gold ten-dollar pieces she gave us, if she is going to know everything we do. So we must mind what we buy," added Catherine with a frown, for she dearly loved to buy nice little things and enjoy them all by herself.

"Let us see—'modesty, obedience, and self-denial.' I think it won't be very hard to behave like angels for one week," said Kate, the oldest and prettiest of the three, looking again at the letter she had read aloud.

"Obedience is always hard to me, and I never expect to be an angel," laughed Kitty, while her black eyes twinkled with mirth and mischief, as she threw down her knitting.

"Self-denial sounds very nice, but I do hate to give up things I want, and that is just what it means," sighed Cathy, who seldom had a chance to try this wholesome virtue in her luxurious home.

"People call me vain sometimes, because I don't pretend to think I'm a fright when I know I'm not. So perhaps Grandma meant the 'modesty' for me," said Kate, glancing at the long mirror before her, which reflected a charming figure, all blue silk, lace ruffles, and coquettish knots of ribbon here and there.

"Of course you can't help knowing you are a beauty, with your blue eyes, yellow hair, and sweet complexion. I should be as vain as a peacock if I were half as pretty," answered Cathy, who mourned over her auburn locks and the five freckles on her rosy cheeks. But she had never looked better than now, in her pale green-and-white costume, with fan and mitts, and the objectionable hair hidden under a big cap that added several years to her age—a thing one does not object to at sixteen.

"Now, *I* don't worry about looks, and as long as I have a good time, it doesn't matter if I *am* as brown as a berry and have a turned-up nose," said brunette Kitty, settling the cherry bows on her flounced apron and surveying with great satisfaction her red silk hose and buckled shoes.

"Won't it be delicious to own a set of real pearls—necklace, earrings, and cross—all on black velvet in a red case, with a great gold 'C' on the outside! So glad our fathers were brothers and named us all for Grandma. Now the letter suits each of us. Young girls can wear pearls, you know. Won't the necklace look well on me?" asked Kate, glancing again at the mirror, as if she already saw the new ornament on her white throat.

"Lovely!" cried both the others, who heartily admired bonny Kate and let her rule over them because she was a little older. "Don't tell anyone about this trial of ours, nor what we do at the fair, and see if Grandma really does know," said Kitty, whose pranks always were found out in some mysterious manner.

"She will—I know she will! Grandma is a very wise old lady, and I do feel sometimes as if she really was a fairy godmother—she knows so well what we want and do and think about, without a word being said," added Cathy, in such an awestricken tone that the others laughed and agreed that they must look well to their ways if they wanted the promised reward.

The fair began next day, and a splendid opening it was, for neither time, taste, nor money had been spared to make the great hall an inviting place. The flower table in the middle was a lovely bower of green, with singing birds, little fountains, and the attendant young ladies dressed as roses of different sorts. At the art table, maidens in medieval costumes made graceful pictures of themselves, and in the café old-fashioned Priscillas and neat-handed Phyllises tripped to and fro, with all the delicacies of the season on their silver salvers. Around the walls were the usual booths, full of gay trifles, and behind them sat the stately matrons who managed the affair, with their corps of smiling assistants, to beguile the money out of the full pockets of the visitors. The admission fee was so high that none but the well-to-do could enter. So no common folk mingled with the elegant crowd that soon filled the hall and went circling around the gay stalls, with a soft rustle of silks, much nodding of plumed bonnets, and a lively rattling of coin, as people bought their last Christmas gifts at double the price asked for them in any shop.

"Isn't it splendid?" whispered the Kit Kat Club, as they stood with their trays waiting for the first customers to appear.

"I'm sure I don't see what harm Grandma could find in this," said Kate, shaking out her skirts and smoothing the golden curls shining on her temples.

"Nor I," cried Kitty, prancing a little to enjoy the glitter of the buckles in her smart shoes.

"Nor I yet," echoed Cathy, as she looked from her cousins to the nine other girls who made up the twelve, and saw in the excited faces of all something which dimly suggested to her more thoughtful mind what Grandma meant.

Just then a party came under the flag-festooned arch, and all the young waiters flew to serve their guests, for now the fun began.

Nothing remarkable happened that first day, and our three were too busy learning their duties and trying to do them well for any thought of pearls or promises. But at night they confided to one another that they never were so tired in all their lives; for their feet ached, their heads were a jumble of orders, and sundry mistakes and breakages much disturbed their peace of mind.

Kitty walked in her sleep that night and waked her mother by rattling the candlestick, evidently under the impression that it was her tray.

Kate kept calling out, "Two vanilla ices! Cup of coffee! Chicken salad for three!" And Cathy got up with a headache, which inclined her to think, for a time at least, that Grandma might be right about young girls at fairs.

But the pleasant bustle soon set spirits dancing again, and praises from various quarters reconciled them to the work, which was not half so much like play as they had supposed. So the cousins strolled about arm in arm, enjoying themselves very much, till the hour for opening the café arrived.

They all three made a discovery this day, and each in a different way learned the special temptation and trial which this scene of novelty and excitement had for them.

Kate saw many eyes follow her as she came and went, and soon forgot to blush when people turned to look, or whispered, "Isn't that a pretty one?" so audibly that she could not help hearing. She was a little shy at first, but soon learned to like it, to feel disappointed if no notice was taken of her, and often made errands about the hall when off duty, that she might be seen.

Kitty found it very hard to be at the beck and call of other people, for she loved her liberty and hated to be "ordered around," even by those she was bound to obey. Just now it was particularly hard; for though the presiding ladies tried to be angelic, the unavoidable delays, disorders, and mishaps at such times worried them, and some were both dictatorial and impatient, forgetting that the little maids were not common biddies, but young ladies, who resented the least disrespect.

Cathy's trial was a constant desire to eat the good things she carried, for in a dainty way she was something of a glutton and loved to feast on sweets, though frequent headaches was the penalty she paid. Such tempting bits of cake, half-eaten jellies, and untouched ices as she had to yield up to the colored women who washed the dishes and ate "de leavin's" with aggravating relish before her eyes! These lost tidbits haunted her even when she took her own lunch, and to atone for the disappointment, she ate so much that her companions no longer wondered that she was as plump as a partridge.

On the third day the novelty had worn off, and they all felt that they would like to sit down and rest. Kate was tired of tossing her curls and trying to look unconscious; Kitty hated the sound of the little bells, and scowled every time she had to answer one; Cathy had a fit of dyspepsia, which spoiled all her pleasure; and each secretly wished the week was over.

"Three more days of it! Do you think we shall hold out?" asked Kate, as they were preparing to go home after a very hard day, for the fair was a great success and had been thronged from opening to close.

"I won't give in as long as I have a foot to stand on, and Mrs. Somerset may glare at me as much as she likes when I smash the dishes," said Kitty, exulting in her naughty little soul over one grand avalanche by which she had distinguished herself that evening.

"I shall if I can, but I don't want to see ice cream nor smell coffee again for a year. How people can stuff as they do is a wonder to me," sighed Cathy, holding her hot head in her cold hands.

"Do you suppose Grandma knows all we have been doing?" said Kitty, thinking of an impertinent reply she had made to the much enduring Mrs. Somerset that day.

"I hope not!" ejaculated Cathy, remembering the salad she

had gobbled behind a screen, and the macaroons now hidden in her pocket.

"She isn't here, but perhaps someone is watching us for her. Wouldn't that be dreadful?" suggested Kate, devoutly hoping no one in the secret had seen her when she stood so long at the art table, where the sun shone on her pretty hair and Miss Wilde's ugly terra-cotta costume set off her own delicate dress so well.

"We'd better be careful and not do anything very bad, for we don't seem to have a chance to do anything particularly good," said Kitty, resolving to smile when called and to try and keep six orders in her head at once.

"I don't believe we shall any of us get the pearls, and I daresay Grandma knew it. Fairs are stupid, and I never mean to tease to help with another," said Cathy dismally, for dyspepsia dimmed even the prospect of unlimited dainties on the morrow and did Grandmama a good turn, as I daresay she expected it would.

"I shall keep on trying. For I do want them very much, and I know what I can do to earn them, but I won't tell," and Kate tucked away her curls, as if done with vanity forever, for the dread of losing the pearls set her to thinking soberly.

Next morning she appeared with only a glimpse of yellow ripples under the lace of her cap, kept in the café, and attended to her work like a well-trained waiter. The others observed it and laughed together, but secretly followed her good example in different ways—Kitty by being very docile and Cathy by heroically lunching on bread and butter.

Kate felt better for the little effort, and when she was sent to carry a cup of tea to Miss Dutton after the hurry was over, she skipped around the back way and never looked to see if anyone's eyes followed her admiringly.

Miss Dutton was a little old maid, whose booth was near the café, in a quiet corner, because her useful articles did not make much show, though many were glad to buy them after wasting money on fancy things.

"Here is a young friend of mine who is longing to stir about. You look very tired. Don't you want to rest here a while and let Alice take your place, my dear?" asked Miss Dutton as she sipped her tea, while Kate affably chatted with a bright little girl, who looked decidedly out of place behind the piles of knit shirts and Shaker socks.

"Yes, indeed, if she likes. Take my cap and apron. Your dress is blue, so they match nicely. Our busy time is over, so you will get along without any trouble. I shall be glad to rest."

As she spoke, Kate stepped behind the table and, when Alice was gone, sat contentedly down under a row of piece bags, dusters, and bibs, well pleased to be obliging in such a convenient manner. Miss Dutton chatted about the fair in her pleasant way till she was called off, when she left her money box and booth in the girl's care till her return.

An old lady came and bought many things, glad to find useful articles, and praised the pretty shop woman for making change so well, saying to her companion as she went away:

"A nice, well-bred girl, keeping modestly in her place. I do dislike to see young girls flaunting about in public."

Kate smiled to herself and was glad to be where she was just then. But a few minutes later she longed to "flaunt about," for there was a sudden stir. Someone said eagerly, "The English swells have come," and everybody turned to look at a party of ladies and gentlemen who were going the rounds, escorted by the managers of the fair.

Kate stood up in a chair to watch the fine people, but without thinking of deserting her post till she saw them going into the café.

"There! I forgot that they were coming today, and now I shall not have the fun of waiting on them. It is too bad! Alice has my place, and doesn't know how to wait, and isn't half so—" She did not finish the sentence aloud, for she was going to say, "pretty as I." "She ought to come back and let

me go. I can't leave till she does. I depended on it. How pro-
voking everything is!" and in her vexation Kate pulled down
a shower of little flannel petticoats upon her head.

This had a soothing effect, for when she turned to put
them up, she saw a square hole cut in the cambric which
parted this stall from the café, and peeping in, she could see
the British lions feed, while a well-dressed crowd looked on
with the want of manners for which America is famous.

"Well, this is some comfort," thought Kate, staring with
all her eyes at the jolly, red-faced gentleman who was order-
ing all sorts of odd things, and the stout lady in the plain
dress who ate with an appetite which did honor to the English aristocracy.

"That is Lord and Lady Clanrobert, and the fine folks only
the people-in-waiting, I suppose. Now, just see Kitty laugh! I
wonder what he said to her. And there is Alice, never doing a
thing at her table, when it ought to be cleared at once. Cathy
takes good care of my lady. *She* knows where the nice things
are and how to set them out. If only I were there, how I
would sail about and show them one pretty girl, at least."

Kate was much too excited to be ashamed of that last
speech, though made only to herself, for at that moment she
saw Miss Dutton coming back, and hastened to hang up the
little petticoats and resume her seat, trying to look as if nothing had happened.

"Now, run if you like, my dear. I'm sorry to have kept you
so long, for I suppose you want to see the grandees. Go and
tell Alice to come back if you are rested," said the old lady,
bustling in with a sharp glance over her glasses.

Kate never knew what put the idea into her head, but she
followed a sudden impulse and turned a selfish disappointment into a little penance for her besetting sin.

"No, thank you. I will stay till she comes, and not spoil her
fun. I've had my share, and it won't hurt me to keep quiet a
little longer," she said quickly, and began to sort red mittens

to hide the color that suddenly came into her cheeks, as if all the forgotten blushes were returning at once.

"Very well, dear. I am glad to keep such a clever helper," and Miss Dutton began to scribble in a little book, as if putting down her receipts.

Presently the crowd came streaming out again, and after making a few purchases, the English party left and peace was restored. Then Alice came flying up in great excitement.

"Oh, it was such fun! The fine folks came to our tables and were so nice. My lady said 'Me dear' to us, and the lord said he had never been so well served in his life and he must fee the waiters. And after they went out, one of the young men came back and gave us each one of these delicious bonbon boxes. Wasn't it sweet of them?"

Kate bit her lips as she looked at the charming little casket, all blue satin, lace, looking glass, and gold filigree on the outside, and full of the most delicate French confectionery; for it was just one of the things young girls delight in, and she found it hard not to say, "I ought to have it, for you took my place."

But Alice looked so proud and pleased, and it was such a trifle, after all, she was ashamed to complain. So she called up a smile and said good-naturedly:

"Yes, it is lovely, and will be just the thing to keep trinkets in when the candy is gone. These elegant boxes are what grown-up young ladies get at Christmas, so you will feel quite grand when you show yours."

She tried to look as usual, but Alice saw that something was amiss and, suddenly thinking what it might be, exclaimed eagerly: "I truly didn't know they were coming when I took your place, and in the flurry I forgot to run to ask if you wanted to go back. Please take the box. You would have had it but for me. Do—I shall feel so much better if you will, and forgive my carelessness."

Kate was naturally generous, and this apology made it all

right, so her smile was genuine as she put the pretty toy away, saying heartily this time:

"No, indeed. You did the work and shall keep the fee. I don't mind now, though I did want to see the fun and felt cross for a minute. I don't wonder you forgot."

"If you won't take the box, you must the candy. I don't care for it, and you *shall* go halves. There, please do, you dear, good-natured thing," cried Alice, emptying the bonbons into a pretty basket she had lately bought, and giving it to Kate with a kiss.

This peace offering was accepted with a good grace, and when she had resumed her cap and apron, Kate departed, carrying with her something sweeter than the bonbons in her basket. For two pair of eyes followed her with an expression far more flattering than mere admiration, and she felt happier than if she had waited on a dozen lords and ladies. She said nothing to her cousins, and when they condoled with her on the loss she had sustained, she only smiled and took a sugarplum from her store, as if determined that no foolish regret should embitter her small sacrifice.

Next day Cathy, in a most unexpected manner, found an opportunity for self-denial, and did not let it slip. She had lightened many a weary moment by planning what she should buy with her ten dollars. Among various desirable things at the fair was a certain green-and-white afghan, beautifully embroidered with rosebuds. It was just ten dollars, and after much hesitation she had decided to buy it, feeling sure Grandma would consider it a useful purchase. Cathy loved cozy warmth like a cat and pleased herself by imagining the delightful naps she would take under the pretty blanket, which so nicely matched the roses on her carpet and the chintz on the couch in her charming room at home.

"I'll have it, for green suits my complexion, as the milkmaid said; and I shall lie and read and rest for a week after all this trotting, so it will be nice to cover my tired feet. I'll go and get it the minute I am off duty," she thought, as she sat waiting for customers during the dull part of the afternoon. Her chair was near the door of the temporary kitchen, and she could hear the colored women talk as they washed dishes at the table nearest her.

"I told Jinny to come 'fore dark and git a good warmin' when she fetched the clean towels. Them pore childern is 'most perished these cold nights, and I ain't been able to git no blankets yet. Rent had to be paid, or out we goes, and work is hard to find these times. So I 'most give up when the childern fell sick," said an anxious-looking woman, glancing from the bright scene before her to the wintry night coming on without.

"'Pears to me things ain't give round even-like. Some of these ladies has heaps of blankets, I ain't a doubt, laying idle, and it don't occur to 'em we might like a few. I wouldn't ask for red-and-blue ones, with 'mazin' fine flowers and things worked on 'em. I'd be mighty thankful for a pair of common ones for three or four dollars, or even a cheap comfortable. My old mammy is with me now, and suffers cruel with her bones, poor creeter, and I can't bear to take my cloak off her bed, so I'm gittin' my death with this old dud of a shawl."

The other woman coughed as she gave a pull to the poor covering over her thin shoulders and cast an envious look at the fur cloaks hanging in the ladies' room.

"I hope she won't steal any of them," thought Cathy, adding pitifully to herself, as she heard the cough and saw the tired faces: "I wonder they don't, poor things! It must be dreadful to be cold all night. I'll ask Mama to give them some blankets, for I know I shall think about the sick children and the old woman, in my own nice bed, if I don't do something."

Here a Topsy-looking girl entered the kitchen and went straight to the fire, putting up a pair of ragged boots to dry and shivering till her teeth chattered, as she warmed her hands and rolled her big eyes about what must have seemed to her a paradise of good things.

"Poor child! I don't suppose she ever saw so much cake in

her life. She shall have some. The sick ones can eat oranges, I know, and I can buy them all without leaving my work. I'll surprise her and make her laugh, if I can."

Up got Cathy, and going to the great refreshment table, bought six fine oranges and a plateful of good, solid cakes. Armed with these letters of introduction, she appeared before the astonished Jinny, who stared at her as if she were a new sort of angel, in cap and apron instead of wings and crown.

"Will you have these, my dear? I heard your mother say the babies were sick, and I think you would like some of our goodies as well as they," she said, smiling, as she piled her gifts in Jinny's outstretched arms.

"Bless your kind heart, miss. She ain't no words to thank you," cried the mother, beaming with gratitude, while Jinny could only show every white tooth as she laughed and bit into the first thing that came handy. "It's like manny from the skies to her, pore lamb. She don't git good vittles often, and them babies will jest scream when they sees them splendid oranges."

As Mrs. Johnson gave thanks, the other woman smiled also and looked so glad at her neighbor's pleasure that Cathy, having tasted the sweets of charity, felt a desire to do more, and, turning to Mrs. Smith, asked in a friendly tone:

"What can I send to your old mother? It is Christmastime, and she ought not to be forgotten when there is such a plenty here."

"A little mess of tea would be mighty welcome, honey. My old mammy lived in one of the fust families down South and is used to genteel ways, so it comes hard on her now. For I can't give her no luxuries, and she's ninety years old the twenty-fust of next Jenniwary," promptly responded Mrs. Smith, seeing that her hearer had a tender heart and a generous hand.

"She shall have some tea and anything else you think she would like. I'll have a little basket made up for her, and tell her I wish her a merry Christmas."

Then, hearing several bells ring impatiently, Cathy hurried away, leaving behind her three grateful hearts and Jinny speechless still with joy and cake. As she went to and fro, Cathy saw the dark faces always smiling at her, and every order she gave was attended to instantly by the willing hands of the two women, so that her work seemed lightened wonderfully and the distasteful task grew pleasant.

When the next pause came, she found that she wanted to do more; for a little food was not much, and the cloak on old Mammy's bed haunted her. The rosy afghan lost its charm; for it was an unnecessary luxury, and four blankets might be got for less than that one small one cost.

"I wonder what they would do if I should give them each five dollars. Grandma would like it, and I feel as if I should sleep warmer if I covered up those poor old bones and the sick babies," thought Cathy, whose love of creature comforts taught her to sympathize with the want of them. A sudden glow at her heart made her eyes fill, her hand go straight to her pocket, and her feet to the desk where the checks were handed in.

"Please change this for two fives. Gold, if you have it— money looks more in pretty, bright pieces," she said, as the lady obeyed, wondering what the extravagant little girl was going to buy now.

"Shall I?" asked Cathy, as she walked away with two shining coins in her hand. Her eye went to the kitchen door, out of which Jinny was just going, with a great basket of soiled towels in one hand and the precious bundle in the other, while her mother was saying, as she pulled the old cape closer:

"Run along, chile, and don't forgit to lay the pieces of carpet on the bed when you tucks up the babies. It's awful cold, and I can't be home till twelve to see to 'em."

That settled the question in Cathy's mind at once, and wishing the fives were tens, she went to the door, held out a hand to either woman, saying sweetly, "This is for blankets. It is my own. Please take it," and vanished before the astonished creatures could do more than take the welcome money and begin to pour out their thanks.

Half an hour afterward she saw the little afghan going off on the arm of Miss Dutton, and smiled as she thought how deliciously warm her old down coverlet would feel when she remembered her investment in blankets that day.

Kitty's trial came on the last night of the fair, and seemed a very hard one at the time, though afterward she was ashamed to have felt it such an affliction. About nine o'clock her mother came to her, saying anxiously:

"The carriage is here, and I want you to go right home. Freddy's cold is so bad I'm afraid of croup. Nurse is away, and Mary Ann knows nothing about it. You do, and I can trust you to watch and send for me if he grows worse. I cannot leave yet, for all the valuable things on my table must first be taken care of. Now go, like a good girl, and then I shall feel easy."

"Oh, Mama, how can I? We are to have a supper at eleven, and I know something nice is to happen—bouquets from the managers, because we have held out so well. Mary Ann will take care of Freddy, and we shall be home by twelve," cried Kitty, in dismay at losing all the fun.

"Now, Kitty, don't be disobedient. I've no time to argue, and you know that dear little boy's life is of more importance than hundreds of suppers. Before midnight is the time to watch, and keep him warm, and give him his pellets regularly, so that he may not have another attack. I will make it up to you, dear, but I shall not have a moment's peace unless you go. Mary Ann is so careless, and Freddy minds you so well. Here are your things. Help me through tonight, and I don't think I will ever undertake another fair, for I am tired to death."

Kitty took off her little cap and put on her hood without a word, let her mother wrap her cloak around her and walk with her to the door of the hall, giving last directions about drafts, spongia, wet bandages, and hot bottles, till she was shut out in the cold with thanks and a kiss of maternal relief. She was so angry that she had not dared to speak, and nothing but her love for her little brother made it possible for her to yield without open rebellion. All the way home she fretted inwardly and felt much ill-used; but when Freddy held out his arms to her, begging her to "tuddle me, 'cause my torp is so bad," she put away her anger and sang the restless child to sleep as patiently as if no disappointment made her choke a bit now and then.

When all was quiet and Mary Ann on guard, Kitty had time to think of her own trials, and kept herself awake imagining the pretty supper, the vote of thanks, and the merry breaking-up in which she had no part. A clock striking ten reminded her to see if Freddy had taken his medicine, and stealing into the nursery, she saw why her mother sent her home. Careless Mary Ann was sound asleep in the easy chair, a door had swung open, and a draft blew over the bed where the child lay, with all the clothes kicked off in his restless sleep and the pellets standing untaken on the table.

"I don't wonder Mama felt anxious, and it's lucky I know what to do. Mary Ann, go to bed; you are of no use. I have had experience in nursing, and I will take care of Master Freddy."

Kitty vented her vexation in a good shake of the girl's stout shoulders and sent her off with an air of importance funny to see. Then she threw herself into her task with all her heart and made the baby so comfortable that he slept quietly, in spite of the cough, with his chubby hand in hers. Something in the touch of the clinging fingers quieted all impatience, the sight of the peaceful face made her love her labor, and the thought that any carelessness might bring pain or danger to the household darling filled her heart with tender fears and a glad willingness to give up any pleasure for his sake. Sitting so, Kitty remembered Grandma's letter and owned that she was right; for many things in the past week proved it, and Mama herself felt that she should be at home.

"I shall not get the pearls, for I haven't done anything good, unless I count this," said Kitty, kissing the little hand she held. "Grandma won't know it, and I didn't keep account of the silly things I have left undone. I wonder if Miss Dutton could have been watching us. She was everywhere with her raffle book, and smiled and nodded at us like a dear old mandarin every time we met."

Kitty's mind would have been set at rest on that point if she could have seen Miss Dutton at that moment, for after a chat with Mama, the old lady had trotted off to her own table and was making the following singular entry in her raffle book:

"C. No. 3. Ordered home; went without complaint; great disappointment; much improved in docility; evidently tried hard all week to obey. Good record."

No one else saw that book but Grandmama, and she read in it three neatly kept records of that week's success, for Miss Dutton had quick eyes, ears, feet, and wits and did her work well, thanks to her peephole and the careless tongues and artless faces of girls who tell secrets without knowing it.

On Christmas morning each of the cousins looked anxiously among her many gifts for the red case with the golden "C" on it. None of them found it, but Kate discovered the necklace in a bonbon box far finer than the one she lost; Cathy found the pretty afghan pinned together with the cross; and on a fresher nosegay than any the managers gave their little maids, Kitty saw the earrings shining like drops of frozen dew. A note went with each gift, all alike, and all read with much contentment by the happy girls, as they owned the justice of the divided reward:

My dear,

The trial has succeeded better than I thought, for each has done well. Each deserves a little prize, and each will, I think, take both pride and pleasure in her share of Grandmama's love and Grandmama's pearls.

BERTIE'S BOX

A CHRISTMAS STORY

"Here's a letter for you, Mama, and please, I want the red picture on it," said little Bertie, as he came trotting into the room where his mother and aunt sat busily putting the last touches to their generous store of Christmas gifts.

"Do read it, Jane; my hands are too sticky," said Mrs. Field, who was filling pretty horns and boxes with bonbons.

"Whom do you know in Iowa?" asked Aunt Jane, looking at the postmark.

"No one. It is probably a begging letter. As secretary of our great charitable society, I often get them. Let us see what it is," and Mrs. Field popped a broken barley-sugar dog into Bertie's mouth to cheer him during the long process of picking off the stamp.

"Well, I never! What will folks ask for next? Just hear this!" exclaimed Aunt Jane, after running her eye over the neatly written page:

Mrs. Field:

Dear Madame—Knowing your kind heart, I venture to hope that you may be willing to help me from your abundant stores. I will state my request as briefly as possible. I am so poor that I have nothing for my two little boys on Christmas. I have seen better days, but my husband is dead, my money is gone. I am sick, alone, and in need of everything. But I only ask some small presents for the children, that they may not feel forgotten at this season of universal pleasure and plenty. Your mother's heart will feel how hard it will be for me to see their disappointment when for the first time in their little lives Santa Claus brings nothing.

Hopefully yours,
Ellen Adams

"Isn't that queer?" said Aunt Jane.

"It is pathetic," answered Mrs. Field, looking from the loaded table before her to the curly head at her knee.

"It's only a new and sentimental way of begging. She says she needs everything and, of course, expects you will send money. I hope you won't be foolish, Anna."

"I shall not send money, but surely out of all this plenty we can spare something for the poor babies, and let them keep their faith in Santa Claus. It won't take long to make up a little bundle, and will be no great loss if this woman has deceived us. My blessed mother used to say it was better to be deceived now and then than to turn away one honest and needy person. I only hope I may not forget all about it in my hurry," and having finished her sweet job, Mrs. Field went away to wash her hands before beginning another.

As they talked, neither of the ladies observed that a pair of large blue eyes were fixed upon their faces, while a pair of sharp little ears took in the story, and a busy little mind thought about it after both had put the subject aside.

Bertie sat thinking for several minutes, while Aunt Jane forgot him in her anxiety over the new cap she was making. At last he got up and walked slowly into the nursery, saying to himself, with a thoughtful face:

"Mama won't remember, and Aunty don't care, and those

poor little boys won't have any Twismuss if I don't 'tend to it. I've got lots of nice things, and going to have more, so I guess I'll give 'em some of the bestest ones."

Full of goodwill but uncertain how to begin, Bertie stood with his hands behind his back, looking about the pleasant room strewn with all manner of half-used-up and broken playthings. A good-sized wooden box in which a little horse had come still stood where he had left it, with two chairs harnessed to it and whip and reins lying near.

"That will do," said Bertie, and fell to work so busily that Aunt Jane heard nothing of him until a loud bang made her jump and call out sharply, "What are you doing, child?"

"Playing Santa Claus, Aunty, and packing my sleigh. Don't you hear the bells wing?" answered Bertie, shaking the reins and cracking the whip, with a sly twinkle in his eye; for he didn't want to be disturbed yet.

"Well, don't get into mischief," and Aunt Jane went on with her cap, just ready for the pink bows.

More bangs followed, and nails were evidently being driven. But Bertie often played carpenter, so no notice was taken, and soon he was busy pasting bits of paper on the box with his own particular "muscilack" pot.

"Now it's all ready, and Mama will be so pleased 'cause I saved her lots of trouble," he said to himself, surveying the bedaubed box with great satisfaction. "I guess I better put it under the bed till I come back. Aunty might see it and say it was clutter," he added, and tugged and shoved until it was safely hidden.

Then he went out for his walk and forgot all about it until the next day.

II

"Where *is* Bertie's best hat? I want to put a new elastic on it and cannot find it anywhere. What ever does the child do with his things?" said Mary, the nurse, fussing about to get her odd jobs done, that she might get off early to her Christmas shopping. There was a great hunt, but no hat appeared until Mary spied a bit of the feather sticking out of a crack in the badly fastened cover of the box under the bed.

"My patience! What a fine mess it will be in, crammed up in that way," scolded Mary, pulling it out and looking around for the hammer.

Aunt Jane was sewing at the window, and Mrs. Field had just come in, with a little parcel in her hand. Both looked on with interest while the lid came off the queer box, stuck full of nails and gay with red and blue labels that would have puzzled the wisest expressman.

Out came the hat, crushed flat, Bertie's best coat, several of his most costly books, a collection of toys, pictures, and sticky rolls of candy, while on the top of all appeared the piece of gingerbread given for lunch the day before.

"What has the dear child been at, I wonder?"

"He said he was playing Santa Claus yesterday when I heard him pounding those nails," answered Aunt Jane, adding severely, "He ought to be whipped for spoiling good things in that way."

"Here he comes. We'll see what his little idea was before we scold him," said Mama, as the familiar little trot was heard coming through the hall.

The moment Bertie's eye fell on the box, the music stopped, and he looked distressed.

"Why, that's mine! What made you spoil it, Mary?"

"Tell me about it, dear," and Mama turned the troubled face up to her own.

"It's for the poor little boys you read about. I was afraid you'd forget them, so I packed it all myself, and I thought you'd be so pleased," cried the boy eagerly.

"So I am, but why put in your nice things, dear, and not ask me about it?"

"You told me always to give the best pieces away, and I

thought they ought to be my very bestest, 'cause the little boys were so poor. Can't it go, Mama?"

Mrs. Field stood silent for a moment, looking from the small parcel in her hand to the overflowing box; then she kissed her little son, saying, with something like tears in her eyes:

"My blessed little Christian, you rebuke your mother and show her what she ought to do—give generously and gladly and trust her fellow creatures as you do. See the difference between our boxes! Mine so small and mean, his full of all his dearest treasures, even the bread out of his mouth. Bertie, I'll fill *your* box with comforts and send it in your name. You shall play Santa Claus in sweet earnest and have all the thanks."

Why Mama hugged him and Aunt Jane sniffed without another word of blame, Bertie did not know or care, but hopping gaily around his box, he cried with a beaming face:

"Yes, fill it cram-full, and let me help. Mama, have lots to eat in it. I know the boys will like that best."

"We will! Get your little wagon, and we will go around picking up all sorts of things for this remarkable box," said Mama, as she led the way to the great closet where her charity stores were kept.

It was a pretty sight, the packing of that box; for Mama kept finding something more to put in, and Bertie played expressman to his heart's content as he dragged the creaking yellow cart to and fro, full of half-worn clothes, toys he was tired of, and things to eat, all for "the poor little boys who hadn't any Twismuss."

"Now a few odds and ends to fill the corners, and it will be ready for Papa to nail up when he comes in to dinner," said Mama, as the last pair of little hose and her own warm wrapper went in.

"I'll send my purple shawl. It makes me look like a lemon, and it will be comfortable for the woman, if she really does need clothing," said Aunt Jane, who had watched the packing and melted in spite of herself.

"Another bit of Christmas work, my little Santa Claus. Warm the cold hearts, open the closed hands, and make us all love and help one another," whispered Mrs. Field, as old Aunty went away to get the shawl.

"I like this play," cried Bertie, patting down the bundles and rejoicing over the goodies he had seen put in.

"It is better to give than to receive, so play away, dear, and fill a bigger box each year," answered Mama, with a hand on the yellow head, as if she blessed it. Here Papa came in, and having read the letter and had a good laugh over Bertie's first box, he was very ready to nail up the second and send it off. He also pulled out his full pocketbook and, after hesitating a moment over a five- and a ten-dollar bill, hastily slipped the latter into an envelope and hid it in the pocket of the wrapper that lay on the top.

"Foolish, I daresay, but I must follow my boy's good example, and hope it is all right," he said, and then went to look up the hammer.

The cover was tightly fastened on, with a plainly written address, and Papa promised to have it sent off at once.

"I wonder what will come of it?" said Mama, as they stood looking at the heavy box.

"I predict that you'll never get a word of thanks," answered Aunt Jane, as if to atone for her generosity.

"You will probably get a letter asking for more," added Mr. Field, half-regretting his ten dollars now that it was too late to change it for a five.

"I know the dear little boys will be awfully glad to get it, and I shall like my goodies better because they have got some too," cried Bertie, untroubled by a doubt and full of happy satisfaction at having shared his comforts with those poorer than himself.

III

It was Christmas Eve, and far off in Iowa, people were making merry all through the great city. Even down among the shabby streets some small festivity was going on, and the little shops were full of working people buying something for tomorrow. But up in one room of an old house sat a woman rocking a sick baby to sleep and trying to sing while tears rolled down her cheeks.

It was a very poor room, with little in it but a table piled with work, a cold stove, one lamp, and an almost empty closet. In the bed were two black heads just visible under the shawl spread over them, and the regular breathing told that Jimmy and Johnny were sleeping soundly, in spite of cold and hunger and the prospect of no Christmas presents tomorrow.

As she rocked, poor Mrs. Adams glanced at the unfinished work on her table and wondered how she should get on without the money she hoped to have earned if Baby had not fallen ill.

Then her eye wandered from two small socks hung up on either side of the fireplace to the two little red apples on the mantel overhead. They were all she could get for Jimmy and Johnny, and even these poor gifts could not go into the stockings until the holes were mended, for neither had any toes left.

"As soon as Baby drops off, I'll mend them, and maybe I can finish a couple of vests if my oil holds out. Then I can get a bit of candy for the poor little lads. Christmas isn't Christmas to children without a taste of sweeties," said the poor mother, looking tenderly at the black heads under the shawl she was shivering without.

As if anxious to help all she could, Baby did "drop off" and, being tucked up on the foot of the bed, slept nicely for an hour, while Mother's fingers worked as fast as cold and weariness would let them.

"No answer to my letter. Well, I hardly expected it, being a stranger, and everyone so busy at this time of year. But it would have been such a comfort just to get a trifle for the poor dears," thought Mrs. Adams, as she sat alone, while the bells rang Christmas chimes and a cheery murmur came up from the wintry streets below.

Just then a bumping was heard on the stairs, a loud rap came at her door, a rough voice said suddenly, "Something for you, ma'am—all paid," and a hurried expressman dumped a big box just inside her door and was gone before she got her breath.

For a minute she thought she must be dreaming, it was all so sudden. Then she was sure that it was some mistake. But there was her name on the muddy lid, and she clasped her hands in speechless delight, feeling that it *must* be the answer to her letter.

Down went the work, and catching up the poker and a flatiron, she had that cover off in about three minutes; and, astonishing to relate, not one of those dear children woke up in spite of the noise.

If the Fields, Aunt Jane, and Bertie could have seen what went on for the next hour, they would have had no doubts about the success of their present, for Mrs. Adams laughed and cried, hugged the bundles, and kissed the kind note Mama had slipped in. She put on the warm wrapper and purple shawl at once and felt as if comfortable arms were around her. But when she put her hand in the pocket of the gown, where something rustled, and found the money, she broke down entirely and, dropping on the floor, fairly hugged the box, sobbing:

"God bless the dear people and keep them safe and happy all their lives!"

Many presents were given that night and many thanks returned, but none was a greater surprise than this one and none more gratefully received. Its coming was like the magic of the fairy tales; for everything seemed changed in a minute, and poor Mrs. Adams felt warm, rich, and happy, with comfortable clothes on her back, ten dollars in her pocket, and in her bosom the kind letter that proved even better than the box that she had generous friends to trust and help her. That cheered her most of all, and when her lamp went out after an hour of real Christmas work and a touching letter to Mrs. Field, she crept to bed with Baby cuddled close to a glad and grateful heart.

IV

"What's that?" said Jimmy, as he woke next morning and heard a roaring in the stove, where usually no fire was kindled until a late hour, to save fuel.

Popping up his head, he gave one astonished stare around the room and then dived to the bottom of the bed, where they usually burrowed to keep warm.

"I say, Johnny, it isn't our room at all. Something's happened, and it's just splendid," he whispered, pulling his brother's hair in his excitement.

"Go 'way! I ain't coming up yet," was the sleepy answer, as the elder boy curled himself up for another nap.

"There's a big fire, and something smells real nice, and there's new clothes all around, and Baby's sitting up in a red gown, and Mother's gone, and our stockings are crammed full—really, truly!"

The last piece of news roused Johnny and sent both scrambling up to sit staring in speechless wonder for several moments.

It was as Jimmy said. A good fire made the air comfortable; something nice sizzled on the stove; a big loaf, a piece of butter, and six eggs appeared upon the table, where mush and molasses were usually seen day after day. On the curtains were pinned little coats and trousers, hats hung on the bedposts, and a row of half-worn boots seemed ready to prance off the window seat. Baby sat bolt upright, as gay as a parrot, in a red flannel nightgown and a blue sacque, with an orange in one hand and a rubber horse in the other. But, most joyful sight of all, two long gray stockings dangled from the mantelpiece, brimful of delightful things that bulged mysteriously and came peeping out at the top.

"Is it Heaven?" whispered Jimmy, awestricken at such richness.

"No, it's Santa Claus. Mother said he wouldn't come, but I knew he *would,* and he has. Isn't it tip-top?" and Johnny gave a long sigh of pleasure, with one eager eye on his stocking and the other on a certain pair of blue knickerbockers with steel buttons.

"Let's get up and grab our presents," proposed Jimmy, and up it was, for out both went like two monkeys, giving Baby a glimpse of their funny nightgowns, made out of an old plaid shawl, gay but warm.

Each seized a stocking and a handful of toys and flew back again to rejoice over the new treasures until Mother appeared, with her arms full of bundles. She too was changed, for she wore a gray gown, with a purple shawl and red hood—so comfortable! Her face shone and her lips smiled, as if all her troubles had flown away. The sad old mother was gone, and a pretty, happy one ran to hug them, saying all in one breath:

"Merry Christmas, my darlings! See all the good things that dear lady sent us; and the blessed little boy helped, and gave the clothes off his back, and played Santa Claus, and all thought of us. Oh, thank 'em! Thank 'em, and kiss me quick, for my heart is full."

Then a grand cuddling went on, with Baby in the midst of it, and no one thought of breakfast till the kettle boiled over and reminded Mrs. Adams that her flock must have something more substantial than sugarplums to eat.

Such fun getting into Bertie's old clothes! They just fitted eight-year-old Johnny, and Jimmy didn't mind if the trousers bagged and the jackets lapped on him. They were new and beautiful to the shabby little fellows, tired of darns and patches, and when both were dressed, they strolled about as proud as two small peacocks.

The poor mother had no fears about dinner, for in the magic box were a pie, a cake, tea, oranges, figs, and nuts; and her morning purchases had laid in a bit of meat, with potatoes, so the Christmas feast was safe, and for one happy day all should have enough.

When breakfast was over and the excited family was about to return to their treasures, Mrs. Adams said, with what the children called her "Sunday look": "Boys, come here and put your hands in mine and say with me, 'God bless our dear little Santa Claus and send him many Christmases as happy as the one he has made for us!'"

Johnny and Jimmy said it very soberly, and then, as if the bottled-up rapture of their boyish hearts must find a vent in noise, they burst out with a shrill shout, to which Baby added a squeal of delight:

"Hurrah for Bertie Field and the jolly box he sent us!"

LITTLE ROBIN

No one called her that till after the Christmas I am going to tell about, and when you have read the story, you will see what a good name it was for her.

Bess was twelve years old—a rosy, bright-eyed little girl who did errands for all the old ladies who lived in the village. There were a good many of them—nice, kind old souls, very busy about their small affairs, very sociable, and very good to the poor; so they were glad to make Bess their messenger and pay her for doing their errands. She lived with her grandmother and liked to earn money, for they were poor and the old woman was getting more feeble every year. But Bess was strong and well, and such a wise, steady child the fussiest old lady could trust her to match wools, carry parcels, or deliver messages without a mistake. Every morning, when all was neat in the little house and Grandma settled comfortably at her knitting, Bess, with her big satchel on her arm, would trot from door to door to get her orders and then go on to the middle of the town for the letters and the various things the old ladies wanted.

In this way she earned a good deal, not always in money,

but in good warm clothes for Grandma and help about the wood and rent. Each old lady did what she could, for none were rich. But among them Bess fared well, and was a happy, useful child, beloved by all for her cheerful face, pretty manners, and faithfulness in everything.

One Christmas Eve she was thinking how well they were getting on as she trudged up the long hill with a basket of pies from Miss Palmer to her friend Mrs. Baker. The sun was setting splendidly, but the wind was very sharp and a bitter-cold night was coming on, with a moon by and by to light the merry sleighing parties. At the minister's gate stood two pretty little children resting after a coast down the bank about three feet high. They were hopping up and down to warm their toes and chattering like magpies, though their little noses were red and they ought to have been safe in the house at that hour.

But the mother was busy trimming the church and the nurse gossiping in the kitchen, so little Arty and Min got into trouble, as we shall see.

"Joe said the Christmas trees came from those woods, and I saw him bring lots on his sled. So if we go up, we can get a dear little one for the dolls and drag it home on *my* sled," said the boy, full of the new idea and longing for a good run in the smooth road, where bells had been jingling gaily all day as sleighs flew to and fro.

"It's pretty far. Would Mama like it?" asked the small girl, eager to surprise her family of dolls with a fine tree, but re-membering certain promises about leaving the garden.

"She wouldn't mind—and we'll get a ride on the first sleigh that comes along. Tuck up on my sled and be ready. I'll hang on and drag you; then we'll go quick and not be a bit tired," answered Arty, looking anxiously for a horse's head to come around the corner.

Bess came instead, and nodded to them as she passed. "Time to go indoors. Run, or Jack Frost will nip your noses," she said, wondering to see them there so late.

"We ain't afraid. We are going to see where Christmas trees grow, and get one for our dollies," called the children, waving their red mittens.

Bess never stopped to talk when doing errands, so she hurried on and left the children waiting for a ride. Before long a sleigh passed with an old man in it, and Arty hung on unobserved, while little Min bumped along on the yellow sled behind. The horse went fast, and soon the runaways were far away on the hilltop. But it was such fun to skim along with jingling bells, to see the trees fly by, to feel that no one knew where they were and that this would be a fine adventure to tell when they got home, that they kept on till the old man discovered them and ordered them off at once.

"Here's a nice road, and over there, seems to me, I see lots of Christmas trees all shining bright," said Arty, as he dragged his sister into the wood along the path made by the sleds of the lumbermen.

"Do they grow with candles on 'em?" asked Min.

"I shouldn't be s'prised if they did. Ours always has candles, and Mother ties on the presents. Anyway, we can play this is a fairy wood and everything is splendid. Now you get off, and we'll run down that nice little path and see if that pretty red is a fire or the sky. I guess these trees are too big for us. We must get a little one and pull it up," directed Arty, feeling much elated with his adventure and bent on exploring the forest, which looked particularly attractive just then, with the green boughs powdered with snow.

So the innocent little souls went scrambling deeper and deeper among the pines toward the grove of small trees, playing they saw giants and fairies by the way. It was warmer in the wood. A squirrel came to welcome them, an owl flew by with its soft cry, as if trying to be agreeable, and they talked, and snowballed, and pulled up a dozen little trees before they found one that suited them. Meantime, the pretty light faded away, and they realized how far from home they were.

"My boots are so tired I can't go anymore. Please pull me on the sled, Arty," said Min, quite used up and rather scared by the shadows that began to fill the corners of the wood.

"I left the sled somewhere, 'cause the runner broke. I guess we won't try to find it, but run right home. It's pretty late, and I'm awfully hungry—ain't you?" answered Arty, trudging stoutly away in what he fancied was the right direction.

"Yes, and I want to see Mama," said Min, with a quaver in her voice suggestive of tears.

"Now, don't you be a baby. If you fret and cry, I'll never take you on a nice tramp again. Take hold of me and come along, and in a minute we'll find the road and run right home."

Arty spoke bravely, but his heart began to fail him, for no path appeared and the winter twilight was darkening fast. His little conscience told him he had done wrong to go so far, and every moment he grew more and more sure that they were lost. Poor Min struggled along in the big rubber boots that burdened her short legs, and after tumbling into holes, slipping off icy stones, and wading through drifts for what seemed hours to her weary little feet, she suddenly stopped short and sobbed out:

"Oh, we're lost! We're lost—and never can find Mama again! I'm so cold and tired and hungry I can't go anymore. Please let me rest, Arty, and find my hanchif."

"Let's both sit down and see about it. Here's a nice log for you. Don't cry, dear. I'll find the way somehow. If I'd known we were going to be lost, I'd have had lots of pebbles in my pocket, like Hop-o'-my-thumb; then we'd be all right. It *is* pretty cold. Wonder how hunters make a fire when they haven't any matches? Seems as if I read about rubbing two sticks. You rest and see me do it, Min. Then we'll be nice and warm with a fire, and wolves and bears won't dare to touch us if we stay all night."

Such a dreadful idea dismayed poor Min, and she cried aloud, while Arty vainly rubbed two green twigs till his fingers were nearly frozen. This disappointment and his sister's dismal wailing, as well as the darkness gathering about them, upset the boy, and after a manful struggle to keep back the tears, he began to cry also, while the little owl hooted mournfully and the cold wind sighed among the pines.

It was a sad sight, the two shivering, sobbing little creatures all alone in the wintry wood, when they should have been safe and warm at home. But no one saw it except the evening star, which peeped through the boughs like a bright eye watching over them.

When all the tears were shed and both were too cold and tired to cry anymore, Arty took heart and tried to carry his sister on his back toward an open place which he fondly hoped was the path. A bad fall into a deep hollow chilled his courage, and after struggling on a little longer, he gave up and sat down again in despair.

"I'm so sleepy! Let's say 'Now I lay me' and go to bylow," said Min with a sob and a gape, as her head fell on Arty's shoulder, top-heavy with weariness, for it was long past her bedtime.

"Come under this tree, where there isn't any snow, and we'll cuddle down and try to be warm till Father comes to find us. I'll take care of you, dear. I ain't afraid of the dark—much."

As he spoke, Arty drew the poor little girl under the wide-spreading boughs of a hemlock and, putting his arms about her, tried not to tremble and start at every sound, or to stare into the gloom with wide eyes full of fear. Min was asleep in a moment, and after a few more penitent tears, Arty dropped off also, just as he had resolved to watch all night. So there they lay, asleep in the wood, where the bitter cold would soon freeze them if no one came to find and save them. But the old tree sheltered them well, the kind star watched over them, and the little owl skimmed softly away to bring a friend of whom they never thought.

Mrs. Baker kept Bess some time, asking about all the news of the village, and, when she went, filled her basket with cookies and gave her a little can of milk for her grandmother.

"I'm afraid I've kept you too long, dear. It grows dark so sudden nowadays. Do take my lantern, so you won't slip and spill the milk. Put the can in the basket; then it will ride stiddy, and you'll have a hand free for the lantern," said the old lady, peering out into the dusk.

Bess did not want the light, as she was used to running over the snow, but to oblige Mrs. Baker, she accepted it, and set out for home. Just as she left the gate, a little dark object on the white road caught her eye farther up the hill, and she went to see what it was, thinking it might be the full purse poor little girls were always finding in the stories she read.

No, it was only a little red mitten. But Bess looked troubled as she turned it over; for on the back was a white "M," and she knew it was one of the pairs Grandma had knit for little Minnie.

"I do believe those naughty babies really did go after a tree. I thought they were only playing. What a fright their folks will be in at home if they did run away! Yes, here is the mark of a sled. I'll run up the hill and see if they did go this way."

Off went Bess, and soon another little mitten told her she was on the track of the runaways, for Min had been so busy holding on she lost her mittens without knowing it. The marks of runners and two small pairs of feet were plainly seen in the snow where the children turned into the wood, and Bess followed the trail, calling as she went, sure that the little things could not have gone far.

Now she was glad of the lantern, for by its light she could

see where the wanderers went; and presently the abandoned sled made her more anxious than ever, for it was evident the children had gone toward a pond nearby. Bess was out of breath, cold, and frightened, but she pressed on, thinking only of the lost babies and their poor mother, for she knew that if the children were out long on such a bitter night, it might cost them their lives.

Soon the little steps turned in a safer direction, and Bess was so glad that she had not got to look for them in that dreadful pond that she cheered up, and ran, and looked, and called, till a faint, far-off cry made her heart beat fast as she hurried toward the sound. A soft, sad wail it seemed, and tears came to her eyes while she paused to listen from time to time, thinking of the dear babies calling for help, alone in the great wood.

"I'm coming, Arty—here's Bess—don't cry, little Min," she shouted, scrambling over logs and through the bushes as the wail grew louder and louder, till she came to an open spot and found nothing but a small owl perched on a bare tree blinking at her light.

Much disappointed and quite exhausted, she sat down to rest, putting the lantern on the ground beside her. Then the good light did its part, for it shone under the hemlock boughs on a little black heap, out of which stuck four small rubber boots plainly seen against the snow. Bess saw them, gave a cry of joy, and ran to wake the children with kisses as she hugged and patted them in her delight. Arty opened his eyes and shivered, but Min lay as cold and still as if she had been a little marble statue.

"She is frozen. She is dead. What shall I do? Oh, what shall I do?" cried Bess in despair, when she had rubbed the purple hands and white cheeks, and lifted the stiff eyelids, and called the child every tender name she could think of.

Arty seemed too sleepy to speak or understand, and poor Bess could only clasp her hands and look about for help, quite heartbroken at the dreadful fear she felt that she had come too late.

As her eyes glanced from the poor baby to the clear, cold sky, asking God to show her what to do, the beautiful star shone on her like a friendly eye and made her think of the one that led the shepherds to the manger where the Christ Child lay that Christmas Eve so long ago.

It comforted her somehow, and gave her new strength and hope. Catching up Min, she went as fast as she could toward a soft light which suddenly began to glimmer not far off. She thought it was the rising moon, but in a moment saw that it was the flame of a fire left by the lumbermen. They had covered it, but the wind had fanned the embers, and one bright flame blazed up to show Bess where lay the help she so much needed.

As fast as her tired feet could go, she hurried to the warm spot, and laying Min on the hemlock boughs where the men sat to eat their dinners, she raked open the fire, threw on some dry chips, and, covering the child with her own cloak, ran back to bring Arty and the basket and the lantern. Up sprang a fine fire, and the blessed warmth began to be felt as the half-frozen children lay in the full light of the blaze, while Bess set the can on the coals, heated the milk, and made Arty drink some.

He was soon awake and, when a cookie was put into his hand, began to eat like a hungry boy and to remember what had happened. He told Bess all about it, while she held Min in her arms, rubbing her till the warmth returned to feet and hands and feeding her with little sips of hot milk till she sighed, "More—nice—more," and lifted her drowsy little head to find the mouth of the can for herself.

Many kisses, cookies, and chips restored the nearly frozen children to life, and then the question was how to get them home. Arty said he could walk, but found his legs so weak and stiff that Bess was afraid to let him try. She could not carry Min so far; the sled was useless; and the nearest house was a long way off. So the wise child decided to leave them where they were, safe by the warm fire, while she ran for help.

Explaining this to the boy, she told him to watch Min—who had fallen asleep again with a cake in her hand—to throw on chips, drink the milk, and not be afraid till she came back. He promised stoutly; but before she had piled up the wood, made the fire safe, and hung the lantern on a tree to mark the place, he had fallen back on the hemlock boughs, worn out, and as fast asleep as his little sister.

"Perhaps it is just as well. He won't take it into his head to run after me and get lost again. I won't be long, and they can't freeze now," said Bess, as she tucked them up under her cloak with their feet to the fire and laid boughs over them to keep the small coverlet from blowing away.

Then, feeling that she had done her best, she ran away to tell the anxious parents that the lost babies were safe. The moon was up now, and as Bess trudged through the wood, its big bright face cheered her up, showed her the way, and seemed to smile approvingly upon the brave little girl.

While she had been doing her part so well, the town had been all astir and people running up and down looking for the minister's children. The poor mother was sure they had fallen in the river, for holes were found near the shore, and marks of little feet. Everything was in confusion at the house, and lanterns were flying to and fro like fireflies as the anxious neighbors looked high and low. No one thought of the great pine wood on the hilltop. It was so far away, and the children never went there, so it was no wonder people felt sure the dear babies had fallen into the water and been drowned.

A crowd of sad-faced men were standing at the gate of the parsonage, and the old ladies were inside crying over the poor mother, who sat as if turned to stone, waiting for her dear dead children to be brought home to her. Suddenly down the road came a little figure running fast, with hood half off, no cloak, and panting breath.

"It's Bess! She's found them!" cried the men, springing to meet her.

At the sight of help all her strength seemed to leave the little girl, and she could only whisper brokenly, as she pointed backward: "Safe—in the wood—by the fire—go quick!" Then she dropped into the strong arms of the man who stood nearest, and never heard the loud cheer that went up, telling the town that the minister's children were found.

Out rushed the startled women, and carried Bess in to be blessed and cried over and comforted by the grateful mother, while the men went off as fast as horses could carry them to the lumber camp, which all knew well.

Bess was quite used up, and could only lie on the sofa and be petted and praised by all the old ladies after word had been sent to Grandma that she was safe.

Soon the chime of the bells came merrily down the long hill, and the runaways were laid in their mother's arms, safe but too sleepy to do anything but cry for bed, where they were speedily put, to dream of owls and cookies, Christmas trees and broken sleds, till next morning.

The minister, who had been away at a wedding, came back in time to hear the story that night and to carry Bess home himself, a very proud and happy little girl. She was quite satisfied with the thanks and praises showered upon her, and thought that would be the end of it. But the old ladies made a fine plan for their pet, and all the next day, in spite of their own dinners and gifts, they prepared for the surprise in the evening.

Good things to eat, warm things to wear, a load of wood, and no end of kind words and wishes were the presents left at the door of the little house that Christmas morning, and Bess felt so rich it didn't seem as if she could bear any more.

But when a note came from Arty and Min asking her to come up and see their tree, she was glad to go, and after she had wrapped Grandma up in the funny, old-fashioned cloak and pumpkin hood she liked to wear, they drove away in style when the big sleigh came for them.

It was early in the evening, on account of the children, who were none the worse for their prank except bad colds and some stiffness in their usually active little legs. They nearly smothered Bess with kisses and hugs, understanding now that they owed their lives to her, and it was sweet to see the proud air with which Arty led her in and the eagerness with which little Min brought an easy chair and nestled into it beside her friend, not to mention the mother's face and the father's handshake as they welcomed her. All the old ladies were there in their best caps, and a flock of children, so there was quite a party to enjoy the tree. But first the minister made a little speech.

"Friends," he said, "we must wait a few minutes while the candles are lighted, so I will tell a story to amuse you."

Then, as the old ladies beamed and nodded till their cap ribbons rustled, and the children pranced in their chairs with impatience, he told the dear old story of "The Babes in the Wood." But he changed it as he went along, and improved it immensely, many of his hearers thought, for he left out the cruel uncle and the bad men altogether; made it winter instead of summer, so there were no blackberries to eat, but cookies and milk; the kind robin covered the babes with hemlock boughs, not leaves; and, best of all, they didn't die, but went home safe and well to a father and mother, who were kept alive for the express purpose of thanking that dear robin.

There was great laughter and clapping among the children, and some tears twinkled out of the eyes of the tender-hearted old ladies as they listened. But everyone shouted when the story ended, and the minister added: "My runaways went to find a Christmas tree, and here is the one good fairies have sent them, not for their dolls, but for the brave, kind friend who saved their lives."

Then the folding doors flew open, and there on a table stood the loveliest little tree ever seen, all shining with candles, golden fruit, pretty gifts, and on the top a great bright star, for Bess had told about the one she saw in the wood when she prayed for help.

All the children took hands and danced about the tree until astonished Bess was ready to go and take the presents hung there for her by these kind people, who were glad to show their gratitude in this pretty way. Among them were a year's rent in an envelope, from the minister; all manner of warm and comfortable things for Grandma; and for Bess a scarlet cloak and hood to replace the old gray one burned and torn that night in the wood.

"Let me keep the little gray one, dear. I love it, for it helped to warm and save my babies; and do you wear this to remember me by," said Mrs. Minister, as she wrapped the pretty cloak around Bess, with a look and touch so soft and loving the little girl felt as if her own mother kissed her.

"Now she looks like Red Riding Hood, but I won't let the old wolf eat her," cried Arty, bound to be her knight forevermore.

"No, I think she looks like the robin redbreast that covered the babes with leaves," began the minister, smiling at her, with his hand on her head.

"Yes, yes, she's the robin—she's the good robin," cried the children, pleased with the fancy.

And after that, Bess was called "Little Robin" by everyone who knew her, and the old ladies were never tired of telling how she earned the name.

LU SING

In Paris, in the year 1879, a daughter was born to one of the sisters of Miss Alcott. But the mother, sad to say, died soon after, and so the little girl was carried overseas to America to be brought up by her aunt, to whom she was a great joy and comfort. In a letter of that time to the editor of St. Nicholas, *Miss Alcott wrote, "I have been so bowed down with grief at the loss of my dear sister May that I have not had a thought or care for anything else. May left me her little daughter for my own, and soon I shall be too busy singing lullabies to one child to write tales for others or go anywhere, even to see my kind friends."*

Miss Alcott wrote a number of stories for her little niece when Lulu was about eight years old. These stories were tied up in little birch-bark covers and were called "Lulu's Library." A number of them were afterward published under that title, but the following story has been kept by Lulu all these years. The readers of St. Nicholas *will be glad to see a new story by the author of* Little Women. *And it will interest them also to know that Miss Alcott herself and little Lulu are two of the characters in "Lu Sing."*

All the principal characters in the story, indeed, are real people, though disguised by Chinese names, and of course the Chinese incidents are entirely fanciful. Little Lulu could not pronounce the names of her two aunts very plainly, so Aunt Louisa became "Ah Wee" and Aunt Anna "Ah Nah." And in the same way the author has introduced Lulu's names of her two cousins as "Ef Rat" and "Jay Rat," while Julia, the name of the governess, became "Ju Huh."

Although "Ah Nah" was extremely fond of tea, she did not own 365 teapots. She was somewhat stout, and always happy and cheerful, and was continually trying to help others. "Ah Wee" usually took the lead in family matters, and those who knew the author of the story will easily recognize her in the character.

The real "Lu Sing," after the death of her aunt, went back to live with her father in Switzerland, and she is today as charming and sweet a girl as could be found anywhere. Her two old cousins, "Ef Rat" and "Jay Rat," are very proud of her.

"Ef Rat"*

Once on a time there lived in China a little girl named Lu Sing, which means "Peach Blossom." She was eight years old and very pretty, with beady black eyes, slanting brows, a pug nose, and a red mouth. Her hair was done in a great bow on the top of her head and seven golden pins stuck in it. She wore robes of pink and blue and yellow and violet silk, with wide sashes of gauze and tiny satin shoes, and had parasols of every color to match.

She lived with two kind aunts, one named Ah Nah and the other Ah Wee, and two cousins, Ef Rat and Jay Rat, and she had a teacher whom she called Ju Huh.

Their home was a beautiful Chinese house, with silver balls on the points of the roof that sang sweetly when the wind blew. It was full of tall silk screens, fans and lanterns,

---

* Frederick Alcott Pratt, son of Alcott's older sister, Anna.

mats of perfumed grass, tea trays and china jars, splendidly embroidered curtains, and gilded dragons made into chairs and sofas.

The cousins were tea merchants, and the old aunts were very rich, so Lu Sing had everything she wanted, and might have been a very happy girl if one of the naughty spirits that fly about everywhere and are called "jinns" in China had not come to trouble her, as we shall see.

She was a good child most of the time, always skipping and singing, and kissing the aunts, and romping with the cousins, as gay as a lark. But she did not like to study, and when Ju Huh got out the ebony tablet and the ivory-covered books and the india ink and the brush and the sheets of rice paper, and struck the brass gong, an hour after breakfast, Lu Sing always began to hear the naughty jinn say, "Don't go! Fret and pout and make a fuss, my blossom, and we will have some fun."

Poor Ju worked long and patiently over Lu Sing, and at last gave up in despair, and could only teach Lu to play on the tom-tom and embroider birds and flowers on bits of silk and satin, as little American girls sew patchwork.

Lu liked the music and the pretty colors, so she did these things pleasantly, and she and the jinn felt very proud to think they had got their own naughty way.

Now, Ah Nah was a dear old soul, as gentle as a dove, and her only fault was a too great love of tea. She had three hundred sixty-five pots—one for each day in the year—and took sips every half hour; for the fire in the copper pan burned all the time, and her pocket was always full of the finest kind of orange pekoe, so she could brew tea at any moment.

Ah Wee did not drink tea, and was always scolding about it, because she was poorly and cross and had to live on bird's-nest soup to cure her "whong-hong tummyfuss," which is Chinese for dyspepsia. Well, the two aunties were much troubled about Lu and her naughty ways, and they tried to think how they could cure her of this last trick. For if she would not study, she would be a dunce, and dunces are shut up in little pens and fed like pigs, but not let out to play like other children. This was such a sad idea that poor Ah Nah cried a cupful of tears over it, and Ah Wee said, with a stamp that smashed two lovely china monsters: "By the Great Dragon and the Sacred Teapot, that child shall be made to mind."

"But how?" said Ah Nah, drying her tears on a pink tissue-paper handkerchief and taking a sip of tea to comfort her.

"We will fly kites, and if that does not do it, we must put her in the river to soak the badness out of her."

Now, flying kites is one way in which the Chinese pray, and putting in the river is the way they punish naughty children. They are shut up in willow cages and kept in the water, all but their heads, till they are so clean and hungry and tired that they promise to be good for a long time, as they hate to be soaked.

When anyone wishes a thing very much, he makes a fine kite, writes on it his wish, and at midnight, when the moon shines, he goes to Wang Choo, or "Windy Hill," and flies the kite till it is out of sight; then he cuts the string and waits to see if it will come down again. If it does, they know that the King of Heaven in the Great Blue Tent says "no" to the wish, and they are very sad. But if the kite never comes down, they are sure the prayer will be answered, and go home singing for joy.

Now the two aunts resolved to make a prayer kite and ask that Lu Sing might grow very good and learn her lessons. So they pasted lovely rose-colored paper on a frame shaped like a star, wrote in silver letters, "Great King, teach our dear child to obey," and one moonlit night, when everyone was asleep, they crept out to fly the kite.

Two funny old ladies, wrapped up in plum-colored cloaks, with gauze veils around their heads, toddled along on their tall slippers, one carrying the kite, the other her dear teapot, so she could refresh herself after the long walk. Nobody but the watchmen with their lanterns and war fans was stirring in the streets. The tea gardens were empty now, the tom-toms and the whong-whong were done beating in the theaters, the dancing girls were asleep on their mats, and the flower boats were floating quietly down the river to the Great Pagoda, to be ready for a feast in the morning.

Away went the old ladies over the bridge, by the china houses, where the silver bells chimed softly in the wind, and up the long road to the top of Wang Choo. A gale always blew there, and kites always went up well. Ah Nah, being fat, held the ball of silken cord, and Ah Wee, being long and thin like a "hoan-hop," or grasshopper, ran with the great kite and sent it sparkling up in the moonlight. Then they sat down to wait till it was out of sight. Up, up, up it went, like a red-and-silver bird, carrying the old aunts' prayer to the Great Blue Tent where the King of Heaven lived. When they could see it no longer, Ah Wee cut the string, and Ah Nah at once made some very strong tea to keep her awake until dawn, for if the kite did not fall before then, it never would.

So there they sat, praying and sipping for three long hours, and little Lu Sing was snugly asleep on her sweet-scented mats under the satin coverlet and never dreamed what trouble the aunties took for her sake. The sky grew pink at last, and the "wik-wak," or lark, began to sing, the lemon flowers to shine like stars among the dark leaves, and the tea pickers to come into the wide fields to gather the leaves with the dew on them.

"Sister, our prayer is heard. We may go home," said Ah Wee, who had sat bolt upright like a Chinese mummy all the time, while dear old Ah Nah nodded and dozed in spite of six pots of tea.

"Praise and thanks to the Holy Crocodile and the Golden Butterfly, who is queen of the air. Let us go." And bundling the little teapot into her pocket, Ah Nah waddled after Ah

Wee, who went stalking down the hill, singing in a cracked voice:

> *Fly, kite, fly fast,*
>   *Like a bird in air.*
> *For the Great King's ear*
>   *Whisper our prayer.*
> *Lu Sing, Lu Sing,*
>   *Our darling child,*
> *Soon, soon shall grow*
>   *Patient and mild.*
>
> *Then beat the whong,*
>   *The tom-tom play,*
> *And all rejoice*
>   *In that glad day.*
> *Boom ho! Bang hi!*
>   *Ching ri do me!*
> *Bum ra! Rum ki!*
>   *Ping, sang, boo, see!*

As the people all along the way heard this lovely song, they popped up their heads, or peeped out of the window, and joined in the chorus, for they knew that a prayer kite had been flown and all was well with somebody.

No one at home but Rox Ha, the housekeeper, knew anything about this night adventure, and the old ladies never said a word. But all day they watched Lu Sing to see if any change took place in her. No; she was very perverse, and would say "pag" when Ju Huh wanted her to say "pug." She also called her teacher a "mush-wag," which means "old fuss," and was a naughty child till school was over. Then she came smiling out to get her lunch of sugared cakes made of melon seeds and plums.

The aunts did not punish her; they waited, hoping some

good "win," or spirit, would come into her heart and make her a better child. But nothing happened till she went to bed, and then no one knew it but Lu Sing. The aunts very early put on the tall blue paper extinguishers which they used as nightcaps, and went to sleep, being wearied after the long night on the hill. Everyone else had retired, and the house was shut up.

Now, Lu Sing had a charming little room with walls like tea trays, all black and gold. A great fan moved to and fro over her head all night, the mats were as fine as silk, and the soft quilts were of satin, full of swansdown.

A splendid screen shut in her bed. It was in four parts: At the head, embroidered on gray satin, was a silver moon and stars; at the foot, on pale pink, a golden sun; on the right a rosy branch of peach blossoms made the white satin lovely; and on the left, upon green, was a crane with long red legs, a black bill, a fiery eye, and feathers that shone like mother-of-pearl. All rich children had screens like this, with the moon, meaning night, at the head; the sun, for morning, at the foot; the flowers, meaning happiness; and the crane, good luck.

A light in the gauze lantern made it bright enough for Lu to see the pretty pictures on her screen, and she often lay staring at them till "Peep Oi" (Old Sleep Man) shut her eyes tight. This night she could not even doze, but kept looking at the crane, for he seemed to be alive. His eyes grew as bright as sparks, his plumes stirred, his tucked-up leg came down, and at last, to her great surprise, his long bill opened, and he said in a rough voice:

"Ha, bad child! Listen to me. I am the Conscience Bird, and when boys and girls won't be good, I come and peck at them. So!"

Here he gave a snap at the bedclothes, and Lu felt a sharp pinch in her arm. It frightened her very much, but she could not stir; and in another minute the crane pecked again, in another place, still harder. Lu tried to call out, but she could not speak, and had to lie still till she was well nipped all over. Then the great bird stopped, and after clashing his dreadful beak to get the down out of it, he said sternly:

"Every night that you are bad, I shall come to peck. But if you are good, I shall tell you stories and bring you nice dreams. Don't tell anyone of this, or I shall peck very hard. Try your best, and see if you are not good by and by. Now go to sleep"; and with two waves of his wings Lu was fast asleep.

When she waked up, she felt it was only a bad dream, for there stood the crane on one long red leg just as usual, never saying a word. But she told no one and really did try that day to behave, for in her heart she knew the Conscience Bird was right, and was afraid he might come and peck again. She expected to be all black-and-blue with pinches, but her rosy, plump little body was not hurt a bit; only on her breast was one red spot like a star. It had never been there before, and Lu thought that must be the place where her conscience lived. So she folded her gauze "tob," or shirt, over it and went to breakfast, very sober, with this strange secret in her heart.

"The good win has driven out the bad jinn, and our prayer is answered. Dear Lu Sing is so sweet today, it must be so," said the old aunts, watching her with their peeping eyes as she went to "sigh book soh," or school, so pleasantly that Ju Huh nearly fell off her seat to see such a smiling child come in and not have to be dragged by the tails of her sash or the knobs on her head. But when Lu said "pug" right off instead of "pag," and "ri ko day," not "day so ki," as she usually did, poor Ju cried for joy.

All day Lu was good; and when everyone gave her nine kisses at bedtime, and the cousins promised her a little palanquin, or carriage, all to herself if she kept on in this lovely way, and the aunties burned spices and sticks of sandalwood before the china gods in the sacred corner to thank the Great King, the little girl lay down on her sweet-smelling mats very happy.

Would the crane come? Yes; soon his eyes began to shine, his pearly plumes to move. Down came the red leg, open went the long bill, and out came a soft voice, saying pleasantly:

"Good child! I am pleased with you, and you shall have a splendid dream to reward you. Go on trying, and by and by it will be easy to be good."

Then the downy wings waved over her, and Lu dreamed all night of birds and flowers, and pretty children, and feasts of bonbons, and fountains of sweet water, and palaces, of jewels, of dolls that talked, and books that never were the same no matter how often you looked at them, and all manner of strange and lovely things.

After that day a great change took place in Lu Sing; and though she had a naughty fit now and then and got a good pecking, she soon began to find that it grew easy to be good; and then fine dreams and charming stories were her reward, for the Conscience Bird kept his word and in a short time was very fond of Lu.

So the time came when the children chose the Summer Queen, as they called the little girl who was to rule over them in all their plays during the vacation. It was always the best little girl, and everyone wanted to be chosen. For it was a great honor, and the fathers and mothers were pleased and proud, and the child's name was put in the papers, and the emperor sent her a present. This year everyone thought it would be Fou Choo, a dear little girl who was loved by all her mates, she was so good and sweet. But the Conscience Bird had his plans, and if Lu had waked up in the night, she would have found him gone from the screen, for he flew to the beds of the other children and in their dreams told them all about her, and how hard she tried to be good, and how pleased the old aunts would be if she should be chosen. The children wagged their heads and talked the matter over, but it could be settled only by votes when the day came.

So all were busy getting ready, for each one had a new dress; and as the little girls in China are named for flowers, they wore the colors that belonged to them, and wreaths of lemon, orange, rose, violet, or lily to match the pretty silk gowns. Lu Sing had a pretty pink robe worked with silver butterflies, nine pearl pins in her hair, all her best necklaces and bracelets, blue velvet shoes, a white silk parasol with silver bells on the points and a coral handle, her best fan, and a wreath of peach blossoms. She looked lovely as she stood all ready on the steps anxiously waiting for the procession to come along.

The two aunts were going in sedan chairs, and the Rat cousins, with their pigtails waving, peacock feathers in their caps, and black satin robes shining with gold dragons, were ready to follow, for everyone went to this picnic.

Soon the *boom! boom!* of the whongs was heard, the sweet toot of the tweedle-dees, and the soft thump of the tom-toms; and the splendid banners came waving down the street— for each child carried one, and all were as gay as rainbows. Fou Choo walked at the head and beckoned Lu Sing to come with her. So Lu ran down and took her hand, and on they marched, two very pretty little girls, one in blue and gold and the other in pink and silver, with the big flags and music going on in front. All the friends followed, and the streets looked as if a flower bed were passing by. Garlands hung on the houses, lanterns were ready to light at dark, and great fans waved to keep the air cool. The emperor and his children stood on the roof of the palace and looked down, and all the little parasols bowed as the little procession passed.

At last they came to the rose garden where the picnic was held and the queen chosen. A great golden basket stood at the foot of a throne made of red roses, and as the children passed by, each dropped in a flower which meant a name.

Then, when all but two were seated on the grass, the flowers were counted, and the child who had the most votes was proclaimed the queen. Everyone watched eagerly, for soon two piles of flowers grew bigger and bigger. One was forget-me-nots and meant Fou Choo, the other peach blossoms and meant Lu Sing. At last the basket was empty, and far the largest pile, as all could see, was the pink one!

"Lu Sing! Lu Sing! All hail the queen!" shouted the children; and the gongs banged, and the music played, the flags waved, and the friends clapped and cheered. Everyone was glad, and Lu Sing was so surprised and pleased that she hid her rosy little face behind her silver fan as she was led by Fou Choo and Lee Wing to receive the crown of white roses and the beautiful little necklace sent by the emperor. Then the feast was held, and games were begun that lasted all day; and at night the long procession of lanterns went winding home as the happy children escorted the queen to her house, sang under her windows, and then left her to be kissed by the proud aunties and cousins before she crept into her little bed to thank the good Conscience Bird, who sang her to sleep with the sweetest song ever heard.

THE EAGLET IN THE DOVE'S NEST

"Bless me, what is that?" cried Mrs. Dove one day, as something fell out of the sky into her nest and nearly knocked little Bill and Coo off the branch where they sat wondering if they would ever be brave enough to fly.

"It is a very ugly bird, Mama," said Bill, one of the young doves, staring with all his eyes at the queer stranger.

"It hasn't any feathers and looks very sad and scared. Do comfort it, Mama," said little Coo, who was the most tender-hearted dove that ever lived.

"Poor thing, it does seem hurt and frightened, but it looks so big and wild and unlike any young bird I ever saw that I am half afraid to go near it," answered Mrs. Dove, peering timidly in.

It was a strange bird, for, though very young, it filled the whole nest; and while the breath was nearly knocked out of its little body by the fall, its gold-ringed eyes were bright and sharp, its downy wings flapped impatiently, and its strong beak snapped, as if ready to bite.

"It is hungry," said Bill, who had a large appetite himself and was always ready to eat.

"Give it that nice berry you brought for me. I can wait," said Coo, glad to help.

Mrs. Dove offered the ripe strawberry, but the stranger refused it with a scream that made the gentle doves quake on their pink legs, it was so fierce and loud.

"I'll go and ask Neighbor Owl to come and tell us what it is and how to take care of it"; and away went Mrs. Dove, after carefully settling her children in the empty nest of a neighbor close by, where they sat staring at the newcomer, who screamed and flapped and flashed its golden eyes at them, as if trying to make them understand who it was.

"Oh, this is a young eagle," said the owl when he came. "You had better push it out of the nest at once, for as soon as it is large enough, it will eat you all up, or fly away without thanking you for your care."

"I cannot turn the poor little bird out of my house to die. Don't you think, if I keep it a little while and am very kind to it, I can make it love us and be happy till it is able to take care of itself?" asked Mrs. Dove.

"Well, I am sure if anyone can, you can. But you know it is hard to tame a wild bird, and eagles are very fierce. This is a golden eagle, the finest kind of all, and probably came from some nest far up in the mountains yonder. I can't imagine how it got here, but here it is, hungry and naked, and you can do as you like about keeping it. Only feed it on worms and bugs, and tame it if possible."

Away flapped the owl, who disliked the light, and evidently thought Mr. and Mrs. Dove very foolish if they kept the wild bird in their nest.

"Let it rest and then send it away," said Bill, who was a prudent fellow.

"No, no, Mama. Keep it and love it, and make it good, and it won't want to hurt us, I know," cried little Coo, ready to take in a hawk or a naughty cuckoo, if they needed help.

"I will think about it, my dears, and meantime get something for it to eat," answered Mrs. Dove, flying away at once; for she was a wise as well as a very kind bird, and when she made up her mind, nothing changed it. She soon came back with a nice fat worm, which her new child snapped up eagerly and screamed for more. Nine times did that kind dove go to and fro, though she was plump and easily tired, before the hungry eaglet was satisfied. Then it put its head under its wing and went to sleep for an hour, and when it woke up, it was in a better temper and answered questions in a shrill small voice very unlike the soft coo of the doves.

"What is your name, my dear?" asked Mrs. Dove, who had taken a nap as well as her guest.

"Golden Eye, but Papa called me Goldy," answered the eaglet.

"Where did you live, love?"

"Far, far away, up among the clouds, in a much bigger nest than this, among the rocks on the mountain."

"Why did you leave it, darling?"

"My mama died, and while Papa was at her funeral, a bad kite stole me and was carrying me away when I pecked so hard he let me drop, and here I am."

"Dear me, dear me, what a sad tale!" sighed Mrs. Dove.

Bill looked up through the pine boughs to see if the bad kite was near, but Coo wiped a tear from her eye with her left wing and hopped nearer, saying:

"Please let poor Goldy stay, Mama, since he has no mother and cannot get back to his home. We will love him dearly and all be so happy he will like to stay till he is grown."

"Yes, dear, I shall keep him and fear no harm. Eagles are noble birds, and if I am kind to this poor thing, his family will be grateful and perhaps spare the lives of all little birds for our sake."

"I shall like to stay here till I can fly, and I will tell my people not to hurt you, for you are kind birds and I love you," said Goldy, putting up his bill to kiss Mrs. Dove; for he was proud to hear his race praised and was touched by the sweetness of his new friends. The little eaglet had a good heart, and it was well he had come to stay for a while with the gentle doves, as we shall see.

All the birds in the wood came to see the stranger, and all said that Mrs. Dove would have a great deal of trouble with him, for it was evident the wild thing was hard to manage and had a fierce temper and a strong will. But Mama Dove would not send him away and, though often discouraged and sad, still clung to her naughty Goldy, sure that, in time, love and patience would tame him.

Bill and Coo were good children and needed little training. Bill liked his own way, but Mama only had to say, "My son, do it to please me and because it is right," and he gave up. Coo was so loving she was easily managed, her faults being of the gentler sort, and a look from Mama was enough to keep her straight.

But oh, dear me! What trials that sweet, plump dove did have with her foster child! If Goldy could not get what he wanted, he would scream and peck, and lie on his back and kick, till he nearly fell out of the tree. He wanted to eat all sorts of indigestible things and, if denied, would throw his dinner to the ground and sulk for hours. He was saucy to Bill and Coo, and put on airs to the other birds who came to see him, and told everyone he was a golden eagle, not a common bird, and someday he would fly away to live in the clouds with his splendid father. That was the naughty side of him. The good side was very sweet, and so it was impossible to help loving him and hoping he would grow up a fine bird after all.

He pitied all poor little creatures, was very generous, and gave away anything he had to give so gladly it was sweet to see him. When in a good temper, he was charming and sat up like a real king, telling tales to the doves and other birds, who loved to look and listen; for soon the down on him changed to feathers of a pretty color, his fine eyes shone, and he learned to talk softly, not to scream, as eagles have to do where the wind blows and thunder growls and water-falls dash.

One wing had been hurt when he fell, and Mama Dove had tied it up with a bit of gold-thread vine so it would not droop and be weak. Long after the other wing was strong and ready to fly, he still wore the bandage, for wise Mrs. Dove felt that she had not done all she could for this wild creature yet, so she did not let him know his wing was well lest he should fly away too soon.

Goldy was improving very fast now, and though in his heart he longed to see his father and go to find his home in the mountains, he loved the doves and was very happy with them.

One day, as he sat alone in the pine tree, a hawk flew by and stopped to ask what he was doing there. Goldy told his story, and the hawk said scornfully:

"You silly bird! Pull off that vine and fly away with me! I'll help you find your father by and by."

Goldy was much excited by this idea, and when the hawk with his strong bill pulled off the bandage, he flapped his wings and found them all right.

With a scream of joy he flew straight up into the sky and went floating around and around, learning to balance himself in the air, to dip and rise, as he had seen other eagles do. The hawk showed him how and hoped to get the eaglet to his nest, where he would keep him till he found his father and made the eagle his friend by restoring his lost child.

Meantime, Mrs. Dove and Bill and Coo came home to find the nest empty and to hear from the linnet that Goldy had gone.

"I told you so," said the owl, with a wise nod. "All your care is wasted, and I am sure you will never see that un-grateful bird again."

But Mama Dove wiped a tear from one of her bright eyes and said gently:

"No, my friend, love and care are never wasted. And even if Goldy does not return, I am glad I was a mother to him, and I am sure he will not forget us, but be better for his stay in the dove's nest."

Coo went to comfort her mother, and Bill hopped to a high branch to see if the runaway was in sight.

"I think I see him far away, skimming about with a bad hawk. What a pity he has such a dangerous guide! He will teach him naughty things and perhaps be cruel to him if he does not obey," said Bill, standing on tiptoe to peer up to where two dark specks were seen in the blue sky.

"Let us all sing loud, and maybe he will hear and come back. I know he loves us and is a dear bird in spite of his pride and self-will and temper," said Mrs. Dove, beginning to coo with all her might.

The other birds set up a chirping, twittering, singing, and calling till the wood was full of music, and a faint, sweet sound went up even to the cloud where Goldy was soaring and trying to look at the sun. He was tired now, and the hawk was cross because he would not go home with him, but wanted to find his father at once, and he had pecked and scolded him till he was afraid. So when the song of the dear wood birds reached him, it sounded like a call of "Come home, darling, come home to us. We all are waiting, we all are waiting." Something seemed to draw him back, and with a sudden sweep he sank down, down, till the hawk dared not follow him any farther, for he saw a farmer with his gun, ready to shoot the thief that had been stealing some of his young chickens.

Glad to be rid of the new friend, Goldy flew back to the old ones, who welcomed him with such a concert it seemed as if they would split their little throats with joy.

"I thought my darling would not leave me without a good-

bye," cooed Mother Dove, as she smoothed the eaglet's ruffled feathers softly with her bill, while her own birds stood
first on one pink leg and then on the other and flapped their
wings for joy.

"I think you tied a cord around my heart as well as around
my wing, and that draws me back to you, dear Mama," said
Goldy, nestling close to the white breast that was so full of
love for him. "I will fly away and enjoy myself sometimes, but
I will always come back and tell my adventures, and if ever I
find my father, I will not go to him till I have said good-bye
and thanked you with all my heart."

So Goldy lived on with the doves, growing strong and
handsome, with golden plumes, keen, bright eyes, and wide
wings that bore him up into the sky, where he gazed at the
sun without winking and was a true eagle, fearless, beautiful,
and wild. But in his heart he still loved the gentle doves, still
tried to be like them in many things, and after every long
flight came back to fold his wings in the pine tree and tell
splendid tales of all he had seen on the green earth and in
the blue sky. The wood birds were never tired of hearing
these tales and would listen with their round eyes fixed on
him, without stirring a feather, even for hours at a time. They
all admired him very much and loved him, too; for, though
so strong, he never hurt them, and if a hawk came near,
he would drive it away and keep the little songbirds safe.
They called him their prince and hoped he would always stay
with them.

But Goldy longed for his home on the mountaintop and
for his father, and the older he grew the stronger grew the
longing; for that quiet life was not natural to a bird meant to
live high among rocks and clouds, to fight the storm, and to
soar up nearer to the sun. So he could not help it, but kept it
to himself till one day, when he had flown far away and
stopped to rest on a great cliff in a wild and lonely place, he
saw a large golden eagle sitting nearby, looking down upon

the world with his keen eye, as if trying to find something. Goldy had never seen so splendid a bird, and ventured to speak to him. He was very gentle to Goldy as the young eagle told his story, to which he listened eagerly. Before he ended, he gave a loud scream of joy, flapped his great wings, and cried, with eyes that shone like jewels:

"You are my lost baby! I have looked far and wide for you, and thought you were dead. Welcome, my dashing son, prince of the air and delight of my heart!"

Then Goldy felt his father's great wings fold about him, the golden plumes press his own, and the brilliant eyes look fondly into his as the king of birds told him about his beautiful mother, his new home far away, and the friends waiting to welcome him to their free life.

He enjoyed it all, but when his father wished to take him there at once, he said gently:

"No, Papa, I must first go and say good-bye to the dear birds who cared for me when I was a poor, helpless, naughty little fowl. I promised, and I cannot grieve them by going away without telling them how happy I am and thanking them."

"And so you shall, and take my thanks also. Give Madame Dove this feather, and tell her no creature that flies will ever harm her while she has the king's plume to show. Make haste, my son, and return as soon as you can, for I cannot spare you long."

Then Goldy flew back and told his happy news, and though the doves were very sorry to lose him, they knew it was best, for his right place was with his royal father. They and other summer birds were soon going south for the winter and would have to leave him, for eagles love snow and wind and storms and do not fly to warm countries in autumn.

Everyone was glad Goldy had found his father, and when the time came for him to go, all gathered to say good-bye. Mrs. Dove was very proud of the golden feather, and Bill and

Coo felt as brave as lions when they stuck it up in their nest like a banner, for it was a great honor to have such a gift from the king of birds.

There was a lively farewell concert, and everything in the wood that could sing joined in it. Even the owl hooted and the hoarse crows cawed, while the mosquitoes hummed and the crickets chirped like mad. Then, with kisses all around, Goldy flew up, up, far out of sight, while the sweet music followed him till he could hear it no longer. But under his wing he hid a little white feather, Mother Dove's last gift to him, which would keep his heart always true and warm.

And the lessons of the gentle bird helped him to rule his temper, guide his will, and make him a comfort to his father, the pride of the mountaintop, and the noblest eagle that ever turned his golden eyes to the sun.

APPENDIX

A GOLDEN WEDDING

[Chapter V of *Moods* (1865)]

Hitherto they had been a most decorous crew, but the next morning something in the air seemed to cause a general overflow of spirits, and they went up the river like a party of children on a merrymaking. Sylvia decorated herself with garlands till she looked like a mermaid; Mark, as skipper, issued his orders with the true Marblehead twang; Moor kept up a fire of fun-provoking raillery; Warwick sang like a jovial giant; while the *Kelpie* danced over the water, as if inspired with the universal gaiety, and the very ripples seemed to laugh as they hurried by.

"Mark, there is a boat coming up behind us with three gentlemen in it, who evidently intend to pass us with a great display of skill. Of course you won't let it," said Sylvia, welcoming the prospect of a race.

Her brother looked over his shoulder, took a critical survey, and nodded approvingly.

"They are worth a lesson, and shall have it. Easy, now, till they pass; then hard all, and give them a specimen of high art."

A sudden lull ensued on board the *Kelpie* while the blue

shirts approached, caught, and passed with a great display of science, as Sylvia had prophesied, and as good an imitation of the demeanor of experienced watermen as could be assumed by a trio of studious youths not yet out of their teens. As the foam of their wake broke against the other boat's side, Mark hailed them:

"Good morning, gentlemen! We'll wait for you above there, at the bend."

"All serene," returned the rival helmsman, with a bow in honor of Sylvia, while the other two caused a perceptible increase in the speed of the *Juanita*, whose sentimental name was not at all in keeping with its rakish appearance.

"Shortsighted infants, to waste their wind in that style, but they pull well for their years," observed Mark paternally, as he waited till the others had gained sufficient advantage to make the race a more equal one. "Now, then!" he whispered a moment after; and as if suddenly endowed with life, the *Kelpie* shot away with the smooth speed given by strength and skill. Sylvia watched both boats, yearning to take an oar herself, yet full of admiration for the well-trained rowers, whose swift strokes set the river in a foam and made the moment one of pleasure and excitement. The blue shirts did their best against competitors who had rowed in many crafts and many waters. They kept the advantage till near the bend. Then Mark's crew lent their reserved strength to a final effort and, bending to their oars with a will, gained steadily till, with a triumphant stroke, they swept far ahead, and with oars at rest waited in magnanimous silence till the *Juanita* came up, gracefully confessing her defeat by a good-humored cheer from her panting crew.

For a moment the two boats floated side by side while the young men interchanged compliments and jokes, for a river is a highway where all travelers may salute each other, and college boys are "Hail fellow! Well met!" with all the world.

Sylvia sat watching the lads, and one among them struck

her fancy. The helmsman who had bowed to her was slight and swarthy, with Southern eyes, vivacious manners, and a singularly melodious voice. A Spaniard, she thought, and pleased herself with this picturesque figure till a traitorous smile about the young man's mouth betrayed that he was not unconscious of her regard. She colored as she met the glance of mingled mirth and admiration that he gave her, and hastily began to pull off the weedy decorations which she had forgotten. But she paused presently, for she heard a surprised voice exclaim:

"Why, Warwick! Is that you or your ghost?"

Looking up, Sylvia saw Adam lift the hat he had pulled over his brows, and take a slender brown hand extended over the boatside with something like reluctance as he answered the question in Spanish. A short conversation ensued, in which the dark stranger seemed to ask innumerable questions, Warwick to give curt replies, and the names Gabriel and Ottila to occur with familiar frequency. Sylvia knew nothing of the language, but received an impression that Warwick was not overjoyed at the meeting; that the youth was both pleased and perplexed by finding him there; and that neither parted with much regret as the distance slowly widened between the boats, and with a farewell salute parted company, each taking a different branch of the river, which divided just there.

For the first time Warwick allowed Mark to take his place at the oar, and sat looking into the clear depths below, as if some scene lay there which other eyes could not discover.

"Who was the olive-colored party with the fine eyes and foreign accent?" asked Mark, lazily rowing.

"Gabriel André."

"Is he an Italian?"

"No, a Cuban."

"I forgot you had tried that mixture of Spain and Alabama. How was it?"

"As such climates always are to me—intoxicating today, enervating tomorrow."

"How long were you there?"

"Three months."

"I feel tropically inclined, so tell us about it."

"There is nothing to tell."

"I'll prove that by a catechism. Where did you stay?"

"In Havana."

"Of course, but with whom?"

"Gabriel André."

"The father of the saffron youth?"

"Yes."

"Of whom did the family consist?"

"Four persons."

"Mark, leave Mr. Warwick alone."

"As long as he answers, I shall question. Name the four persons, Adam."

"Gabriel senior; Dolores, his wife; Gabriel junior; Catalina, his sister."

"Ah, now we progress. Was Señorita Catalina as comely as her brother?"

"More so."

"You adored her, of course?"

"I loved her."

"Great heavens, what discoveries we make. He likes it, I know by the satirical glimmer in his eye; therefore, I continue. She adored you, of course?"

"She loved me."

"You will return and marry her?"

"No."

"Your depravity appalls me."

"Did I volunteer its discovery?"

"I demand it now. You left this girl believing that you adored her?"

"She knew I was fond of her."

"The parting was tender?"

"On her part."

"Iceberg! She wept in your arms?"

"And gave me an orange."

"You cherished it, of course?"

"I ate it immediately."

"What want of sentiment! You promised to return?"

"Yes."

"But will never keep the promise?"

"I never break one."

"Yet will not marry her?"

"By no means."

"Ask how old the lady was, Mark?"

"Age, Warwick?"

"Seven."

Mark caught a crab of the largest size at this reply and remained where he fell, among the ruins of the castle in Spain which he had erected with the scanty materials vouchsafed to him, while Warwick went back to his meditations.

A drop of rain roused Sylvia from the contemplation of an imaginary portrait of the little Cuban girl, and looking skyward, she saw that the frolicsome wind had prepared a practical joke for them in the shape of a thundershower. A consultation was held, and it was decided to row on till a house appeared, in which they would take refuge till the storm was over. On they went, but the rain was in greater haste than they, and a summary drenching was effected before the toot of a dinner horn guided them to shelter. Landing, they marched over the fields, a moist and mirthful company, toward a red farmhouse standing under venerable elms with a patriarchal air which promised hospitable treatment and good cheer—a promise speedily fulfilled by the lively old woman who appeared with an energetic "Shoo!" for the speckled hens congregated in the porch and a hearty welcome for the weather-beaten strangers.

"Sakes alive!" she exclaimed. "You be in a mess, ain't you? Come right in and make yourselves to home. Abel, take the menfolks up chamber, and fit 'em out with anything dry you kin lay hands on. Phebe, see to this poor little creeter, and bring her down lookin' less like a drownded kitten. Nat, clear up your wittlin's, so's't they kin toast their feet when they come down; and Cinthy, don't dish up dinner jest yet."

These directions were given with such vigorous illustration, and the old face shone with such friendly zeal, that the four submitted at once, sure that the kind soul was pleasing herself in serving them, and finding something very attractive in the place, the people, and their own position. Abel, a staid farmer of forty, obeyed his mother's order regarding the "menfolks"; and Phebe, a buxom girl of sixteen, led Sylvia to her own room, eagerly offering her best.

As she dried and re-dressed herself, Sylvia made sundry discoveries, which added to the romance and the enjoyment of the adventure. A smart gown lay on the bed in the low chamber, also various decorations upon chair and table, suggesting that some festival was afloat; and a few questions elicited the facts. Grandpa had seven sons and three daughters, all living, all married, and all blessed with flocks of children. Grandpa's birthday was always celebrated by a family gathering. But today, being the fiftieth anniversary of his wedding, the various households had resolved to keep it with unusual pomp, and all were coming for a supper, a dance, and a "sing" at the end. Upon receipt of which intelligence Sylvia proposed an immediate departure; but the grandmother and daughter cried out at this, pointed to the still-falling rain, the lowering sky, the wet heap on the floor, and insisted on the strangers' all remaining to enjoy the festival and give an added interest by their presence.

Half promising what she wholly desired, Sylvia put on Phebe's second-best blue gingham gown, for the preservation of which she added a white apron, and, completing the whole with a pair of capacious shoes, went down to find her party and reveal the state of affairs. They were bestowed in the prim best parlor, and greeted her with a peal of laughter, for all were *en costume*. Abel was a stout man, and his garments hung upon Moor with a melancholy air; Mark had disdained them and, with an eye to effect, laid hands on an old uniform, in which he looked like a volunteer of 1812; while Warwick's superior height placed Abel's wardrobe out of the question; and Grandpa, taller than any of his seven goodly sons, supplied him with a sober suit—roomy, square-flapped, and venerable—which became him and with his beard produced the curious effect of a youthful patriarch. To Sylvia's relief, it was unanimously decided to remain, trusting to their own penetration to discover the most agreeable method of returning the favor; and regarding the adventure as a welcome change after two days' solitude, all went out to dinner prepared to enact their parts with spirit.

The meal being dispatched, Mark and Warwick went to help Abel with some outdoor arrangements; and begging Grandma to consider him one of her own boys, Moor tied on an apron and fell to work with Sylvia, laying the long table which was to receive the coming stores. True breeding is often as soon felt by the uncultivated as by the cultivated; and the zeal with which the strangers threw themselves into the business of the hour won the family and placed them all in friendly relations at once. The old lady let them do what they would, admiring everything and declaring over and over again that her new assistants "beat her boys and girls to nothin' with their tastiness and smartness." Sylvia trimmed the table with common flowers till it was an inviting sight before a viand appeared upon it; and hung green boughs about the room, with candles here and there to lend a festal light. Moor trundled a great cheese in from the dairy, brought milk pans without mishap, disposed dishes, and caused Nat to cleave to him by the administration of surreptitious tidbits and jocular suggestions; while Phebe tumbled about in everyone's way, quite wild with excitement, and Grandma stood in her pantry like a culinary general, swaying a big knife for a baton as she issued orders and marshaled her forces, the busiest and merriest of them all.

When the last touch was given, Moor discarded his apron and went to join Mark. Sylvia presided over Phebe's toilet and then sat herself down to support Nat through the trying half hour before, as he expressed it, "the party came in." The twelve years' boy was a cripple, one of those household blessings which, in the guise of an affliction, keep many hearts tenderly united by a common love and pity. A cheerful creature, always chirping like a cricket on the hearth as he sat carving or turning bits of wood into useful or ornamental shapes for such as cared to buy them of him, and hoarding up the proceeds like a little miser for one more helpless than himself.

"What are these, Nat?" asked Sylvia, with the interest that always won small people, because their quick instincts felt that it was sincere.

"Them are spoons—'postle spoons, they call 'em. You see, I've got a cousin what reads a sight, and one day he says to me, 'Nat, in a book I see somethin' about a set of spoons with a 'postle's head on each of 'em. You make some and they'll sell, I bet.' So I got Gramper's Bible, found the picters of the 'postles, and worked and worked till I got the faces good; and now it's fun, for they do sell, and I'm savin' up a lot. It ain't for me, you know, but Mother, 'cause she's wuss'n I be."

"Is she sick, Nat?"

"Oh, ain't she! Why, she hasn't stood up this nine year. We was smashed in a wagon that tipped over when I was three years old. It done somethin' to my legs, but it broke her back and made her no use, only jest to pet me and keep us all kind of stiddy, you know. Ain't you seen her? Don't you want to?"

"Would she like it?"

"She admires to see folks, and asked about you at dinner, so I guess you'd better go see her. Look a-here, you like them spoons, and I'm a-goin' to give you one. I'd give you all on 'em if they wasn't promised. I can make one more in time, so you jest take your pick, 'cause I like you and want you not to forget me."

Sylvia chose Saint John, because it resembled Moor, she thought; bespoke and paid for a whole set, and privately resolved to send tools and rare woods to the little artist, that he might serve his mother in his own pretty way. Then Nat took up his crutches and hopped nimbly before her to the room where a plain, serene-faced woman lay knitting, with her best cap on, her clean handkerchief and large green fan laid out upon the coverlet. This was evidently the best room of the house, and as Sylvia sat talking to the invalid, her eye discovered many traces of that refinement which comes through the affections. Nothing seemed too good for "daughter Patience"; birds, books, flowers, and pictures were plentiful here, though visible nowhere else. Two easy chairs beside the bed showed where the old folks oftenest sat; Abel's home corner was there by the antique desk covered with farmers' literature and samples of seeds; Phebe's workbasket stood in the window; Nat's lathe in the sunniest corner; and from the speckless carpet to the canary's clear water glass, all was exquisitely neat, for love and labor were the handmaids who served the helpless woman and asked no wages but her comfort.

Sylvia amused her new friends mightily, for, finding that neither mother nor son had any complaints to make, any sympathy to ask, she exerted herself to give them what both needed, and kept them laughing by a lively recital of her voyage and its mishaps.

"Ain't she prime, Mother?" was Nat's candid commentary when the story ended and he emerged red and shiny from the pillows where he had burrowed with boyish explosions of delight.

"She's very kind, dear, to amuse two stay-at-home folks

like you and me, who seldom see what's going on outside four walls. You have a merry heart, miss, and I hope will keep it all your days, for it's a blessed thing to own."

"I think you have something better, a contented one," said Sylvia, as the woman regarded her with no sign of envy or regret.

"I ought to have. Nine years on a body's back can teach a sight of things that are wuth knowin'. I've learnt patience pretty well, I guess, and contentedness ain't fur away, for though it sometimes seems ruther long to look forward to, perhaps nine more years layin' here, I jest remember it might have been wuss and if I don't do much now, there's all eternity to come."

Something in the woman's manner struck Sylvia as she watched her softly beating some tune on the sheet, with her quiet eyes turned toward the light. Many sermons had been less eloquent to the girl than the look, the tone, the cheerful resignation of that plain face. She stooped and kissed it, saying gently:

"I shall remember this."

"Hooray! There they be—I hear Ben!"

And away clattered Nat, to be immediately absorbed into the embraces of a swarm of relatives who now began to arrive in a steady stream. Old and young, large and small, rich and poor, with overflowing hands or trifles humbly given, all were received alike—all hugged by Grandpa, kissed by Grandma, shaken half breathless by Uncle Abel, welcomed by Aunt Patience, and danced around by Phebe and Nat till the house seemed a great hive of hilarious and affectionate bees. At first the strangers stood apart, but Phebe spread their story with such complimentary additions of her own that the family circle opened wide and took them in at once.

Sylvia was enraptured with the wilderness of babies and, leaving the others to their own devices, followed the matrons to "Patience's room" and gave herself up to the pleasant tyranny of the small potentates, who swarmed over her as she sat on the floor, tugging at her hair, exploring her eyes, covering her with moist kisses, and keeping up a babble of little voices more delightful to her than the discourse of the flattered mamas, who benignly surveyed her admiration and their offspring's prowess.

The young people went to romp in the barn; the men, armed with umbrellas, turned out en masse to inspect the farm and stock and compare notes over pigpens and garden gates. But Sylvia lingered where she was, enjoying a scene which filled her with a tender pain and pleasure, for each baby was laid on Grandma's knee, its small virtues, vices, ailments, and accomplishments rehearsed, its beauties examined, its strength tested, and the verdict of the family oracle pronounced upon it as it was cradled, kissed, and blessed on the kind old heart which had room for every care and joy of those who called her "Mother." It was a sight the girl never forgot, because just then she was ready to receive it. Her best lessons did not come from books, and she learned one then as she saw the fairest success of a woman's life while watching this happy grandmother with fresh faces framing her withered one, daughterly voices chorusing good wishes, and the harvest of half a century of wedded life beautifully garnered in her arms.

The fragrance of coffee and recollections of Cynthia's joyful aberrations at such periods caused a breaking-up of the maternal conclave. The babies were borne away to simmer between blankets until called for. The women unpacked baskets, brooded over teapots, and kept up a harmonious clack as the table was spread with pyramids of cake, regiments of pies, quagmires of jelly, snowbanks of bread, and gold mines of butter—every possible article of food, from baked beans to wedding cake, finding a place on that sacrificial altar.

Fearing to be in the way, Sylvia departed to the barn, where she found her party in a chaotic Babel; for the offshoots had been as fruitful as the parent tree, and some four dozen young immortals were in full riot. The bashful roosting with the hens on remote lofts and beams; the bold flirting or playing in the full light of day; the boys whooping, the girls screaming, all effervescing as if their spirits had reached the explosive point and must find vent in noise. Mark was in his element, introducing all manner of new games, the liveliest of the old, and keeping the revel at its height; for rosy, bright-eyed girls were plenty, and the ancient uniform universally approved. Warwick had a flock of lads about him absorbed in the marvels he was producing with knife, stick, and string; and Moor a rival flock of little lasses breathless with interest in the tales he told—one on each knee, two at each side, four in a row on the hay at his feet, and the boldest of all with an arm about his neck and a curly head upon his shoulder, for Uncle Abel's clothes seemed to invest the wearer with a passport to their confidence at once. Sylvia joined this group and partook of a quiet entertainment with as childlike a relish as any of them, while the merry tumult went on about her.

The toot of the horn sent the whole barnful streaming into the house like a flock of hungry chickens, where, by some process known only to the mothers of large families, everyone was wedged close about the table; and the feast began. This was none of your stand-up, wafery, bread-and-butter teas, but a thoroughgoing, sit-down supper, and all settled themselves with a smiling satisfaction, prophetic of great powers and an equal willingness to employ them. A detachment of half-grown girls was drawn up behind Grandma as waiters; Sylvia insisted on being one of them and proved herself a neat-handed Phillis, though for a time slightly bewildered by the gastronomic performances she beheld. Babies ate pickles, small boys sequestered pie with a velocity that made her wink, women swam in the tea, and the men, metaphorically speaking, swept over the table like a swarm of locusts, while the host and hostess beamed upon one another and their robust descendants with an honest pride which was beautiful to see.

"That Mr. Wackett ain't eat scursely nothin', he jest sets lookin' round kinder 'mazed like. Do go and make him fall to on somethin', or I shan't take a mite of comfort in my vittles," said Grandma, as the girl came with an empty cup.

"He is enjoying it with all his heart and eyes, ma'am, for we don't see such fine spectacles every day. I'll take him something that he likes and make him eat it."

"Sakes alive! Be you to be Mis' Wackett? I'd no idee of it, you look so young."

"Nor I. We are only friends, ma'am."

"Oh!" and the monosyllable was immensely expressive as the old lady confided a knowing nod to the teapot, into whose depths she was just then peering. Sylvia walked away wondering why persons were always thinking and saying such things.

As she paused behind Warwick's chair with a glass of cream and a round of brown bread, he looked up at her with his blandest expression, though a touch of something like regret was in his voice.

"This is a sight worth living eighty hard years to see, and I envy that old couple as I never envied anyone before. To rear ten virtuous children, put ten useful men and women into the world, and give them health and courage to work out their own salvation, as these honest souls will do, is a better job done for the Lord than winning a battle or ruling a state. Here is all honor to them. Drink it with me."

He put the glass to her lips, drank what she left, and, rising, placed her in his seat with the decisive air which few resisted.

"You take no thought for yourself and are doing too much. Sit here a little, and let me take a few steps where you have taken many."

He served her and, standing at her back, bent now and

then to speak, still with that softened look upon the face so seldom stirred by the gentler emotions that lay far down in that deep heart of his; for never had he felt so solitary.

All things must have an end, even a family feast, and by the time the last boy's buttons peremptorily announced, "Thus far shalt thou go and no farther," all professed themselves satisfied, and a general uprising took place. The surplus population were herded in parlor and chambers, while a few energetic hands cleared away and, with much clattering of dishes and wafting of towels, left Grandma's spandy-clean premises as immaculate as ever. It was dark when all was done, so the kitchen was cleared, the candles lighted, Patience's door set open, and little Nat established in an impromptu orchestra, composed of a table and a chair, whence the first squeak of his fiddle proclaimed that the ball had begun.

Everybody danced; the babies, stacked on Patience's bed or penned behind chairs, sprawled and pranced in unsteady mimicry of their elders. Ungainly farmers, stiff with labor, recalled their early days and tramped briskly as they swung their wives about with a kindly pressure of the hard hands that had worked so long together. Little pairs toddled gravely through the figures, or frisked promiscuously in a grand conglomeration of arms and legs. Gallant cousins kissed pretty cousins at exciting periods and were not rebuked. Mark wrought several of these incipient lovers to a pitch of despair by his devotion to the comeliest damsels and the skill with which he executed unheard-of evolutions before their admiring eyes; Moor led out the poorest and the plainest with a respect that caused their homely faces to shine and their scant skirts to be forgotten. Warwick skimmed his five years' partner through the air in a way that rendered her speechless with delight, and Sylvia danced as she never danced before. With sticky-fingered boys, sleepy with repletion but bound to last it out; with rough-faced men who paid her paternal compliments; with smart youths who turned sheepish with that white lady's hand in their big brown ones, and one ambitious lad who confided to her his burning desire to work a sawmill and marry a girl with black eyes and yellow hair. While, perched aloft, Nat bowed away till his pale face glowed, till all hearts warmed, all feet beat responsive to the good old tunes which have put so much health into human bodies and so much happiness into human souls.

At the stroke of nine the last dance came. All down the long kitchen stretched two breathless rows—Grandpa and Grandma at the top, the youngest pair of grandchildren at the bottom, and all between fathers, mothers, uncles, aunts, and cousins, while such of the babies as were still extant bobbed with unabated vigor, as Nat struck up the Virginia Reel, and the sturdy old couple led off as gallantly as the young one who came tearing up to meet them. Away they went, Grandpa's white hair flying in the wind, Grandma's impressive cap awry with excitement, as they ambled down the middle, and finished with a kiss when their tuneful journey was done, amid immense applause from those who regarded this as the crowning event of the day.

When all had had their turn and twirled till they were dizzy, a short lull took place, with refreshments for such as still possessed the power of enjoying them. Then Phebe appeared with an armful of books, and all settled themselves for the family "sing."

Sylvia had heard much fine music, but never any that touched her like this, for, though often discordant, it was hearty, with that undercurrent of feeling which adds sweetness to the rudest lay and is often more attractive than the most florid ornament or faultless execution. Everyone sang as everyone had danced, with all their might—shrill children, soft-voiced girls, lullaby-singing mothers, gruff boys, and strong-lunged men. The old pair quavered, and still a few indefatigable babies crowed behind their little coops.

Songs, ballads, comic airs, popular melodies, and hymns came in rapid succession. And when they ended with that song which should be classed with sacred music for association's sake, and, standing hand in hand about the room with the golden bride and bridegroom in their midst, sang "Home," Sylvia leaned against her brother with dim eyes and a heart too full to sing.

Still standing thus when the last note had soared up and died, the old man folded his hands and began to pray. It was an old-fashioned prayer, such as the girl had never heard from the bishop's lips—ungrammatical, inelegant, and long. A quiet talk with God, manly in its straightforward confession of shortcomings, childlike in its appeal for guidance, fervent in its gratitude for all good gifts and the crowning one of loving children. As if close intercourse had made the two familiar, this human father turned to the Divine, as these sons and daughters turned to him, as free to ask, as confident of a reply, as all afflictions, blessings, cares, and crosses were laid down before Him and the work of eighty years submitted to His hand. There were no sounds in the room but the one voice, often tremulous with emotion and with age, the coo of some dreaming baby, or the low sob of some mother whose arms were empty, as the old man stood there, rugged and white atop as the granite hills, with the old wife at his side, a circle of sons and daughters girdling them around, and in all hearts the thought that as the former wedding had been made for time, this golden one at eighty must be for eternity.

While Sylvia looked and listened, a sense of genuine devotion stole over her. The beauty and the worth of prayer grew clear to her through the earnest speech of that unlettered man, and for the first time she fully felt the nearness and the dearness of the Universal Father, whom she had been taught to fear, yet longed to love.

"Now, my children, you must go before the little folks are tuckered out," said Grandpa heartily. "Mother and me can't say enough toe thank you for the presents you have fetched us, the dutiful wishes you have give us, the pride and comfort you have allers ben toe us. I ain't no hand at speeches, so I shan't make none, but jest say, ef any 'fliction falls on any on you, remember Mother's here toe help you bear it; ef any worldly loss comes toe you, remember Father's house is yourn while it stans, and so the Lord bless and keep us all."

"Three cheers for Gramper and Grammer!" roared a six-foot scion as a safety valve for sundry unmasculine emotions, and three rousing hurrahs made the rafters ring, struck terror to the heart of the oldest inhabitant of the rat-haunted garret, and summarily woke all the babies.

Then the good-byes began; the flurry of wrong baskets, pails, and bundles in wrong places; the sorting out of small folk too sleepy to know or care what became of them; the maternal cluckings and paternal shouts for Kitty, Cy, Ben, Bill, or Mary Ann; the piling into vehicles, with much ramping of indignant horses unused to such late hours; the last farewells, the roll of wheels, as one by one the happy loads departed and peace fell upon the household for another year.

"I declare for't, I never had sech an out-an'-out good time sense I was born intoe the world. Ab'ram, you are fit to drop, and so be I. Now let's set and talk it over along of Patience 'fore we go toe bed."

The old couple got into their chairs, and as they sat there side by side, remembering that she had given no gift, Sylvia crept behind them and, lending the magic of her voice to the simple air, sang the fittest song for time and place—"John Anderson, My Jo." It was too much for Grandma: The old heart overflowed, and reckless of the cherished cap, she laid her head on her "John's" shoulder, exclaiming through her tears:

"That's the cap sheaf of the hull, and I can't bear no more tonight. Ab'ram, lend me your hankchif, for I dunno where mine is, and my face is all of a drip."

Before the red bandanna had gently performed its work in

Grandpa's hand, Sylvia beckoned her party from the room and, showing them the clear moonlit night which followed the storm, suggested that they should both save appearances and enjoy a novel pleasure by floating homeward instead of sleeping. The tide against which they had pulled in coming up would sweep them rapidly along, and make it easy to retrace in a few hours the way they had loitered over for three days.

The pleasant excitement of the evening had not yet subsided, and all applauded the plan as a fit finale to their voyage. The old lady strongly objected, but the young people overruled her; and being reequipped in their damaged garments, they bade the friendly family a grateful adieu, left their more solid thanks under Nat's pillow, and reembarked upon their shining road.

All night Sylvia lay under the canopy of boughs her brother made to shield her from the dew, listening to the soft sounds about her: the twitter of a restless bird, the bleat of some belated lamb, the ripple of a brook babbling like a baby in its sleep. All night she watched the changing shores, silvery green or dark with slumberous shadow, and followed the moon in its tranquil journey through the sky. When it set, she drew her cloak about her and, pillowing her head upon her arm, exchanged the waking for a sleeping dream.

A thick mist encompassed her when she awoke. Above the sun shone dimly, below rose and fell the billows of the sea, before her sounded the city's fitful hum, and far behind her lay the green wilderness where she had lived and learned so much. Slowly the fog lifted, the sun came dazzling down upon the sea, and out into the open bay they sailed, with the pennon streaming in the morning wind. But still with backward glance the girl watched the misty wall that rose between her and the charmed river, and still with yearning heart confessed how sweet that brief experience had been, for though she had not yet discovered it, like—

The fairy Lady of Shalott,
She had left the web and left the loom,
Had seen the water lilies bloom,
Had seen the helmet and the plume,
And had looked down to Camelot.

A GOLDEN WEDDING

[Chapter VII of *Moods* (1882)]

Hitherto they had been a most decorous crew, but the next morning something in the air seemed to cause a general over-flow of spirits, and they went up the river like a party of children on a merrymaking. Sylvia decorated herself with vines and flowers till she looked like a wood nymph; Max, as skip-per, issued his orders with the true nautical twang; Moor kept up a fire of fun-provoking raillery; Warwick sang like a jovial giant; the *Kelpie* danced over the water, as if inspired by the universal gaiety, and the very ripples seemed to laugh as they hurried by.

"This is just the day for adventures. I hope we shall have some," said Sylvia, waving her bulrush wand, as if to conjure up fresh delights of some sort.

"I should think you had enough yesterday to satisfy even your adventurous soul," answered Max, remembering her for-lorn plight the night before.

"I never have enough! Life was made to enjoy, and each day ought to be different from the last; then one wouldn't get so tired of everything. See how easy it is. Just leave the old behind and find so much that is new and lovely within a

258

few miles of home. I believe in adventures, and mean to go and seek them if they don't come to me," cried Sylvia, looking about her, as if her new kingdom had inspired her with new ambitions.

"I think an adventure is about to arrive, and a very stirring one, if I may believe those black clouds piling up yonder." And Warwick pointed to the sky where the frolicsome west wind seemed to have prepared a surprise for them in the shape of a thundershower.

"I shall like that. I'm fond of storms and have no fear of lightning, though it always dances around me, as if it had designs upon me. Let it come; the heavier the storm the better. We can sit in a barn and watch it rave itself quiet," said Sylvia, looking up with such an air of satisfaction the young men felt reassured, and rowed on, hoping to find shelter before the rain.

It was after lunch, and refreshed by the cooler wind, the deepening shadows, the rowers pulled lustily, sending the boat through the water with the smooth speed given by strength and skill. Sylvia steered, but often forgot her work to watch the faces rising and falling before her, full of increasing resolution and vigor, for soon the race between the storm and the men grew exciting. No hospitable house or barn appeared, and Max, who knew the river best, thought that this was one of its wildest parts, for marshes lay on one hand and craggy banks on the other, with here and there a stretch of hemlocks leaning to their fall as the current slowly washed away the soil that held their roots. A curtain of black cloud edged with sullen red swept rapidly across the sky, giving an unearthly look to both land and water. Utter silence reigned as birds flew to covert and cattle herded together in the fields. Only now and then a long, low sigh went through the air like the pant of the rising storm, or a flash of lightning without thunder seemed like the glare of angry eyes.

"We are in for a drenching, if that suits you," said Max,

turning from the bow where he sat, ready to leap out and pull the boat ashore the instant shelter of any sort appeared.

"I shall just wrap my old cloak about me and not mind it. Don't think of me, and if anything does happen, Mr. Warwick is used to saving me, you know."

Sylvia laughed and colored as she spoke, but her eyes shone and a daring spirit looked out at them, as if it loved danger as well as his own.

"Hold fast then, for here it comes," answered Adam, dropping his oar to throw the rug about her feet, his own hat into the bottom of the boat, and then to look beyond her at the lurid sky, with the air of one who welcomed the approaching strife of elements.

"Lie down and let me cover you with the sail!" cried Moor anxiously, as the first puff of the rising gale swept by.

"No, no, I want to see it all. Row on, or land, I don't care which. It is splendid, and I must have my share of it," answered Sylvia, sending her hat after Warwick's and sitting erect, eager to prove her courage.

"We are safer here than in those woods, or soaking in that muddy marsh, so pull away, mates, and we shall reach a house before long, I am sure. This girl has had the romance of roughing it; now let us see how the reality suits her." And Max folded his arms to enjoy his sister's dismay, for just then, as if the heavens were suddenly opened, down came a rush of rain that soon drenched them to the skin.

Sylvia laughed and shook her wet hair out of her eyes, drank the great drops as they fell, and still declared that she liked it. Moor looked anxious, Warwick interested, and Max predicted further ills like a bird of evil omen.

They came, whirlwind and rain—thunder that deafened, lightning that dazzled, and a general turmoil that for a time might have daunted a braver heart than the girl's. It is one thing to watch a storm, safely housed, with feather beds, non-conductors, and friends to cling to—but quite another thing to be out in the tempest, exposed to all its perils, tossing in a boat on an angry river, far from shelter, with novelty, discomfort, and real danger to contend with.

But Sylvia stood the test well, seeming to find courage from the face nearest her; for that never blanched when the sharpest bolt fell, the most vivid flash blinded, or the gale drove them through hissing water, and air too full of rain to show what rock or quicksand might lie before them. She did enjoy it in spite of her pale cheeks, dilated eyes, and clutching hands, and sat in her place silent and steady, with the pale glimmer of electricity about her head, while the thunder crashed and tongues of fire tore the black clouds, swept to and fro by blasts that bowed her like a reed.

One bolt struck a tree, but it fell behind them; and just as Moor was saying, "We must land; it is no longer safe here," Max cried out: "A house! A house! Pull for your lives, and we will be under cover in ten minutes."

Sylvia never forgot that brief dash around the bend; for the men bent to their oars with a will, and the *Kelpie* flew like a bird, while with streaming hair and smiling lips the girl held fast, enjoying the rapture of swift motion, for the friends had rowed in many waters and were masters of their craft.

Landing in hot haste, they bade Sylvia run on, while they paused to tie the boat and throw the sail over their load, lest it should be blown away as well as drenched.

When they turned to follow, they saw the girl running down the long slope of meadow, as if excitement gave her wings. Max raced after her, but the others tramped on together, enjoying the spectacle, for few girls know how to run, or dare to try. So this new Atalanta was the more charming for the spirit and speed with which she skimmed along, dropping her cloak and looking back as she ran, bent on outstripping her brother.

"A pretty piece of energy. I didn't know the creature had so much life in her," said Warwick, laughing as Sylvia leaped a brook at a bound and pressed up the slope beyond, like a hunted doe.

"Plenty of it. That is why she likes this wild frolic so heartily. She should have more of such wholesome excitement and less fashionable dissipation. I spoke to her father about it and persuaded Prue to let her come," answered Moor, eagerly watching the race.

"I thought you had been at work, or that excellent piece of propriety never would have consented. You can persuade the hardest-hearted, Geoffrey. I wish I had your talent."

"That remains to be seen," began Moor. Then both forgot what they were saying to give a cheer as Sylvia reached the road and stood leaning on a gatepost panting, flushed, and proud, for Max had pressed her hard in spite of the advantage she had at the start.

They found themselves, a moist and mirthful company, before a red farmhouse standing under venerable elms with a patriarchal air which promised hospitable treatment and good cheer—a promise speedily fulfilled by the lively old woman, who appeared with an energetic "Shoo!" for the speckled hens congregated in the porch and a hearty welcome for the weather-beaten strangers.

"Sakes alive!" she exclaimed. "You be in a mess, ain't you? Come right in and make yourselves to home. Abel, take the menfolks up chamber, and fit 'em out with anything dry you kin lay hands on. Phebe, see to this poor little creeter, and bring her down lookin' less like a drownded kitten. Nat, clear up your wittlin's, so's't they kin toast their feet when they come down; and, Cinthy, don't dish up dinner jest yet."

These directions were given with such vigorous illustration, and the old face shone with such friendly zeal, that the four submitted at once, sure that the kind soul was pleasing herself in serving them, and finding something very attractive in the place, the people, and their own position. Abel, a staid farmer of forty, obeyed his mother's order regarding the "menfolks"; and Phebe, a buxom girl of sixteen, led Sylvia to her own room, eagerly offering her best.

As she dried and re-dressed herself, Sylvia made sundry discoveries, which added to the romance and the enjoyment of the adventure. A smart gown lay on the bed in the low chamber, also various decorations upon chair and table, suggesting that some festival was afoot; and a few questions elicited the facts. Grandpa had seven sons and three daughters, all living, all married, and all blessed with flocks of children. Grandpa's birthday was always celebrated by a family gathering. But today, being the fiftieth anniversary of his wedding, the various households had resolved to keep it with unusual pomp, and all were coming for a supper, a dance, and a "sing" at the end. Upon receipt of which intelligence Sylvia proposed an immediate departure; but the grandmother and daughter cried out at this, pointed to the still-falling rain, the lowering sky, the wet heap on the floor, and insisted on the strangers all remaining to enjoy the festival and give an added interest by their presence.

Half promising what she wholly desired, Sylvia put on Phebe's best blue gingham gown, for the preservation of which she added a white apron, and, completing the whole with a pair of capacious shoes, went down to find her party and reveal the state of affairs. They were bestowed in the prim best parlor, and greeted her with a peal of laughter, for all were *en costume*. Abel was a stout man, and his garments hung upon Moor with a melancholy air; Max had disdained them and, with an eye to effect, laid hands on an old uniform, in which he looked like a volunteer of 1812; while Warwick's superior height placed Abel's wardrobe out of the question; and Grandpa, taller than any of his seven goodly sons, supplied him with a sober suit—roomy, square-flapped, and venerable—which became him and with his beard produced the curious effect of a youthful patriarch. To Sylvia's relief, it was unanimously decided to remain, trusting to their own penetration to discover the most agreeable method of returning the favor; and regarding the adventure as a welcome change after two days' solitude, all went out to dinner prepared to enact their parts with spirit.

The meal being dispatched, Max and Warwick went to help Abel with some outdoor arrangements; and begging Grandma to consider him one of her own boys, Moor tied on an apron and fell to work with Sylvia, laying the long table which was to receive the coming stores. True breeding is often as soon felt by the uncultivated as by the cultivated, and the zeal with which the strangers threw themselves into the business of the hour won the family and placed them all in friendly relations at once. The old lady let them do what they would, admiring everything and declaring over and over again that her new assistants "beat her boys and girls to nothin' with their tastiness and smartness." Sylvia trimmed the table with common flowers till it was an inviting sight before a viand appeared upon it; and hung green boughs about the room, with candles here and there to lend a festal light. Moor trundled a great cheese in from the dairy, brought milk pans without mishap, disposed dishes, and caused Nat to cleave to him by the administration of surreptitious tidbits and jocular suggestions; while Phebe tumbled about in everyone's way, quite wild with excitement, and Grandma stood in her pantry like a culinary general, swaying a big knife for a baton as she issued orders and marshaled her forces, the busiest and merriest of them all.

When the last touch was given, Moor discarded his apron and went to join Max. Sylvia presided over Phebe's toilet and then sat herself down to support Nat through the trying half hour before the party arrived. The twelve years' boy was a cripple, one of those household blessings which, in the guise of an affliction, keep many hearts tenderly united by a common love and pity. A cheerful creature, always chirping like a cricket on the hearth as he sat carving or turning bits of wood into useful or ornamental shapes for such as cared to buy them of him, and hoarding up the proceeds like a little miser for one more helpless than himself.

"What are these, Nat?" asked Sylvia, with the interest that always won small people, because their quick instincts felt that it was sincere.

"Them are spoons—'postle spoons, they call 'em. You see, I've got a cousin what reads a sight, and one day he says to me, 'Nat, in a book I see somethin' about a set of spoons with a 'postle's head on each of 'em. You make some and they'll sell, I bet.' So I got Gramper's Bible, found the picters of the 'postles, and worked and worked till I got the faces good; and now it's fun, for they do sell, and I'm savin' up a lot. It ain't for me, you know, but Mother, 'cause she's wuss'n I be."

"Is she sick, Nat?"

"Oh, ain't she! Why, she hasn't stood up this nine year. We was smashed in a wagon that tipped over when I was three years old. It done somethin' to my legs, but it broke her back and made her no use, only jest to pet me and keep us all kind of stiddy, you know. Ain't you seen her? Don't you want to?"

"Would she like it?"

"She admires to see folks, and asked about you at dinner, so I guess you'd better go see her. Look a-here, you like them spoons, and I'm a-goin' to give you one. I'd give you all on 'em if they wasn't promised. I can make one more in time, so you jest take your pick, 'cause I like you and want you not to forget me."

Sylvia chose Saint John, because it resembled Moor, she thought; bespoke and paid for a whole set, and privately resolved to send tools and rare woods to the little artist, that he might serve his mother in his own pretty way. Then Nat took up his crutches and hopped nimbly before her to the room where a plain, serene-faced woman lay knitting, with her best cap on, her clean handkerchief and large green fan laid out upon the coverlet. This was evidently the best room of the house, and as Sylvia sat talking to the invalid, her eye discovered many traces of that refinement which comes through the affections. Nothing seemed too good for "daughter Patience"; birds, books, flowers, and pictures were plentiful here, though visible nowhere else. Two easy chairs beside the bed showed where the old folks oftenest sat; Abel's home corner was there by the antique desk covered with farmers' literature and samples of seeds; Phebe's workbasket stood in the window; Nat's lathe in the sunniest corner; and from the speckless carpet to the canary's clear water glass, all was exquisitely neat, for love and labor were the handmaids who served the helpless woman and asked no wages but her comfort.

Sylvia amused her new friends mightily, for, finding that neither mother nor son had any complaints to make, any sympathy to ask, she exerted herself to give them what both needed, and kept them laughing by a lively recital of her voyage and its mishaps.

"Ain't she prime, Mother?" was Nat's candid commentary when the story ended and he emerged red and shiny from the pillows where he had burrowed with boyish explosions of delight.

"She's very kind, dear, to amuse two stay-at-home folks like you and me, who seldom see what's going on outside four walls. You have a merry heart, miss, and I hope will keep it all your days, for it's a blessed thing to own."

"I think you have something better, a contented one," said Sylvia, as the woman regarded her with no sign of envy or regret.

"I ought to have. Nine years on a body's back can teach a sight of things that are wuth knowin'. I've learnt patience pretty well, I guess, and contentedness ain't fur away; for though it sometimes seems ruther long to look forward to, perhaps nine more years layin' here, I jest remember it might have been wuss and if I don't do much now, there's all eternity to come."

Something in the woman's manner struck Sylvia as she watched her softly beating some tune on the sheet, with her quiet eyes turned toward the light. Many sermons had been less eloquent to the girl than the look, the tone, the cheerful resignation of that plain face. She stooped and kissed it, saying gently:

"I shall remember this."

"Hooray! There they be—I hear Ben!"

And away clattered Nat to be immediately absorbed into the embraces of a swarm of relatives who now began to arrive in a steady stream. Old and young, large and small, rich and poor, with overflowing hands or trifles humbly given, all were received alike—all hugged by Grandpa, kissed by Grandma, shaken half breathless by Uncle Abel, welcomed by Aunt Patience, and danced around by Phebe and Nat, till the house seemed a great hive of hilarious and affectionate bees. At first the strangers stood apart, but Phebe spread their story with such complimentary additions of her own that the family circle opened wide and took them in at once.

Sylvia was enraptured with the wilderness of babies and, leaving the others to their own devices, followed the matrons to "Patience's room" and gave herself up to the pleasant tyranny of the small potentates, who swarmed over her as she sat on the floor, tugging at her hair, exploring her eyes, covering her with moist kisses, and keeping up a babble of little voices more delightful to her than the discourse of the flattered mamas, who benignly surveyed her admiration and their offspring's prowess.

The young people went to romp in the barn; the men, armed with umbrellas, turned out en masse to inspect the farm and stock and compare notes over pigpens and garden gates. But Sylvia lingered where she was, enjoying a scene which filled her with a tender pain and pleasure; for each baby was laid on Grandma's knee, its small virtues, vices, ailments, and accomplishments rehearsed, its beauties examined, its strength tested, and the verdict of the family oracle pronounced upon it as it was cradled, kissed, and blessed on the kind old heart which had room for every care and joy of those who called her "Mother." It was a sight the girl never forgot, because just then she was ready to receive it. Her best lessons did not come from books, and she learned one then as she saw the fairest success of a woman's life while watching this happy grandmother with fresh faces framing her withered one, daughterly voices chorusing good wishes, and the harvest of half a century of wedded life beautifully garnered in her arms.

The fragrance of coffee and recollections of Cynthia's joyful aberrations at such periods caused a breaking-up of the maternal conclave. The babies were borne away to simmer between blankets until called for. The women unpacked baskets, brooded over teapots, and kept up a harmonious clack as the table was spread with pyramids of cake, regiments of pies, quagmires of jelly, snowbanks of bread, and gold mines of butter—every possible article of food, from baked beans to wedding cake, finding a place on that sacrificial altar.

Fearing to be in the way, Sylvia departed to the barn, where she found her party in a chaotic Babel; for the offshoots had been as fruitful as the parent tree, and some four dozen young immortals were in full riot. The bashful roosting with the hens on remote lofts and beams; the bold flirting or playing in the full light of day; the boys whooping, the girls screaming, all effervescing as if their spirits had reached the explosive point and must find vent in noise. Max was in his element, introducing all manner of new games, the liveliest of the old, and keeping the revel at its height; for rosy, bright-eyed girls were plenty, and the ancient uniform universally approved. Warwick had a flock of lads about him, absorbed in the marvels he was producing with knife, stick, and string; and Moor, a rival flock of little lasses, breathless with interest in the tales he told—one on each knee, two at each side, four in a row on the hay at his feet, and the boldest of all with an arm about his neck and a curly head upon his shoulder, for Uncle Abel's clothes seemed to invest the wearer with a passport to their confidence at once. Sylvia joined this group and partook of a quiet entertainment with as childlike a relish as any of them, while the merry tumult went on about her.

The toot of the horn sent the whole barnful streaming into the house like a flock of hungry chickens, where, by some process known only to the mothers of large families, everyone was wedged close about the table; and the feast began. This was none of your stand-up, wafery, bread-and-butter teas, but a thoroughgoing, sit-down supper, and all settled themselves with a smiling satisfaction prophetic of great powers and an equal willingness to employ them. A detachment of half-grown girls was drawn up behind Grandma as waiters; Sylvia insisted on being one of them, and proved herself a neat-handed Phillis, though for a time slightly bewildered by the gastronomic performances she beheld. Babies ate pickles, small boys sequestered pie with a velocity that made her wink, women swam in the tea, and the men, metaphorically speaking, swept over the table like a swarm of locusts, while the host and hostess beamed upon one another and their robust descendants with an honest pride which was beautiful to see.

"That Mr. Wackett ain't eat scursely nothin'; he jest sets lookin' round kinder 'mazed like. Do go and make him fall to on somethin', or I shan't take a mite of comfort in my vittles," said Grandma, as the girl came with an empty cup.

"He is enjoying it with all his heart and eyes, ma'am, for we don't see such fine spectacles every day. I'll take him something that he likes and make him eat it."

"Sakes alive! Be you to be Mis' Wackett? I'd no idee of it, you look so young."

"Nor I. We are only friends, ma'am."

"Oh!" and the monosyllable was immensely expressive as the old lady confided a knowing nod to the teapot, into whose depths she was just then peering. Sylvia walked away wondering why persons were always thinking and saying such things.

As she paused behind Warwick's chair with a glass of new milk and a round of brown bread, he looked up at her with his blandest expression, though a touch of something like regret was in his voice.

"This is a sight worth living eighty hard years to see, and I envy that old couple as I never envied anyone before. To rear ten virtuous children, put ten useful men and women into the world, and give them health and courage to work out their own salvation, as these honest souls will do, is a better job done for the Lord than winning a battle or ruling a state. Here is all honor to them. Drink it with me."

He put the glass to her lips, drank what she left, and, rising, placed her in his seat with the decisive air which few resisted.

"You take no thought for yourself and are doing too much. Sit here a little, and let me take a few steps where you have taken many."

He served her and, standing at her back, bent now and then to speak, still with that softened look upon the face so seldom stirred by the gentler emotions that lay far down in that deep heart of his.

All things must have an end, even a family feast, and by the time the last boy's buttons peremptorily announced, "Thus far shalt thou go and no farther," all professed themselves satisfied, and a general uprising took place. The surplus population were herded in parlor and chambers, while a few energetic hands cleared away and, with much clattering of dishes and wafting of towels, left Grandma's clean premises as immaculate as ever. It was dark when all was done, so the kitchen was cleared, the candles lighted, Patience's door set open, and little Nat established in an impromptu orchestra, composed of a table and a chair, whence the first squeak of his fiddle proclaimed that the ball had begun.

Everybody danced; the babies, stacked on Patience's bed or penned behind chairs, sprawled and pranced in unsteady mimicry of their elders. Ungainly farmers, stiff with labor, recalled their early days and tramped briskly as they swung their wives about with a kindly pressure of the hard hands that had worked so long together. Little pairs toddled gravely through the figures, or frisked promiscuously in a grand conglomeration of arms and legs. Gallant cousins kissed pretty cousins at exciting periods and were not rebuked. Max wrought several of these incipient lovers to a pitch of despair by his devotion to the comeliest damsels and the skill with which he executed unheard-of evolutions before their admiring eyes. Moor led out the poorest and the plainest with a respect that caused their homely faces to shine and their scant skirts to be forgotten. Warwick skimmed his five years' partner through the air in a way that rendered her speechless with delight, and Sylvia danced as she never danced before. With sticky-fingered boys, sleepy with repletion but bound to last it out; with rough-faced men who paid her paternal compliments; with smart youths who turned sheepish with that white lady's hand in their big brown ones; and one ambitious lad who confided to her his burning desire to work a sawmill and marry a girl with black eyes and yellow hair. While, perched aloft, Nat bowed away till his pale face glowed, till all hearts warmed, all feet beat responsive to the good old tunes which have put so much health into human bodies and so much happiness into human souls.

At the stroke of nine the last dance came. All down the long kitchen stretched two breathless rows—Grandpa and Grandma at the top, the youngest pair of grandchildren at the bottom, and all between fathers, mothers, uncles, aunts, and cousins, while such of the babies as were still extant bobbed with unabated vigor, as Nat struck up the Virginia Reel, and the sturdy old couple led off as gallantly as the young one who came tearing up to meet them. Away they went, Grandpa's white hair flying in the wind, Grandma's impressive cap awry with excitement, as they ambled down the middle and finished with a kiss when their tuneful journey was done, amid immense applause from those who regarded this as the crowning event of the day.

When all had had their turn, and twirled till they were dizzy, a short lull took place, with refreshments for such as still possessed the power of enjoying them. Then Phebe appeared with an armful of books, and all settled themselves for the family "sing."

Sylvia had heard much fine music, but never any that touched her like this, for, though often discordant, it was hearty, with that undercurrent of feeling which adds sweetness to the rudest lay and is often more attractive than the most florid ornament or faultless execution. Everyone sang as everyone had danced, with all their might—shrill children, soft-voiced girls, lullaby-singing mothers, gruff boys, and strong-lunged men. The old pair quavered, and still a few indefatigable babies crowed behind their little coops. Songs, ballads, comic airs, popular melodies, and hymns came in rapid succession. And when they ended with that song which should be classed with sacred music for association's sake, and, standing hand in hand about the room, with the golden bride and bridegroom in their midst, sang "Home," Sylvia leaned against her brother with dim eyes and a heart too full to sing.

Still standing thus when the last note had soared up and died, the old man folded his hands and began to pray. It was an old-fashioned prayer, such as the girl had never heard from the bishop's lips—ungrammatical, inelegant, and long. A quiet talk with God, manly in its straightforward confession of shortcomings, childlike in its appeal for guidance, fervent in its gratitude for all good gifts and the crowning one of loving children. As if close intercourse had made the two familiar, this human father turned to the Divine, as these sons and daughters turned to him, as free to ask, as confident of a reply, as all afflictions, blessings, cares, and crosses were laid down before Him and the work of eighty years submitted to His hand. There were no sounds in the room but the one voice, often tremulous with emotion and with age, the coo of some dreaming baby, or the low sob of some mother whose arms were empty, as the old man stood there, rugged and white atop as the granite hills, with the old wife at his side, a circle of sons and daughters girdling them around, and in all hearts the thought that as the former wedding had been made for time, this golden one at eighty must be for eternity.

While Sylvia looked and listened, a sense of genuine devotion stole over her. The beauty and the worth of prayer grew clear to her through the earnest speech of that unlettered man, and for the first time she fully felt the nearness and the dearness of the Universal Father, whom she had been taught to fear, yet longed to love.

"Now, my children, you must go before the little folks are tuckered out," said Grandpa heartily. "Mother and me can't say enough toe thank you for the presents you have fetched us, the dutiful wishes you have give us, the pride and comfort you have alers ben toe us. I ain't no hand at speeches, so I shan't make none, but jest say, ef any 'fliction falls on any on you, remember Mother's here toe help you bear it; ef any worldly loss comes toe you, remember Father's house is yourn while it stans, and so the Lord bless and keep us all."

"Three cheers for Gramper and Grammer!" roared a six-foot scion, as a safety valve for sundry unmasculine emotions, and three rousing hurrahs made the rafters ring, struck terror to the heart of the oldest inhabitant of the rat-haunted garret, and summarily woke all the babies.

Then the good-byes began; the flurry of wrong baskets, pails, and bundles in wrong places; the sorting out of small folk too sleepy to know or care what became of them; the maternal cluckings and paternal shouts for Kitty, Cy, Ben, Bill, or Mary Ann; the piling into vehicles, with much ramping of indignant horses unused to such late hours; the last farewells, the roll of wheels, as one by one the happy loads departed and peace fell upon the household for another year.

"I declare for't, I never had sech an out-an'-out good time sense I was born into the world. A'bram, you are fit to drop, and so be I. Now let's set and talk it over along of Patience 'fore we go to bed."

The old couple got into their chairs, and as they sat there side by side, remembering that she had given no gift, Sylvia crept behind them and, lending the magic of her voice to the simple air, sang the fittest song for time and place—"John Anderson, My Jo." It was too much for Grandma: The old heart overflowed, and reckless of the cherished cap, she laid her head on her "John's" shoulder, exclaiming through her tears:

"That's the cap sheaf of the hull, and I can't bear no more tonight. A'bram, lend me your hankchif, for I dunno where mine is, and my face is all of a drip."

Before the red bandanna in Grandpa's hand had gently performed its work, Sylvia slipped away to share Phebe's bed in the old garret; lying long awake, full of new and happy thoughts, and lulled to sleep at last by the pleasant patter of the rain upon the roof.

PREFACE

[*Moods* (1882)]

When *Moods* was first published, an interval of some years having then elapsed since it was written, it was so altered, to suit the taste and convenience of the publisher, that the original purpose of the story was lost sight of and marriage appeared to be the theme, instead of an attempt to show the mistakes of a moody nature, guided by impulse, not principle. Of the former subject a girl of eighteen could know but little, of the latter most girls know a good deal; and they alone among my readers have divined the real purpose of the book in spite of its many faults and have thanked me for it.

As the observation and experience of the woman have confirmed much that the instinct and imagination of the girl felt and tried to describe, I wish to give my first novel, with all its imperfections on its head, a place among its more successful sisters; for into it went the love, labor, and enthusiasm that no later book can possess.

Several chapters have been omitted, several of the original ones restored; and those that remain have been pruned of as much fine writing as could be done without destroying the youthful spirit of the little romance. At eighteen, death seemed the only solution for Sylvia's perplexities; but thirty years later, having learned the possibility of finding happiness after disappointment and making love and duty go hand in hand, my heroine meets a wiser, if less romantic, fate than in the former edition.

Hoping that the young people will accept the amendment and the elders will sympathize with the maternal instinct which makes unfortunate children the dearest, I reintroduce my firstborn to the public which has so kindly welcomed my later offspring.

L. M. Alcott
Concord
January 1882

ROMANCE OF CHICAGO, THE RUINED CITY

THROUGH THE FIRE

["Through the Fire" appeared anonymously in the January 13, 1872, issue of *Frank Leslie's Chimney Corner* as an installment in "Romance of Chicago, the Ruined City," described as "a series of thrilling tales of the Chicago conflagration" in the magazine's promotional announcement. Evidence indicates that "Through the Fire" may well be one of Alcott's fugitive stories. Alcott lists the title in her ledger among the works for which she received payment in 1869, and the amount paid indicates that the tale was in all likelihood sold to Frank Leslie, who published the bulk of Alcott's thrillers. But the Chicago fire occurred on October 8–10, 1871. The chronology suggests that the original story was revised to exploit the public's interest in the fire. Whether Alcott herself took part in the revision is unclear, but it seems unlikely that she did, as she apparently stopped writing for Leslie's publications sometime in 1869. The matter of authorship is further complicated by the magazine's claim that the contributors to the "Romance of Chicago, the Ruined City" series were "talented writers, actual residents of the stricken city." But given Leslie's penchant for sensationalism, that claim is not above suspicion. With these caveats duly stated, the text is presented here in the interest of Alcott scholarship.]

It never would have happened but for the fire! But for that, I should now be the miserable wife of—

But let me tell you just how it was. I was a very gay girl—ah, how long ago it seems! My father was rich; we lived in an elegant house in North Chicago. I never knew a care or a want from my cradle, till that awful day.

Let me see—I had known Robert Leonard since we were children and went to school together. In those days we were fast friends. He always drew me on his sled and carried my books home for me.

But as I grew older, all that was dropped, of course. His family was poor; not beggars—perfectly respectable and all that—but his father was in some trade or other, his sister taught in Dearborn Seminary, and he—Robert himself—when he finished school, went into a dry goods store on State Street—as a clerk!

Of course, as Mama said, it wasn't at all proper for me to know him after that. And though I always spoke pleasantly to him when I met him, which made sister Laura very angry, yet I saw him very seldom, and I didn't think much about him.

I had been very busy, too, all the summer and fall. In the first place, I had a gay time at Saratoga and Newport. We had a nice party, and I declare I hardly had time to sleep while we were gone. Then, when we came home, of course I had heaps of shopping to do—all my winter clothes to select and have made. Madame Jordan had finished my wardrobe, and I did have such lovely dresses! Even Laura couldn't find a word of fault with them.

But let me go on. Just as I was ready for the winter's gaiety—and we intended to have a gay winter in Chicago, I can tell you: parties, opera, concerts, and clubs—just then Chester Carleton began to get very particular in his attentions.

I wasn't much surprised, for he'd been attentive all summer. His family was part of our traveling party. And to tell the honest truth, I wondered he hadn't offered himself before—so many lonely chances he'd had. But it was understood in both families that the thing was to be. So when he asked me to go driving with him that pleasant September evening, I had a sort of presentiment what would come of it. So had Laura, for as I left the hall, she whispered:

"Now, behave yourself, Kate, and settle it up right with Chester. You know what's expected of you."

So I did, well enough. His father was rich—so was mine. We went in the same circle in society. He was unexceptional in his life—at least as much so as any young man. Of course I don't mean any puritanical standard. We don't expect that of young men in society, you know. But he was gentlemanly, and it was expected; and I was quite resigned to be Mrs. Carleton.

So when we were driving quietly along South Park Avenue, behind his superb horses—he always did drive the most stylish horses in town, and that was one reason why I liked him—he made some sentimental speeches and finally asked me to be his wife.

I laughed carelessly and said I supposed I would—he must ask Father.

Then he gave me such a magnificent ring—a diamond solitaire. I never did see such a beauty!

I put it on and felt glad the matter was settled; and then we talked over arrangements, and Chester wanted me to be married very soon. He said we'd take a trip South and be back to open a house on the Avenue before the season commenced. And as soon as spring opened, we'd go to Europe for a year or two.

I didn't care particularly about Europe, for I'd spent years and years there already. And after all, there isn't any place so nice for a young lady as New York or Chicago.

But then, I wouldn't be a young lady, he said, but a married lady.

Somehow that jarred on my nerves, and I could hardly believe it. Of course I expected to be a married lady, but I hadn't really thought of it, and I couldn't help looking at him, to see how I should like his looks as my husband.

Well, he was well dressed and gentlemanly, and I couldn't expect too much of young men, Mama always told me. The stuff one sees in novels, about splendid, heroic young men, whom one must look up to and love, isn't a bit like life. I never could find one, if I spent my life hunting, Laura said. So I gave up thinking about that long ago. I was quite satisfied with Chester.

I went home and told Laura it was all settled; and Chester went in and talked to Father; and before we went to Mrs. Alcott's reception that evening, the whole thing was arranged, and I was to be married on the tenth of October.

Before that day, what centuries of agony I had gone through! How my youth was blasted on my brow in one instant!

But I haven't got to that.

Madame Jordan had her hands full again. Laura sent to Paris for the wedding dress—honiton over satin.

I didn't have much fun that month. I was every minute wanted to fit a dress, or to say how I'd have this done, or to shop, or something.

Then I had to go to horrid furniture stores and such places without end, to select the things for our house. It was to be furnished before we went. I got awful tired. But we did pick out elegant things, and I knew my house would be as fine as any on the Avenue.

At last the whole was done, every dress made, and everything ready in the house, and it was Sunday night before the wedding day. Chester came over in a very pious mood and asked me to go to church. So we went to St. James's—it was near—and we looked over the same prayer book, and I really felt very good, and that it was a serious matter to marry.

I asked Chester if he thought we cared enough about each other to be married. He laughed at me and told me that none but clodhoppers married for love nowadays, that comfortable dispositions and plenty of money—"tin," he called it—were worth all the moonshine lovers ever talked.

I remembered—somehow I couldn't help it—one day, about a year before. Robert Leonard and I chanced to meet on the lakeshore in Lincoln Park. I had got separated from my friends, and sat there waiting for them. We talked together, and he got sentimental over our school days.

Privately, I will confess that I've always had a little sentimental feeling myself about those days, for he really seemed to be a very noble boy; and in all the novels I had read, I never met a hero who seemed to be better or nobler than Robert.

But what could I do? Mama would shut me up if she suspected it; Laura would be horrified; the world would be shocked; and I—what *could* I do? I couldn't even imagine how poor people lived. I had a horror of them.

Honestly, now, what was there left for a girl brought up as I had been but to strangle any such thought that came into her heart and politely let him know that he was presuming?

I don't like to speak of it, for he really didn't propose; only I feared he would say too much, so I laughed away serious thoughts. I guess he understood, for he grew quiet and got so pale I was frightened.

He never was sentimental again, though, to be sure, we did not meet often.

Well, as I said, I couldn't help thinking of some noble and tender things he said about love, that Chester laughed at. But I didn't think of it long, for Chester had brought me a queenly set of diamonds, and never told me till we came home from church.

As we went home, we heard the bell strike for fire. Chester counted the strokes.

"Oh, it's way off in the West Side!" he said carelessly, and I soon forgot all about it.

When he went home, and I went to the door to say good night, the fire looked quite bright, and Chester said:

"That's a pretty big fire. I'm glad it's on the West Side. There's such a wind, it might spread if it was this side of the river."

Ah, well, let me linger over that night, for that was the last day of my girlhood. The morrow's sunset saw me a woman— a woman of sorrow and awful memories that never till my dying day will fade from my mind.

I went to bed about eleven. At four or five I awoke and, seeing it quite light in my room, hurriedly rose to look out. My windows looked east—I could see nothing.

I seized a long waterproof cloak from my closet, slipped my feet into slippers, and went into Laura's room, which faced the south.

Oh God, can I ever tell what I saw! One fearful glare—one horrid shower of sparks and burning brands—one deafening roar of flames and wind.

Death stood before me in horrid form.

I seized Laura, I shouted to Father, I rushed frantically over the house calling everybody.

The world was on fire!

Father gave one glance at the window. It was evident that the whole South Side—the business part of the city—was burning. There was his wealth. He was old. He gave one fearful groan and began to cry and wring his hands.

Laura began coolly to pack her treasures. I could not leave the window.

"Kate," she said, "go and pack up your clothes. Think of your wedding outfit! Pack it up."

I heard her mechanically, but I never gave it a thought.

"I'll get another," I said, "if I ever want one."

Now commenced a noise and confusion of wagons and carts, carriages, drays, wheelbarrows, perambulators, every available vehicle. People on foot by thousands—millions, it seemed to me—passed by; loads of furniture, piles of trunks, wagons full of women and children; the whole world was running away.

And above all rose the horrible roar of the fire and the whistle of the wind. Shall I ever hear the wind again and not remember that horrible night?

The servants packed their things and left, Laura got her dresses packed, Mama hid the silver—what she could get in— in a box, and Father did nothing but moan and cry.

I could not think. I forgot my diamonds. I never thought I was not dressed. I gave no heed to Laura. I seemed to be in a dream. I could only think, "Why do they bother me? The world is burning up!" I thought of the verse in the Bible, where the awful day was predicted.

But it was coming too near. Mama began to be anxious to get away from the house. Father and one servant who had not run away got the horses harnessed to the carriage, and we all got in—Mama and Laura on the back seat; Father and I on the front; Laura's trunk up by Henry, the man; and Mama's box under the seat.

First we thought we'd drive toward the river—and we did, for a block or two. But the smoke and fire got so thick, the horses reared and plunged and Mama screamed to turn around.

Henry turned around as quickly as he could for the crowd, and then we started to go over a bridge into the West Side.

Such crowds, such horror in the faces, such reckless brutality in the drivers, such horrid language, such selfishness, such cruelty!

As we neared the bridge, teams and foot passengers got thicker. Loads, carelessly thrown on, constantly fell off. A splendid mirror slipping off and crashing before our horses' feet frightened them so, they became almost unmanageable. Mama, white with terror, clutched me so, I could scarcely breathe. Father saw nothing, and Laura stood up, holding on her trunk.

Finally, two heavily loaded teams stuck on the bridge.

"For God's sake," screamed Mama, "let us get out! I shall die in here!"

"How would you be better on foot?" said Laura. "Sit still! Once over the bridge, the danger is over."

"But to get over—" said poor Mama.

She ended with a shriek as a brutal truck driver crashed past us, smashing both our wheels and knocking down a man who was trying to get by!

I couldn't look at the man. I turned sick. But there was now no question about us. We had no more a carriage—we must go on foot.

Hastily getting out, we abandoned the carriage, but not till Laura got her trunk down, with my help. Then we rushed for the sidewalk, while the horses plunged madly into the crowd.

I don't know how we got along. Laura dragged her trunk —I don't think she ever lifted ten pounds before. I dragged Father, who seemed to be in a stupor. Mama had hard work to get herself along.

We couldn't get over the bridge—we turned north on a side street. Before we had gone a block, we met a rough man.

"Where did you steal that trunk?" he said rudely to Laura.

"I did not steal it," said Laura, with dignity. "It is my own."

"No, it isn't! It's mine," said he, snatching it away from her.

Then Laura forgot her dignity and gave one scream. And he—he—*struck her!*

I never heard another sound from her. That broke her heart, I do believe. She grew white to her lips and dragged herself along as if she was a log.

The next scream was from Mama.

"Oh, dear, I left the silver box in the carriage—and all my diamonds!"

"Well, it's burned up by this time—like all the rest," said Father, and we plodded on.

After hours of walking, with blistered feet and aching heads; after having our clothes on fire more than once, till we were almost in rags; after unheard-of and unspeakable trials and fatigues, we reached the open prairie, northwest of the city—or where the city was.

Brokenhearted and desolate, we threw ourselves on the ground. Hundreds, and thousands, were there before us. Old and helpless, sick and babies, all were there in crowds. Without a blanket to cover them or anything to sit on, they sat and lay in groups.

There we sat, hopeless, from Monday afternoon, the ninth of October—that date is burned into my brain—till Tuesday morning. A rain came down and soaked us through, and then I remembered I was not dressed. Many suffered, and some died, on that prairie that night.

In the morning kindhearted people came to us from the city, and then we learned that the West Division was not burned. Thankfully we accepted the offer of an honest German to ride to town in his wagon. It was an express wagon; it had no seat but the driver's. We put Mama up by him, and we huddled together on the floor.

Thus we rode into Chicago!

Our driver asked where we wanted to go. Pertinent question! Where could we go? Every friend we had was homeless as ourselves. Every house that my father owned, and from which he drew his income, was burned. So far as the present was concerned, we were beggars.

"Where can we go?" said Mama's white lips, while Father moaned and Laura said nothing.

"I think I know of an empty room where you can stay a

while," said the driver. "It ain't no great shakes of a place, but it's a room."

"Of course we'll go anywhere," said I, "till we can think."

He drove up to a dirty-looking grocery, and up a dark and greasy flight of stairs he led us, ushering us at last into a dingy, black, fearful room. I didn't know there could be such a horrible room in the world. Father sank at once on the floor. Mother sat down on a windowsill, and Laura stood looking on the street.

Then we all remembered our gnawing hunger.

"Father," I spoke, "give me some money, if you have any. I'll get something to eat."

Mechanically he took out his purse and gave it to me. Eagerly I counted the money. Just twenty-two dollars between us and starvation. I kept the purse, and found my way downstairs into the grocery below. There, with many qualms, I bought some bread and crackers.

And it was my wedding day!

Oh, let me draw a veil over this day. Let me not tell how I tramped around to get a few necessities together. I, who had shopped like a princess last week—or was it last century!

Enough that night found us with at least food sufficient— such as it was—and straw to lie on. And the next day I found the blessed Relief Headquarters, in a church, and got some clothes, for I had worn my waterproof only, over my nightdress, till then.

No one could do anything but me. Father was like a child, Mother was really ill, and Laura couldn't be roused to care for anything, not even her meals.

Let me pass over the few days till I found more comfortable rooms and we had moved in them; till we had a few articles of furniture and bedding from the quantities our generous citizens and villagers were pouring in; and till we were regularly supplied with food, which I brought myself from the relief rooms.

Now what was to be done? Naturally, in my trouble, I thought of Chester.

"As soon as I let him know," I said to myself, "he will come over and tell us what to do. The care and responsibility are more than I can bear. His home was not burned, being in the eastern part of the city. Our new house, furnished completely from attic to cellar, was not burned. His business is not injured. Perhaps," I thought, "he will think best to be married at once, though I have no wardrobe, and go at once to keeping house—taking the family, of course, till Father can turn around."

So a ray of comfort stole into my darkness, and I wrote him a note on a sheet of paper I bought at a grocer's.

Nearly a week after I sent it—by private hand, for we had no post office—and when I was beginning to get sick with despair, he came.

I never realized the difference between our past and present condition till he came into that dark, low room—faultlessly dressed, fragrant with perfume, nicely barbered, and daintily gloved—while I had on a calico dress made for one shorter than I, no collar, hair twisted up in a knot, coarse shoes.

"Why, really," he said, "you had a sad time, didn't you, now? Who'd have thought the fire we noticed, Miss Ellis," turning to me, "would have burned you out of house and home?"

"Yes, and everything else," groaned Father.

"Surely, Mr. Ellis, it isn't so bad as that?" he said, smiling.

"Indeed it is!" I said savagely, for his smoothness irritated me. "Every cent of income is gone. We're living on the Relief Society, and shall, till I get work."

"Till—you—get—work!" he ejaculated slowly.

"Yes. You don't think I'll sit down and be fed, as long as I have hands to work?"

"Your hands don't look much like work," he said, glancing at them.

I glanced, too, and saw his ring. He saw it, too. I saw his color change slightly.

"Since things have changed so," I said impetuously, "perhaps you had better take this little piece of property!" and I offered him the ring.

I felt that I must test him at once.

"Well, just as you say, Miss Ellis," he said, taking the bauble. "Things *have* changed very much since last Sunday night."

"Well, good morning!" was my next remark.

He was evidently glad to go, for he said: "Since I can't do anything to help, perhaps I'd better go."

And he went.

I didn't break my heart, for, after all, I didn't love him; but I started on my search for work.

The first question everywhere asked me was, "What can you do?"

Sure enough—what could I do? Not teach; I didn't know enough, though I had graduated at Madame Chegarie's. Not sew; I never learned. Not cook; I knew still less of that. I could stand behind a counter and sell goods, and faithfully I tried to get that work.

Alas, there were other thousands of girls wanting employment who were experienced. After two weeks' daily effort I came home one night in weary-hearted despair.

Father sat in his chair moaning, as he did all the time now. Mother lay in the next room, wasting away to death—I knew it. Laura, as usual, sat by the window.

Tired as I was, I knew I must get tea—if we had any. So I hastily made some and gave a little to Father and Mother, with crackers. And when I had done, I sat down on the only vacant chair—a wooden one, such as I never sat on before— laid my head on the back of it and gave way to my first fit of tears.

It seems that the flood so long pent up had accumulated,

and it came with uncontrollable force. I don't remember much what happened, and I suppose I must have become insensible; for when I came back to consciousness, somebody was trying to lift me from the floor.

He did lift me, and set me in the chair, and then came low, soothing words.

"Don't, now, dear Kate, give way so! Tell me what it is— let me help you! Oh, Kate, why are you so brokenhearted?"

When I still could not reply, or control myself at all, came the tender whisper:

"My darling—my darling! You'll kill me if you don't speak."

I felt warm kisses on my hands, and I opened my eyes to see—Robert Leonard.

"Thank God!" he cried fervently. "I thought you would die, Kate! Why, what is it, dear?"

I tried to collect myself. He seemed to be unconscious of the tenderness of his words, but I felt a hot flush on my face, and he dropped my hand.

"Forgive me! I forgot myself, I was so alarmed."

He walked to the window and then came back.

"Now, I am so glad to have found you! I've been looking ever since the fire," he said. "And I've got a comfortable place for you."

"Why, you were burned out, too!" I said.

"Yes, of course, but I have taken a furnished house, and Mother and Nellie are there. I have my salary yet, for the house I am with opened for business a week after the fire. I insist on your accepting my hospitality till you can look about you."

I began to murmur dissent, but he would not hear.

"I know how your father is situated. He'll be all right after a while, but at present he is helpless. I see," he added, in a lower tone, "he needs care and help—your mother, too—and you—"

His voice changed, and he seemed to choke.

"Robert Leonard," I said, with sudden impulse, "do you care for me here, now, in this dress—a beggar?"

He answered warmly:

"I love you more than ever in my life before, Kate, and I can't remember when I didn't love you."

"Then, if you'll take me as I am, Robert, I will be your true wife and love you all my life!"

"But, Katie," he said tenderly, while an eager joy shone in his face, "I don't want to take advantage of your situation. You are excited now. I'm afraid you might regret—"

"I'm not excited," I went on. "The years of agony I've been through in these past days have shown me the bottom of men's hearts—have opened my eyes to everlasting truth and honor. You were right when you talked of love and honor that day, and I was an impertinent girl when I told you your whole salary wouldn't pay my maid. I hate myself when I think of it! And I shall never forgive myself till I can add somewhat to your happiness, my noble friend!"

Robert brought a clergyman to that room in half an hour, and we were married.

He took us all home, my noble, generous husband; made us all welcome, helped Father onto his feet again, cured up Mother, consoled Laura—with another wardrobe; and thus, one month from that fearful day, I believe I'm the happiest woman in Chicago, burned out or not burned out. And to think that but for the fire, I should now be the wife of Chester Carleton!

Robert had my photograph taken in my wedding dress, and calls it "a relic of the fire."